Rose in the Desert

K.M. Daughters

Cover Art by *Nicola Martinez*

White Rose Publishing, a division of Pelican Ventures, LLC
www.pelicanbookgroup.com PO Box 1738 *Aztec, NM * 87410
Contact Information: titleadmin@pelicanbookgroup.com

White Rose Publishing Circle and Rosebud logo is a trademark of Pelican Ventures, LLC

Publishing History
First White Rose Edition, 2020
Paperback Edition ISBN 978-1-5223-0252-0
Electronic Edition ISBN 978-1-5223-0251-3
Published in the United States of America

Dedication

For Mary and her Son.

What People are Saying

4½ Stars..."Fantastic, A Keeper."
~RT Book Reviews on Rose of the Adriatic

Miracles really do happen in this character-driven story by the writing team behind Daughters. The strength of faith and love prevail in this well-crafted book. Matt and Anna will capture your heart.

~Donna Brown

Part I.

The Parchment

Prologue

Valselo, Croatia

Anna pursued the exuberant toddler down the cobbled walk that bisected the lush, back lawn. Fit from daily jogs, her rapid pulse owed more to nerves than exertion.

"*Dragi jedan*, dear one, wait for Momma!" she shouted.

The little girl giggled in response as she dashed headlong toward the stone perimeter wall surrounding Anna's rose garden.

"Ruža, *please* be careful."

Her daughter approached the eight-foot-high wall at full tilt and leapt catlike directly at the obstacle in her path. Wedging chubby fingers and rubber-tipped sneakers into the stones' crevices, Ruža clung to the slippery surface like a sunny-haired lizard child.

"I climb wall," she declared as she stretched a tiny arm high above her head and lifted one leg upward, scrabbling her shoe on the stone façade for a foothold.

Her heartbeat drumming in her ears, Anna

plucked the intrepid Ruža off the wall and clasped the baby in her arms. The anxiety plaguing Anna since she had awakened that morning approached panic. Trembling, Anna shifted Ruža to ride on her left hip and unlocked the iron garden gate with a shaky hand.

Freeing the baby to romp along the pebbled path that meandered between the forest of exquisite, white rosebushes in bloom, Anna sank down on the stone bench, vigilant and uneasy. Overheated, although dressed in a light sundress on the mild summer's day, Anna couldn't shake the nagging, unnerving foreboding. *Mother, why am I so fearful?* No answer came from her heavenly mentor. Anna's inner mounting anxiety ballooned like rising dough.

"Oh!" Ruža hollered as she spun around and sprinted back to Anna.

Alarm pierced Anna at the frightened expression on Ruža's face.

"The bee buzzed my ear."

Relieved, Anna sighed and gently brushed silken curls away from the two-year-old child's ear. "He didn't sting you, did he?"

Ruža wagged her head and accepted her mother's gentle kiss. "I go play."

Watching her baby's antics while meditating in the miraculous rose garden, lush with undying blooms, usually comprised the serene highpoint of Anna's days. That special place epitomized peace, love, healing, and divinity to her. There the Marian visionary, to whom pilgrims from all over the world fondly referred to as the "Rose of the Adriatic," had prayed, dreamed, offered heartfelt gratitude, and counted her many blessings.

Unable to do anything but worry, Anna grappled

with the utterly foreign sensation. She had received daily communications from the Mother of God since she was a child until Our Lady had imparted seven secrets concerning the fate of the world, and then the daily visits ceased. Thank God, Our Lady still returned to her each year on her wedding anniversaries. During thousands of conversations, Gospa had graced her with the absolute truth of God's love and salvation through His Son. Anna had lived her adult life devoid of fear, having the Queen of Heaven as her guide and protector.

The unearthly, perfect roses blooming in the garden perfumed the air with heavenly aroma. Their beauty and purity reflected the qualities of the celestial gardener who tended Anna's miracle flowers. Our Lady of the Roses, Gospa, the Blessed Virgin, had gifted Anna with the garden. From the harvest of "immortal" roses, the Lord had bestowed hundreds of miracles of conversion, as well as physical and spiritual healings.

"Papa!" Ruža shouted, drawing Anna's gaze toward the garden gate.

Matt emerged through the entryway, beaming at his girls.

"How's my rosebud today?" he boomed as he squatted down, open armed.

Ruža's comical, trundling gait prompted Anna's smile. *Matt is here. Everything will be all right.*

Matt swept the baby off her feet and stood, cradling her in his arms and nuzzling her neck.

Anna rose off the bench to greet him, warmed by the loving gleam in his sky-blue eyes. However, his soft kiss and the strong arm that drew her into his embrace didn't fully comfort her and failed to allay her mysterious disquiet.

"You're tense, love," he said, narrowing his eyes. "Something's wrong."

At the risk of upsetting their daughter, Anna hedged, "Perhaps." She chuckled and then added, "Ruža scared me when she tried to climb the garden wall. Didn't you, dear one?"

Unperturbed, Ruža trained innocent, wide brown eyes at her father. "I climb now, Papa?"

Matt tossed back his head and let loose a delighted hoot. He bussed a kiss on the baby's cheek and set her down. "No climbing the wall, rosebud. You might fall and get hurt."

"OK, Papa."

A chill coursed through Anna. *Is Ruža's safety the reason I'm so nervous today? Dear God, please send Your angels to guard and protect my baby.*

Matt clasped Anna's hand and led her to the bench. "She's speaking English today? My poor Anna, you're outnumbered in this family," he teased.

"For three days in a row now, she abandons Croatian. My English has improved since I married my American doctor and became a mother."

Matt brushed the back of Anna's hand with a soft kiss. "Your English is perfect."

His penetrating gaze was clinical, characteristic of his acute intelligence, his M.D., and Ph.D. degrees. "Doctor-Doctor" Matt Robbins never missed a thing.

"But you're not yourself today, love. I don't think I've ever seen that expression on your face. What's troubling you? Did our little rose really scare you that much?"

"No...yes..." Anna shook her head. "Everything confuses me today. I was frightened and a little amused, too. Seeing her try to go up the wall made me think of your first visit here. Remember how you climbed the garden wall to steal a rose, so you could analyze it and prove that I was a big liar?"

Matt chuckled. "I do remember every second with you." He smiled sheepishly. "I poked and prodded and tested you. You passed the lie detector test with flying colors."

"Colors fly?"

He gently rotated her hand and kissed the palm. "That means you weren't a liar, and I was a skeptical scientist. I confessed what I was up to that night before I resorted to thievery. And, *eventually*...I believed."

"Yes." The heaviness around her heart lightened, remembering all that led her to fall in love with the man who made her dreams come true.

"And I married the most extraordinary woman on the planet and have been graced beyond measure. Just look at our little miracle," he said, grinning from ear to ear.

Ruža sat in the dirt, inspecting a smooth stone. She peered at the rock and spun it around in her hands as if deciphering its composition.

"She is so like you," Anna remarked.

Matt smiled, his eyes twinkling as he gazed at their daughter. "Maybe in some things. But, thank God, she looks just like you. Beautiful. Those soft brown eyes melt me every time. And she has your shiny, honey-blonde hair. We'll have to beat the boys off with a big stick when she's grown."

"I don't understand," Anna said. "You'd strike her suitors?"

He turned his attention to Anna and gazed deeply into her eyes. "I love you," he said.

Anna's spirits lifted, thrilled at the expression in her husband's sparkling eyes that mirrored their abiding love. "I love you, too."

Giving her hands a squeeze, he asked, "Feel better now?"

More at ease, she replied, "Yes, thank you. I feel foolish."

"Good."

She knitted her brows and he chuckled.

"Good that you feel better...not that you feel foolish," he clarified. Stretching out his legs, he relaxed on the bench. "Aren't you going to ask why I'm home in the middle of the day?"

Widening her eyes, she joked, "Because you missed me too terribly to bear it."

He beamed a smile and replied, "There's that. But...Anna you won't believe it. All five terminally ill patients at *Mir* House were spontaneously cured! It was magnificent. I wish you had been there to see it. Harry and I are left with nothing to do."

An obscure dread colored Anna's elation at the unprecedented, wondrous news. Her thoughts whirled as she considered this event's possible connection to her lingering apprehension all day.

Matt's voice muted in her consciousness.

"There's a procession up Gospa Hill planned this evening," he said. "I thought we could hike up Salvation Mountain now for reflection and thanksgiving. Just us three..."

"Anna. Come."

The sweet, beloved voice she knew so well blotted out earthly reality, and Anna shot off the bench.

"What? Anna!" The shock in Matt's voice penetrated the haze.

Breaking into a run Anna shouted, "Our Lady comes. Matt. Quick. Bring the baby. The chapel..." Her breath ragged, Anna raced out of the garden on a bead for the back door. The baby squawked from behind her, apparently protesting her father's depriving her of playtime, as Anna flung open the screen door. Continuing to run, Anna sped through the kitchen toward the little apparition chapel in her home. Nothing mattered except the coming communion with her Mother. And surely, she would receive an explanation of the undiagnosed fearfulness that had gripped her throughout the day.

Panting, Anna bumped into the kneeler at the front of the chapel and fell to her knees on the red vinyl cushion. She raised her eyes, focused on the wall of the chapel above the carved wood crucifix and began reciting the rosary. Brilliant white light radiated in front of her eyes, and all other physical sensations receded as if she were transported beyond earth. Anna fixated on a spot above the altar, rewarded when Our Lady of the Roses appeared, smiling. Joyfully beaming and indescribably beautiful, Our Lady floated on a puffy cloud. Anna's spirit soared.

But confusion and trepidation tarnished her usual ecstasy during apparitions. Anna mouthed the inaudible query, "Mother, are you angry with me?"

"My dear child, at our last meeting, I told you I would come on your next anniversary. Do not think that you have done something wrong that requires me to visit you today. You have accepted with all your heart the plan that my Son and I have. Be happy because I am your mother and I love you with all my heart. Anna, thank you for having responded to my Son's invitation, for persevering and remaining close to

Him until He completes that which He asks of you."

"Oh, Mother. It has been my greatest joy. I have missed you terribly. Thank you so much for coming to me sooner."

"I have told you during our years together about the secrets, dear child."

Anna's pulse raced, remembering the details of the prophesied, monumental, world occurrences that Gospa had entrusted to her. "Yes, Mother. You have spoken of the wishes of The Most High."

"It is time, Anna. I have prepared you for your role, and I will be with you. The Most High will reveal his plan for the world as I have instructed you, Elizabeta, and Josip. Make preparations. You must travel to inform my Son's shepherd, the priest. In three days, this priest shall bear testimony that I have spoken for the Most High, foretelling the forthcoming universal sign, and the events to follow."

"Are the spontaneous healings at Mir House today related?"

"Nothing is impossible for our Lord. What follows will be far more indisputable."

Anna gasped as terror seized her. "Mother, I'm so afraid that I'm unworthy to be your emissary. What if I fail and the chastisement results?"

"You have nothing to fear, my dear, dear child. My Son and I will never leave you. I love you. Thank you for having responded to my call." The brilliant light surrounding Gospa dimmed and then extinguished.

Anna stared numbly at the spot on the pastel-colored wall of the chapel where moments before Our Lady was visible. Shuddering, Anna covered her face with her hands and burst into tears.

Matt's hoarse sobs and Ruža's wails permeated her

trance. She raised her head and trained tear-filled eyes on her husband and daughter.

In the last row of pews, the crying baby strained toward her, wriggling in Matt's lap. Open-mouthed, her husband stared straight ahead as tears streamed down his face.

Petrified, Anna raced toward him, her arms outstretched. "Matt, what is it?" she shrieked.

"I..." He lifted Ruža up into her arms, his penetrating, stricken expression filling her with terror.

Pressing her daughter to her chest, she hung over Matt.

His eyes huge, Matt blurted out, "How have you stood it all these years?"

Anna sat next to Matt and roved her gaze over his body from the top of his head to his shoes, investigating a physical cause for the pained expression on his face. Satisfied that he wasn't injured, she secured the baby on her lap with one arm and touched her free hand to his knee. "Tell me what you mean," she urged.

"I saw her." He wagged his head. "Dear God, I saw her."

Stunned, she exclaimed, "You did? Did you hear our conversation?"

"No. But she spoke to me." He inhaled deeply and then huffed out a breath. "She said, 'You must show Anna the way. She knows nothing of the world beyond the village. She is safe with you, dear child. And you are safe with me. Remember, I'm your mother. Thank you for responding to my call.'" He shifted in his seat and faced her. "Anna, I can't fathom this. How have you stood it all these years?"

"I…" She frowned. "I love her…"

Matt rounded his eyes. "Oh, I know. Now I know fully. What I mean is how can you stand it when she leaves?"

Smiling, Anna nodded her head. "Ah. It's easier now. Because I have you."

Matt brushed a hand over Ruža's silken crown and then cupped the side of Anna's face tenderly. "I must show you the way. I don't know what she means."

"We're going to the desert. In America," Anna retorted.

"All right." He dragged a hand through his curly crop of sandy hair. "Why?"

"The secrets. I wrote them on a parchment. Now I have to deliver the parchment to a priest Our Lady has chosen. He will bear witness that future occurrences and the signs in the desert were foretold." Anna rose unsteadily, hefting her child in her embrace.

Matt stood and encircled his strong arms around her waist.

She gazed up into his eyes and smiled. "First stop is Chicago. Maybe we'll have time to visit with your parents."

1

Chicago Suburbs
Three Days Later

Susie Mulligan twisted her long hair behind her head and lifted the damp ponytail away from the nape of her neck. With her nose inches from the oscillating fan on her desk, she closed her eyes and spent a few frustrated seconds hoping for a cooling effect. Pathetic. The open window hadn't done a thing to lower the temperature in the room either, and the humid air hung heavy and smothering—an annoying steam bath.

I don't know why the old cheapskate won't break down and buy an air conditioner. None of my friends have to sweat like me.

Releasing the hank of hair, she wagged her head and freed a cascade of raven curls down over her shoulders. She squinted at her reflection in her makeup mirror and continued outlining her eyes with a smoky black kohl pencil. She plucked a tissue out of the box, blotted sweat off her upper lip, and then applied dual, generous smears of pink, cherry-flavored gloss to her full lips. Clenching her teeth, she jack-o-lantern grinned into her mirror, checked for pink smudges on the enamel, and then tossed the gloss into her backpack.

She held her breath listening for her parents' stirrings. Silence at last.

I didn't think they'd ever go to sleep tonight. I'm sixteen years old and they still treat me like I'm ten. I have every right to go out at night.

All her friends had cool parents who let them date and stay out until midnight, but not her strict, dinosaur parents. They deserved her sneaking around behind their backs.

And, thank goodness, at least they're heavy sleepers.

The rhinestone-encrusted iPhone vibrated on the bed's purple and pink striped comforter. Scooping up the phone, she read, "Jail break tonight?" She laughed at Spike's text.

"Oh, yeah. Give me 15," she typed in response.

"Pick u up usual place," came his reply.

"C U there. Flash lights."

She stuffed the phone into her backpack and checked the side pouch. Good. She had a lighter and cigarettes. Pulling out the pack, she counted its contents. Only three left. She added the two she had snatched after dinner from her father's stash. He never missed one or two.

Although it was tempting to nab an entire pack, she had wisely resisted. He had grounded her for a month after a pack went missing from his carton, and he had figured out that she was the only possible culprit. That stung.

After she cast one last glance in the mirror, she eased open her bedroom door and stepped gingerly out into the dark hallway, barefooted. Toting her strappy sandals in one hand, she tiptoed down the stairs, scurried through the kitchen, and exited the back door. She unfastened the lock on the knob and carefully latched the door closed behind her.

Ah, freedom! She wanted to shout out the sentiment and wake her next-door neighbor. Wouldn't that old biddy, Mrs. Jarvis, have a fit?

Self-preservation won over spite, and she hurried straight back through her yard toward the tree line. She avoided trampling her mother's plants as she ducked under low hanging branches at the property line and halted to slip on her shoes. Tramping along the narrow access pathway that cut through the trees, she quickened her pace on the downward slope and emerged out onto the Illinois Prairie Path, her chest heaving in the cloying, humid air.

Strolling at a lazy pace, she rummaged in the side pouch of her backpack and dug out a cig and the lighter. She hung the backpack over one shoulder by the strap, lit up, took a deep drag, and sputtered a cough at the searing sensation in her throat. The next drag was nice and smooth.

Satisfied, Susie continued smoking while she traveled the path cloaked in darkness, the flare of burning tobacco from each puff a tiny lamp in front of her. She reached the mouth of a clearing as the crosswalk on the two-lane street came into view about ten yards ahead. Lingering in the shadows, she smoked the cigarette down to the filter, tossed the butt on the ground, and stamped it under her heel. Antsy with anticipation and the nicotine high, she waited impatiently for the flash of headlights signaling Spike's approach.

Suddenly, the creepy sensation that someone watched her sent a chill through her, and the hairs on her arms stood on end. She spun around and called out, "Not funny, Spike."

Expecting Spike to stride into view any second wearing a wise-guy expression on his handsome face, Susie's chest constricted as she peered into the shadows. Despite her growing anxiety, she boomed, "I'm not kidding, Spike. Knock it off."

****

He kneaded his brow and gazed at the girl backlit by the streetlight on the corner.

Who's Spike? Why can't they just leave me alone? Constantly taunting me. Look at this one. Another tramp.

Instinctively ducking behind a tree trunk at the sound of her first outburst, he had a perfect view of the detested interloper. At that hour and after all the frustration on the job, he chose that route purposely, yearning for solitude.

"Spike, if you don't come out right now, I'm going home. I mean it," she called, her voice shrill.

Careful what you wish for, big mouth. I can send you home really quick.

He stepped from behind the tree out onto the path and approached her with his head bent.

"Get away from me," she whined, her voice plaintive.

"Excuse me," he muttered, intending to pass her, cross the street, and leave the little nuisance behind.

"What are you doing sneaking up on me like this?" She blocked his path, fists balled on her hips, her voice dripping with accusation.

They all have vile attitudes. But he'd let it ride. *Keep walking. She isn't worth it.*

Refusing to rise to the bait, he slipped his hands in his pockets, gazed downward, and replied wearily, "Miss, I'm not sneaking up on you. I'm on my way home from work."

"Really? Where do you work dressed like that? A tuxedo?"

He actually shared her apparent distaste for his required uniform and almost smiled. Gazing at her, the disdain he perceived on her sullen face had him narrowing his eyes, sizing her up. "How old are you?"

"I'm sixteen, not that it's any of your business, you creep," she spat out.

"What's a young girl like you doing out alone so late? You should be home in bed."

She ignored him, shrugged a shoulder to slide the strap of a backpack down over her arm, and unzipped it.

Extracting a cell phone from the bag, she flicked a glance at him and sneered, "What are you looking at?" She turned her attention to the phone.

As if his blood boiled in his veins, scalding fury seethed inside. *This insolent brat ruined my life.* His eyes blurred as he fished inside the right pocket of his jacket, fingering the cotton glove. He fisted his hand and jammed his knuckles into the glove's mouth. *You should have left me alone.*

His rage exploded into action as he whipped his hand out of his pocket and landed a perfect upper cut into her windpipe. She emitted a guttural grunt and dropped on to the dirt. He unclenched his fist and wriggled his fingers into the glove. Grasping her ankle, he dragged her lax body farther away from the apron of light beyond the clearing as he jutted his left hand into his pocket and grasped his other glove.

Releasing her foot, he slipped on the left-hand glove and then dove at her prone body, aiming both hands at her neck, thumbs extended. He landed in a straddle on her chest, jarring his knees upon impact with the ground. But the additional deadly blow he dealt to her windpipe compensated nicely for his discomfort.

Her hands clawed lamely at his fingers as he leveraged his body weight into the stranglehold. Her feet kicked out. Choking whimpers gurgled in her throat.

Not so full of yourself now, are you?

He squeezed harder. As her hands fell away and thumped on the ground, he interpreted the gurgling sound she emitted, "Why?"

"You know why," he said through clenched teeth as he mustered all his strength to choke her into permanent silence. "Did you think you could ruin my life and just walk away?"

Her body shuddered beneath him, and she expelled her last breath on a long, "O," as if she finally understood.

He sat back on his haunches atop her lifeless body.

"I hope you do understand," he whispered. "You're to blame...not me."

Rising slowly, he wagged his head. He removed his gloves, stuffed them into his pockets, and ambled away from the girl toward home. A car's engine rumbled in the distance.

He broke into a sprint, racing full out to reach the shelter of the tree-lined path on the far side before the approaching car appeared. Headlights flashed on the road ahead, and he pulled up short of the clearing and reversed direction.

A phone illuminated in the darkness and buzzed vibrations in the dirt in front of him. He ran forward, gazed down at the phone, and read the text. "Where are you?"

In hell. He stomped his boot on the device, smashing it to pieces. *Right where she belongs.*

2

Chicago Gold Coast

"Which one should I pack? The red or the black?" Bernadette dangled two sleeveless tops on her fingertips for her husband's inspection.

"The red one," Glen said without raising his eyes from the open book in his hands.

"Really?" She placed the blouses down on the satin comforter at the foot of their bed and began folding the red one. "I was leaning toward the black, and I'd have bet you'd choose that one, too."

"Nope. Definitely go with red," he repeated, his nose in the book.

"You're not even looking, Dr. Foster."

She grinned as his gaze met hers.

"I don't need to, darling," he said. "You know my preference is for you to wear color, especially red. It's vibrant like you. You wear enough black on the job."

"I wore an olive-green blazer during this morning's broadcast," she joked.

"I stand corrected." His crooked smile lit up his

handsome face. Even after six years of marriage, she desired her brilliant man with the same passionate intensity as she had since their first encounter in the studio—one of the rare times she had been tongue-tied beginning an interview.

He plopped the book in his lap and leaned back against the headboard, obviously luxuriating in their king-sized bed. Bernadette sighed as she placed the red shirt in the suitcase. She'd much rather spend a rare, long weekend with her sexy husband than jet off tomorrow for a four-day hen party with her best friends.

Glen wiggled his eyebrows suggestively. "Why don't you come to bed? You can finish up in the morning."

She gave him a melancholy smile. "I'd love to, but I need to finish packing and then go straight to sleep. As it is, I'll only have a few hours rest. I'll wake up at the crack of dawn, so I can stop at the studio on the way to the airport."

Glen hung over the book again absorbed in the thick reference tome in his lap. "Why exactly are you abandoning me this weekend?" he posed absently.

Bernadette rolled her eyes and chuckled. "I've told you a dozen times, Glen. The Belles are partying in Vegas. It's Laci's bachelorette party."

He snorted a laugh. "Really, Bern, isn't that whole Belles of St. Mary's thing a little juvenile?"

Faking a pout, she protested, "Of course not. The four of us have been proud Belles since Marlo came up with the nickname. I can't remember when exactly. We've known each other since kindergarten at St. Mary's Academy. I don't think we've missed a year watching The Bells of St. Mary's at Christmas time."

"Yeah, well. You know my opinion of Christmas and saints…Mary or otherwise."

She steered clear of the topic of his research scientist, steadfast atheism and said, "The trip sounded like a great idea when Tina suggested Las Vegas to Laci for the blowout shindig she insists on having for her bachelorette party. But now I just wish I could stay home with you."

"Tina? I'm surprised that weird husband of hers is letting her out of his sight."

"Don't be mean. Ramon's not weird." She considered a gentler adjective to describe the man and came up empty. Maybe he is weird. "He's gone through a hard time," she said diplomatically. "Personally, I think he's clinically depressed."

"I'm not being mean. I'm stating a fact. Believe what you want, but there's something off with that man. I think he's more disturbed than depressed. But I don't really want to talk about him right now."

Her eyes widened as Glen vaulted out of the bed, folded her in his arms, and kissed her dizzy. In the next instant, he stalked into her walk-in closet, leaving her off-center and woozy. "I'll help you pack, so you can come to bed sooner."

Not a bad idea.

Metal hangers clinked together as he flung blouses and slacks out the closet door.

Bernadette burst out laughing as she snatched the clothes on the fly and then circled her arms around Glen's waist, affecting a wardrobe ceasefire.

He leaned back into her embrace and kissed the side of her neck, sending delicious thrills through her.

"You've convinced me. I'll pack in the morning. Race you."

She scampered across the room and dove onto the bed, Glen on her heels.

Her cell phone chirred and danced vibrations atop the cherry wood bedside table.

"Ignore it," he said.

"I'm sorry I have to answer it."

Silent, Glen lay flat on the bed.

Regretting that she hadn't turned the cellphone off earlier, she reached out her right hand, nabbed the phone off the table, and swung her legs over the side of the bed. She glimpsed over her shoulder and again said, "I'm sorry," before she connected the call.

He rolled over to his side of the bed, picked up his book, and remarked thinly, "You're always sorry, darling." His frosty tone completely eradicated earlier playfulness.

Glancing at the caller ID display, she swiped to answer. "This better be life or death, Benny."

"Death it is," her cameraman responded. "Crime scene on the main stem of the Prairie Path nearest the city. Teenager, female victim. Might be the Strangler again. I'm pulling up in front of your building now."

"I'll be outside in five." She disconnected the call and hopped off the bed.

"Is it life? Or death?" Glen posed sarcastically.

Pocketing the phone, she faced him. "Another young girl was found strangled. I want to be first press member on the scene."

Glen frowned. "I'm sorry. I shouldn't have been flippant."

Bernadette skirted the bed and cupped his face in her hands. "I really am sorry that I can't be with you right now." She kissed him tenderly. "I promise I'll make it up to you," she said.

"I'll remember where we left off." He beamed a smile. "Make sure you wake me when you get home."

She couldn't resist a tiny bit of mild sarcasm of her own. "Thank you for always accepting my sincere apologies."

Humor danced in his eyes as she gave him a quick peck on the lips, grabbed her tote, and raced out of the room.

Outside, Benny sat behind the wheel of the idling, TV station's truck at the curb in front of the building awning. She rushed through the revolving door, bolted toward the truck, yanked open the passenger door, and climbed inside.

Bernadette slammed the door shut as forward acceleration thrust her back into the seat. At 2:00 AM, the deserted city streets afforded a quick trip across town. Fifteen minutes later, they arrived in the general area of the crime Benny had learned about by monitoring police scanner transmissions.

A cyclone of swirling blue lights visible through a thick stand of trees ahead pinpointed their destination. Benny parked behind the coroner's van, and they burst out of the truck simultaneously. Bernadette hung her credentials lanyard around her neck and met Benny at the rear of the vehicle. He hoisted his equipment out of the truck, slammed shut the cargo doors, and trailed Bernadette over lumpy terrain through a gap in the trees.

Specter blue reflections of the squad cars' lights glistened off the thin sheen of perspiration on her arms as she ducked under a plastic ribbon of yellow police tape hung between two trees.

"Benny, please don't record footage until we get the OK from Detective Corello," she cautioned. "He won't let us run anything without CPD sanction."

"You're the boss," Benny replied, his voice upbeat.

Bernadette recognized the powerful figure of a man in the shadows on the edge of a pool of halogen lights. "Joe," she called out to the detective who leaned a shoulder against a tree trunk.

He focused on an area of lower ground off the far side of the path where the ME's team congregated. Shoving upright off the tree, he faced in her direction and then stalked rapidly toward her. As he neared Bernadette, his scowl became glaringly apparent. "Give me a break, Bern," he said. "I want you to leave. You think we strung up the tape for nothing?"

The cop eyed Benny's camera. "No footage, Benny."

"Hello to you, too, Detective Corello," Benny quipped.

Joe snorted.

"Another one?" Bernadette interjected, ignoring Joe's reprimand. She didn't need to elaborate, having trespassed on similar scenes where Joe had headed the dead-end investigation of recent serial murders.

At his somber head nod, she pulled a notebook and pen out of her tote prepared to document any tidbits he'd care to toss her.

"Yeah, another one." He pinched the corners of his eyes with a thumb and forefinger. "And we've got nothing. No witnesses. No prints or DNA. This guy is a phantom."

"Or gal?"

"My money is on a guy. I can't see a woman having enough power. The damage to the victims' windpipes was so extensive that we're talking brute strength. He practically broke all their necks." Joe wagged his head, grimacing. "These murders are personal and filled with insane rage, but I can't find a connection between the victims."

"Have you identified the body yet?"

"Susan Mulligan. She lives a few blocks away on Garden Street. Her boyfriend…" Joe pointed to a boy smoking a cigarette while seated in the gutter beyond the clearing, "…called it in. She was supposed to meet him over there by the pedestrian crossing."

"Is he a suspect?" Bernadette gazed at the kid.

His hands shook as if palsied while he attempted to light another cigarette off the end of the one he was smoking.

"I'm not officially ruling him out yet, but my gut says no. I haven't gotten his whole story. He was shaking so much when we pulled in that I called an ambulance, and then I called his parents. The paramedics cleared him but said he's in shock. I'm waiting for his parents to come hold his hand before we question him any further. He's only seventeen and his girlfriend, Susan Mulligan, was only sixteen. Like the other vics."

"The Sweet Sixteen Strangler strikes again," Bernadette concluded as she stowed her notebook.

"Really, Bern, do you guys have to give lunatic serial killers catchy names? It drives the whole force nuts."

That stung a little since she had come up with the moniker for the murderer who had preyed on five, counting this one, sixteen-year-old girls the past few months. Her boss loved it, and Bernadette had enjoyed a burst of pride when prime time newscasters used the catch phrase in reporting developments. Defensive at Joe's criticism, she shrugged her shoulders. "Have to keep the audience tuning in, Joe. OK to release the name of the victim when we tape the segment?"

"Go ahead. Her family's been informed."

"Anything else you need me to say on camera?" She rested her hand gently on his arm.

The grating sound from the teeth of a zipper running its track caught her attention. Joe trained red-streaked eyes on the backs of the MEs in motion as they hunkered down on the far side of the path, surely encasing Susan Mulligan in a body bag.

Bernadette averted gazing at the proceedings. Tears brimmed at the thought of another wasted young life. Nightmares after viewing the last victim, frozen in death, her body unnaturally hung over the bottom of a playground slide continued to haunt her dreams.

Joe gazed at her. "Just report the usual, Bern." He heaved a sigh and added, "The police are following up on all leads... Give out the hotline number again. I've got nothing, lady. When I do, I'll give you a call."

"Thanks, Joe. Are you done here? Looks like you can use some sleep."

"Soon. You better go get some shut-eye yourself." He chuckled. "Hearing all the plans my bride has for the weekend, you'll need it."

"I'll bet. Laci's been planning this party since the day you proposed."

"Take care of her. I don't buy that 'what happens in Vegas, stays in Vegas' stuff." He grinned, gave her a bear hug, and then sauntered over to the forensics team.

"Let's get set up," she said, smiling at Benny and then surveying the area.

A vaporous fog blanketed patches of

undergrowth, and the thick line of trees on either side arched over the path.

Claustrophobia enveloped her in the gloomy, funereal atmosphere, sending chills through her despite the dense, muggy air. "Not here, Benny. We don't have enough light." She improvised, ready to take flight. "How about back out by our truck?" Already in motion toward the police tape, she said, "We'll button this up for the five thirty opening broadcast."

Benny at her side, she scooted under the yellow tape and proceeded toward the truck.

"Good shot over there, Bernadette," Benny said, pointing at a spot on the empty street.

Positioning her in the middle of the road in front of the coroner's van, he hefted the camera on top of his right shoulder and switched on the spotlight. As he readied the shoot, Bernadette squinted between the trees and detected the advance of the forensics team. If they timed it right, the body would be loaded into the van as they taped.

Benny folded the fingers of his left hand into the shape of a gun, flicked his wrist backward, and then pointed the "barrel" at Bernadette. Go.

"Good morning, Chicago. While we slept, the Sweet Sixteen Strangler claimed the life of another teenage girl, his fifth victim. Susan Mulligan was supposed to meet her boyfriend for a date last night. When she was late, her boyfriend investigated, and to his horror, he discovered her lifeless body along the main stem of the Illinois Prairie Path. The Chicago Homicide Division is tirelessly canvassing the area and pursuing leads. If you have any information that might assist the investigation and hopefully lead to the apprehension of the Sweet Sixteen Strangler, a CPD hotline is available for your use. Please call the hotline or text your return phone number to the numbers listed below on the television screen. You can also contact the department via the CPD website. The police will keep your identity confidential. This is Bernadette O'Neal for Now Chicago. Stay safe, Chicago."

Benny switched off the spotlight.

Bernadette blinked until the spots in her eyes disappeared. She drifted to the truck and relaxed in the passenger seat while Benny stowed his gear in the back.

He bounded to his door, jumped into the driver's seat, and switched on the ignition.

Checking her watch, she said, "Gee, we have to be in the studio in a couple hours."

"You don't have to come in on your day off. I've got everything I need."

"Really? You're the best. Thanks."

"No big deal. You'd do the same for me."

****

Inside her condo, Bernadette tiptoed down the hallway to her bedroom. A sliver of light gleamed under the closed door. Pleasantly surprised, she opened the door and found Glen wide awake and still buried in his book.

"You waited up for me?"

She noticed the closed suitcase on the Persian rug outside her closet. "And you finished my packing?"

"I had a chance to catch up on some reading. And as to your packing, my darling, I may have had an ulterior motive." He cast her a wicked grin.

Sexy beyond belief.

Beaming at him, she asked, "Have I told you lately how much I love you?"

"A man can never hear it enough."

His wide smile and the suggestive glimmer in his eyes held her in thrall. "You're amazing. How did you know what to pack?"

"You'll be away four nights, so I packed enough for eight. I thought the math worked."

She hooted a laugh. "Sounds about right, thank you. I think I'll put all this extra time to good use. Back in a sec."

In the master bathroom Bernadette slipped into silk pajamas and deposited her clothes in the hamper. After washing her face and brushing her teeth, she spritzed on Glen's favorite scent and hurried to join her husband.

As she neared the side of the bed, he lifted the sheet in invitation. She scooted into bed and nestled in his arms.

The phone rang.

"Don't you dare," he whispered in her ear.

"I don't hear anything," she said.

3

New York City

Summer rain pelted the penthouse apartment's floor to ceiling windows. Central Park blurred into an aerial view of hazy globes of lamplight and shrouded, black-green treetops.

"Just what I need," Marlo muttered as she gazed through the windows.

A vivid crack of incandescent lightening flashed followed by a crescendo of thunder.

Tapping the flight number on her computer keyboard, she hit Go.

She slouched in her chair waiting for the status to appear on her screen, the blue bar on the address line inching from left to right like a barometer of her mounting despair. On time.

"Yeah, right," she grumbled. *They'll wait until I get to the airport, and then they'll post the delay in maddening little increments.*

Her two designer suitcases and matching carry-on stood on the Brazilian cherry wood floor next to the massive mahogany doors that entered out into her private hallway and elevator. Hugely distracted after she had confirmed her suspicions before dinner, she had packed in a frenzy. Now she had no idea what the suitcases contained.

Marlo left her seat and plopped down onto the hardwood floor, cross-legged, her knees resting against the windowpane.

Fishing the thermometer-like stick out of her hoodie's pocket, she stared at the two pink lines. They hadn't disappeared. If anything, the lines appeared darker. Five identical test sticks displaying two pink stripes in little oval windows lay in the bottom of the bathroom trashcan.

Gazing at her indistinct reflection in the glass, she pressed her hands on her still flat stomach. Tears streamed down her pale cheeks like the raindrops that cascaded down the windows, rivers of tiny diamonds.

She swiped away tears and twisted her trademark blue-black, waist-length hair into a knot. Snapping a scrunchy off her wrist, she fastened a messy bun on the top of her head.

Hollow and aching, she had never missed her mother more. Two years had passed since her mom had succumbed to breast cancer, leaving her only child alone. Her non-existent father had abandoned her mother before Marlo was born.

"I'm sorry, Mama," she whispered. "I just can't have a baby now. Don't hate me for what I have to do."

Her mom had raised Marlo Catholic, instilling her values in her daughter with unwavering conviction. Abortion was murder. How many times had she heard that definition from her mother's lips at the kitchen table? Repeatedly, her mother had assured her that no matter what the circumstances, if Marlo ever became pregnant out of wedlock, despite the taboo of premarital sex, she should turn to her mother for help.

But you couldn't give me the kind of help I need. Am I selfish?

Maybe, but recently her wildest dreams had seemingly come true. All the years of rejection had ended. Now she could pick and choose which offers to accept. Marlo Waters counted among the most sought-after fashion models in the world.

Supermodels are clothes hangers, not fat baby factories.

In three weeks, she intended to travel to Milan for fashion week and then jet to Paris. She couldn't afford to sacrifice her figure to pregnancy and didn't have room in her life for a baby.

Unfolding her cramped, long legs from the lotus position, she rose and stalked to her computer, tossing the early pregnancy test down on the desktop. She googled abortion clinics in New York City, propped her left elbow on the desk, and slumped toward the monitor, her chin cupped in her left hand.

Two million search results.

Deciding to call her gynecologist for a referral in the morning before boarding her flight, she checked the digital time display on her computer screen. She was surprised to find that it already was morning per the readout: 1:13 AM.

Her frenetic pregnancy test taking had frittered away the entire evening.

The flight departed at 6:00 AM, so she needed to be at check-in by four thirty. Allowing time for a shower, makeup application and dressing, plus the half hour travel time to the airport, about an hour and a half remained for sleep—if she could nod off the minute her head hit the pillow.

Sighing, she checked her flight again and set up a text notification for updates on departure and gate changes.

The latch on her front door clicked, and she jumped in her seat. Training her eyes on the opening door, she perched on the edge of her chair, her pulse racing.

Irritation replaced fright when Leo barged into the foyer, his briefcase slung over his shoulder.

His eyes widened as his gaze lit on her, and he gave a start, nearly slamming his hand in the door on its backswing. "What are you doing up?" He dropped his briefcase on the floor. "You shouldn't scare me like that."

His accusing tone infuriated her. "Excuse me. This is my home, remember?"

She slid the pregnancy test off the desk, slipped it into her pocket, and stood facing him. "What are you doing here in the middle of the night? Especially since you thought I was asleep."

Having provided him a key to her apartment expressly for emergencies, she considered how she might ask him to return it and still remain friends. She couldn't permit him to waltz into her home uninvited.

"I have smashing news, and I thought I'd surprise you when you woke. I planned to tag along in the limo and review things with you on the ride to the airport. Figured I'd stretch out on the couch until you got up." He pecked a kiss on her crown. "Why aren't you slumbering instead of at the computer so late, luv?"

His fake British accent and odd word choice grated on her nerves. *Who says slumbering? Really…he's Leo Weinstein from Brooklyn not David Beckham.*

"You look so tired. Are you up to snuff?" Knitting

his brow, he tipped a finger under her chin and scrutinized her face, concern evident in his mellow brown eyes.

"I'm fine, just exhausted. It's been a pretty hectic month." She rubbed her drooping eyelids.

He pecked a soft kiss on her cheek. "My poor, dear heart. I know how hard you work."

Leo genuinely cared about her. Since their first meeting at the restaurant where they worked, they had forged a solid bond. She was a first-time waitress, scared to death after moving from Chicago to New York City; he was a busboy after dropping out of Columbia at the end of his freshman year. They were a team: the photographer and the model, aspiring to succeed in the international fashion business. And they had exceeded their own lofty expectations.

If it weren't for Leo, she would still work at the restaurant, and vice versa. Instead, their fateful collaboration had launched two skyrocketing careers. Leo had created Marlo's first professional portfolio, which she had nervously presented during an agentless interview for a start-up sports magazine. The owner not only had hired her as their first cover model but had also insisted on hiring her portfolio photographer as well. Six years ago, Leo did the entire photo shoot for the landmark edition of *Sports Unlimited* that had consistently edged out similar competitors every year since. Overnight, the duo was in demand.

"Why don't you go lie down for a while? I'll wake you in a couple hours." He stretched out on the beige leather sectional, propping his feet with a jarring thud on the fragile and ridiculously expensive glass-topped, coffee table.

"No use," she replied, narrowing her eyes and surveying the table.

Relieved when she didn't detect a chip, or worse yet, a crack, she continued, "I don't have a couple of hours, and I'll never fall asleep now. I'll doze on the plane."

"Well, good luck with that. You think Bernadette, the inquisitor, will give you a moment's peace? The reporter in her will want to know the who-what-where of your life. And goody two-shoes, Tina, will bend your ear, singing the praises of her deadbeat husband, trying to convince herself more than you that she really is happy with him."

Leo detested the Belles. Her mom had thought that he was jealous of anyone usurping his top spot on Marlo's list of friends.

"And don't get me started on Laci," he droned. "Tell me again—where does she get all the money she runs through like water? Poor Joe, how will he support her life style on a cop's salary?" He wagged his head and reflected light gleamed off his bald, smooth-shaven pate.

"Are you done tearing my friends apart?"

Drifting toward the windows, she observed the receding storm. The downpour reduced to lazy dribbles, streaking the outside of the glass. She stood massaging her stiff neck.

"Honestly, Marlo, I don't think you see them for who they truly are."

"They're my lifelong friends, Leo. That's all I need to know. Sure, they have faults. Don't we all?" Absently, she pressed a hand over her lower abdomen. *I've set the morality bar pretty low myself.* "I love them in spite of their failings, just like they ignore mine…and love me."

"You, luv, have no bloody faults." He hopped off the sectional, swaggered jauntily toward her, and wrapped his arms around her.

Listless, she grumbled, "Knock off the phony accent, Leo. I'm not in the mood."

"I don't want to argue with you," he retorted, his Brooklyn accent resurrected. "Are you mad at me for something?"

"Sorry. You didn't do anything. I'm just out of sorts," she mumbled, peering up at him. His gaze was tender. For those few seconds, Marlo's decision to secretly abort their baby warred with her fondness for him.

"How about I pour us a glass of wine?" he tossed out over his shoulder, in motion toward the kitchen. "We can go over the paperwork I brought now, and then I'll leave you alone."

Marlo collapsed on the couch, prickly with self-recrimination. *I can't tell him the real reason I'm so argumentative. He never needs to know. He doesn't want a baby any more than I do.*

"I love this wine. Where did you get it? I've searched for this vintage in all the wine shops on Fifth Avenue ever since we got back from Argentina." He brought over an open bottle and placed two goblets on the coffee table. After half filling both glasses, he handed one to her.

"It found me." She set the goblet down on the coffee table. "Yesterday I found a case at my front door when I returned from the designer fitting."

"Lucky you. This is ambrosia." He took a seat next to her on the sofa and swilled ruby liquid around the bowl of the goblet.

"Take a few bottles. I called Patricia to thank her, and she invited us to stay with her the next time we're on location there. I told her we might take her up on the offer next summer."

"Can you believe it, babe? Look at us, hobnobbing with winery owners. What a hoot. Life is good, and it's about to get much, much better." Setting his glass down on the coffee table, he left his seat and retrieved his briefcase.

"How could it possibly get any better?" She sat erect, keenly following his movements.

Leo ceremoniously opened his briefcase, rummaged his hand inside, and then produced a clipped stack of papers with a flourish.

"We sold it. They loved the pilot."

"No way. Are you kidding me?" Marlo jumped up and pirouetted around the living room.

"Take The Money and Runway is a go." He grinned from ear to ear. "You'll be the most famous model on TV. And I get my chance to produce. Is this unreal or what?"

She smooched his cheek and then flung her arms around him. "You are the best! Thank you, thank you, thank you," she sang.

Beaming at her, he rattled off further details, "They bought the entire fourteen episodes with an option for fourteen more if the ratings for the first season are where they want them." Pausing, he took a swig of wine. Smacking his lips, he added, "And…the best part. No cable for us, babe. Major network *and* primetime all the way."

"Wow. We should be celebrating at the most expensive restaurant in New York."

"We will as soon as you get back from Las Vegas."

"I wish I didn't have to go."

"Then don't go."

"I can't get out of it. Laci would never forgive me. She's poured a fortune into this weekend."

"I don't understand. Don't the bridesmaids throw the bachelorette party?"

"Usually. But Laci has dreamed of this for years, and she wants to control every detail. First class all the way. Bernadette and I have repeatedly pressed her to let us chip in. No way could Tina afford to do that. So far, Laci hasn't budged on the issue. It'll be one extravagant party. I can't even begin to imagine how lavish the wedding will be."

"Not to risk another argument, but how can Laci afford burning money like this? Her job couldn't possibly pay enough for four first-class airfares. And the price of four suites at the most opulent hotel in the country is astronomical. Don't get me started on her designer clothes."

"I've never asked her about money. Her dad is a doctor, and she's his only child. After her parents' divorce he tried to buy Laci's love. I guess he's still trying. Anyway. It doesn't matter. I have to go whether I want to or not."

Marlo chatted with Leo about the new show for a half hour. Thrilled at this game-changer opportunity, she had the second-wind energy to read through the paperwork twice. Invigorated, she showered and dressed, her spirits soaring. When she exited her bedroom ready to leave, Leo was fast asleep on the couch, hugging the contract to his chest.

Gazing at him tenderly, her heart swelled and tears brimmed. Shaking off the sensation, she reminded herself what was at stake. The hormones raging in her bloodstream had to be responsible for her weepiness. *I need to deal with this and...*

She rejected the line of thought, determined to ignore reality the next few days. After Vegas, she'd handle her predicament, put it behind her, and return to normal. A thrilling future lay ahead.

Treading lightly, she advanced to the door, eased it open, and consecutively deposited her bags out in the hallway before leaving the apartment.

Outside, the limo driver raced around the car to open the door for her. While he loaded her luggage, she fished her phone out of her purse, intending to call Laci to advise her that she was on her way. But remembering the time difference, she changed her mind and decided to delay calling until at the gate.

Knowing Laci, she was probably already at the airport waiting for Bernadette and Tina, even though it was only 3:00 AM there.

Lazing in the leather seat, she grinned as the driver steered the car away from the curb. She missed the Belles, and she'd make the most of their reunion. Too much time had passed since they were all together.

4

The alarm blared, rousting Bernadette out of a delicious, deep sleep. Groggy and bleary-eyed, she silenced the buzzer, rose out of bed robotically, and stumbled into the bathroom.

"Do you want me to drive you to the airport?" Glen called out.

"Thanks, honey, but you can go back to sleep. I reserved a car. We're all meeting at O'Hare."

After a quick shower, she banded her shoulder-length hair in a ponytail and applied minimal makeup. By the time she finished dressing, Glen was snoring a racket, so she kissed his cheek softly and rolled her suitcase out into the hall.

She exited her building and discovered that the limo hadn't yet arrived. Pacing on the sidewalk, she scanned the thin stream of traffic approaching along Lake Shore Drive, her cell phone in hand. Glancing at the phone to check the time, she noticed the voicemail indicator. Smiling at the memory of the reason she had declined answering the call last night, she tapped the voicemail icon and listened to the message, expecting to hear one of the Belles' voices.

Surprised when her boss's baritone sounded instead, her interest was piqued.

"Hey, Bern, Chuck Barton. Great work on the Strangler segment. Benny has it ready to run in the morning. I know you're off for the next few days, but something came across my desk that's perfect for you. A priest claims that the world needs to prepare to hear God speak. He's involved with supposed visionaries in Valselo, a speck of a village near the Adriatic Sea. I know you're probably thinking, why me? Maybe you know the priest? His name is Father Mark McKenzie, and he's the pastor at your old Catholic school. Church of St Mary. No rush. Let me know if you want to follow up on this. Have fun."

Hmm. No. The name doesn't sound familiar. But Tina has to know him since she teaches there. Poor thing works for a kook.

A pang of guilt stabbed Bernadette at her unflattering description of a priest. She had drifted away from practicing her religion and couldn't remember the last time she had entered any church. Had Glen's atheism influenced her? *Probably those devout Muslims who killed my father killed my opinion of organized religion more than Glen ever could.*

Regardless, she still believed in God and the notion that He planned to "speak" intrigued her as a journalist and a former Catholic. The limousine braked at the curb in front of her and she jumped into the car. While the driver handled her bag, she tapped contacts, selected Tina's number, and connected the call.

****

Tina wielded a spatula, stirring the scrambled eggs, diced green peppers, and chorizo mixture that cooked in two large skillets on the stove. Humming softly, she gave a start when her cell phone rang. Dumping the spatula on the stovetop, she dove for the bleating phone that shimmied vibrations on the countertop, intent on silencing the strident tones.

She checked the caller ID and connected the call, whispering, "Hold on a sec." With two rapid flicks of her wrist, she lowered the gas on the burners and then bustled into the bathroom, gently closing the door behind her. "Hey, Bernie," she said in a near whisper. "I'm so excited I'm tingly."

Bernadette chuckled. "You've got to get out more, sweetie."

Grinning at her reflection in the mirror, Tina closed the toilet lid and sat down on the commode. "We're going to have so much fun. I can't wait."

"Me, too," Bernie agreed. "Where are you? You sound like you're in a cave."

"In the bathroom."

"Oops. Call me back when you're done."

Tina giggled. "I'm not using it. What's up?"

"Why are you whispering?"

"I don't want to wake Ramon until I finish making his breakfast." She popped up and placed a hand on the doorknob. "I better get back to the stove before I burn his eggs and make him mad. Why are you calling? You're still going, aren't you?"

"Yep. I'm already in the car. I hate that you're such

a slave to your husband, by the way."

"I know. I know." She sighed. "See you at the airport?"

"Sure. I'm glad I left early. The Edens is a nightmare. Quick question? Do you know Father Mark McKenzie?"

"Of course. He's our pastor. Why?"

"My boss wants me to investigate his recent announcement that God is going to speak to the world. Is this guy all right in the head?"

Tina widened her eyes. "Gosh, Bernie. He's brilliant. I don't think I've ever met such a truly holy man. What's this all about?"

"I don't know yet, but thanks for the feedback. We'll talk more when I see you, OK?"

"You bet. See you at the gate."

"Uh-uh. After you're through security, go to the VIP lounge. I'll clear all the Belles to meet there."

Delighted anticipation coursed through her. "Oh, that's wonderful. I'll see you later."

Smiling, she disconnected the phone and opened the bathroom door. Zipping out into the hall, she collided with her husband.

"Ouch," he complained. "Watch where you're going." Scowling, he rubbed his arm.

Tina's stomach sank at Ramon's frown and unappealing appearance. He wore loose, tie-string, plaid pajama bottoms slung low on his hips. His belly bulged under a faded, navy blue and orange Chicago Bears T-shirt. His straight, black hair badly needed a trim, and his breath was as sour as the expression on his face. He trained dull brown eyes on her, effectively deflating her joyful mood. Ramon had changed dramatically from the handsome, romantic Latin lover who had stolen her heart ten years ago. She couldn't remember the last time he had actually smiled.

Swallowing to clear the lump in her throat, she touched his arm tenderly. "I'm so sorry. Do you need ice for that?"

"No," he grumbled, lumbering toward the kitchen. "Who was on the phone?"

"Bernadette. She's on her way to the airport," she replied hurrying to the stove.

A chair scraped behind her, and she winced at the heavy thud that sounded. Evidently, Ramon had plopped down into his seat.

Wrapping a potholder around a skillet handle, she carried one pan to the table and ladled spicy, butter-scented eggs onto his plate. Her mouth watered. But she resisted spooning out another plate of eggs, determined to continue her so-far, vain attempt to starve off the ten pounds she had gained since high school before donning a bathing suit in Las Vegas.

He forked up a mouthful of eggs and groused, "I can't believe you're still going on this stupid trip. How can you leave me like this?"

The walls of the tiny studio apartment closed in on her, and she shut her eyes, praying for patience.

"It's only for a few days," she said evenly as she toted the skillet back to the stove.

Reaching inside a cabinet, she took out four storage containers and filled each equally with eggs.

Tina opened the refrigerator door and stacked the containers on the middle shelf. "I made your breakfasts in advance. See, here, amor?" She opened the freezer compartment and waited for her husband to glance in her direction. Gazing into his upturned eyes, she faked a smile and ignored his deadpan expression. "I froze all your dinners, too. All you have to do is defrost them and heat them in the microwave."

Ramon dropped his gaze and wagged his head. "I need you here with me. I'm no good without you. You know that, Tina. I've gotten so much better with you home since the school year ended. I wouldn't leave if you needed me."

Her gut twisted with frustration at his endless moaning and refusal to act like a grown man. No matter how many times she had coddled him, encouraged him, and strained to devise a strategy that he'd embrace to forget past struggles and just move on, she had made no progress. Since he had forsaken his teaching job, she supposed he wouldn't allow her to enjoy her teaching career, either.

Taking a seat at the table opposite him, she placed her elbows on the tabletop and propped her chin on her hands. "I think you should make an appointment with Janice Morgan at Chicago Crest while I'm gone. She's probably there every day during summer school hours."

He narrowed his eyes. "Why in the world would I want to do that?"

"I think what you really need to do is to accept her offer of reinstatement and go back to teaching in the fall. You hate working at my brother's theatre. You have to quit. It's time to forget the whole nightmare."

Ramon hung his head in his hands.

The kitchen clock ticked in the silence. Itching to flee, take a break, and have some carefree fun for a change, Tina eyed her suitcase on the mustard-colored, shag carpet near the door.

He dropped his hands and leveled his gaze at her. The anguish on his face aged him ten years. Huffing out a sigh, he said, "Don't you think I *want* to pretend none of this happened? But I can't. How can I go back to teaching at Chicago Crest High or anywhere else? The molestation accusation will always haunt me."

"The accusation was false, Ramon. She admitted she was lying and Janice offered you full reinstatement with tenure. Nothing did happen to you in retrospect. You don't have to pretend anything. I don't know what to say to get through to you anymore."

"I won't go back there. I'll be a target for the rest of my life."

"Then apply to some other school. I can recommend you at St. Mary's. They'd hire you in a minute if a spot opens up."

"My good name has been tainted."

"Then change our name from Hernandez to Castillo. We can use my maiden name. Ramon, you can't let a malicious prank paralyze you."

Tears welled in his eyes in response.

The encompassing heartsickness of her lackluster life with Ramon threatened to swamp her. *For better, for worse. For richer, for poorer. In sickness and in health.*

She had thought she had weathered the worst. And she had bitterly swallowed "the poorer" without complaint, although she still mourned the loss of their house to foreclosure and forced herself on a daily basis to accept living in their cramped, rented apartment smothered by Ramon's oppressive neediness. If she continued to think of Ramon's state as sickness, maybe she could remain true to her wedding vows— somehow find a way toward "better."

"I don't want to move out of state, but if that's what it takes for you to be hopeful again, I'm willing to do that," she said.

Hanging his head in his hands again, he mumbled, "No, no."

Powerless to offer other alternatives, she sagged in her seat and counted the minutes until she could leave for the airport. She needed reprieve from constantly exhibiting false optimism to counterbalance his self-pity. Antsy, she shoved her chair back from the table and stood, staring at the crown of his head. "We've been over this a thousand times, amor," she said softly. "Maybe it will be good for you to have some quiet time this weekend to think about your plans for the future."

He groaned and then begged, "Please, stay. I don't want to be alone."

Convinced that it was about time he acted like an adult, she responded breezily, "I'll be a phone call away if you want to talk. You can go over to Mamá and Papá's house every day if you want company. Or even Felipe's house if you aren't sick of seeing him at work. Your family isn't that far away in Bloomington."

"We can't afford the gas."

Exasperated, she rolled her eyes and conceded, "All right, so stay local. The point is you aren't alone, and you can have all the company you want."

"Your family can't stand me. They think I'm a pervert."

No, they think you're breaking my heart. "They know you're not a pervert. They never believed the accusations, and just like me, they weren't the least surprised when she recanted." Tina drifted over to the stove, picked up the skillets, and deposited them in the sink. Twisting the metal stopper closed, she turned on the faucet and spritzed some detergent into the pans.

As the basin filled, she caught her reflection in the window over the sink framed by the cheerful, yellow curtains Mamá had sewn to brighten her new home. Worry lines marred her smooth, olive skin, but overall, she was pleased with the way she looked. She had carefully applied makeup that morning, having time to spare after rising before dawn. Her excitement about the trip had precluded sleep, and she didn't sleep much any night due to Ramon's constant banging around when he returned from work.

He, however, didn't seem to have any trouble sleeping, evidenced by the snoring racket he made moments after his jostling plummet into bed every night.

Ah, well. I'll sleep like a baby tonight beneath zillion thread count sheets in my luxurious bed in the amazing Decadence Hotel.

The smell of soap bubbles and a waft of humidity from the hot dishwater ended her daydreaming. She plunged her hands into the suds and vigorously cleaned the pans. Her cell phone rang and she sprang for it, dripping water on the floor. She swiped a hand on the dishtowel hanging on the oven door handle and then connected the call. "Hey, Laci. Are you on your way already?" she asked, eyeing Ramon slumped at the table.

"No, that's why I'm calling, Teen. Joe was on a case all night, and he just left his apartment to pick me up. I'm only half packed. Do you think Ramon would drive you the airport?"

"Hmmm, I don't know, Lace."

Tina's stomach clenched as her spirits nosedived. Escaping the house solo was challenging enough. Parlaying a ride with her dejected husband would constitute a diplomatic miracle.

"I was counting on you," Tina reminded her.

"I know. I'm so, so sorry. I just don't think I can pull off swinging by your house and still make the flight."

Maybe I can catch Bernadette and hitch a ride in her limo. No matter what, I'm getting out of here.

"Don't worry. I'll see you there. Bernadette said to meet in the V.I.P. lounge."

"Awesome. Thanks, Teen. I don't know what I'd do if we all weren't together this weekend."

Ending the call, Tina searched contacts and selected Bern's cell.

Ramon remained silent and unmoving in his seat.

She wondered if he had fallen asleep and hoped he had. But since he wasn't snoring, she doubted it. When Bernadette answered she blurted out, "Bern, is there any way you could ask your driver to head here and take me to the airport with you?"

"Uh...let me see," she replied.

Muffled conversation sounded, and Tina tapped her foot, praying that a solution was at hand.

"Yep," Bernadette said. "Did Laci stand you up?"

"She's running late, and so is Joe. She said he was out all night."

"I know. I was there, too. We're on our way. Figure twenty minutes or so."

Smiling, Tina responded, "Thank you so much."

Satisfied, she returned to the sink and finished washing the pans. "Ramon, I'm going to use the washroom before I leave, OK?"

No answer.

She ambled down the hall toward the bathroom. When she emerged, Ramon stood in the hallway.

He furrowed his brows and barked, "You're still leaving? After I begged you to stay?"

"Please…"

His hand shot out, and he grasped her upper arm. Searing pain stole her breath, and anger at the affront roared through her. "You're hurting me. Let me go!" She jerked her arm away and dislodged his hand. Panting, she stared at his face.

His jaw slackened, and the aggression seemed to seep out of him like a deflating balloon. He flung his arms around her and clasped her to his chest, plastering her mouth against his shoulder. "I'm sorry. I'm sorry," he chanted, his voice quivering. "I love you so much. You're my world. We've never been apart."

Was it wrong to long for a bit of freedom? Her throat clogged as a myriad of emotions cascaded through her. *Dear God, forgive me. I just need a break.*

"You're my rock. I love you," he said leaning heavily against her.

"I love you, too," she whispered, gently disengaging from the cloying embrace. Smiling, she touched his cheek and gazed deeply into his eyes. "You're not being fair, Ramon. Laci is counting on me to be there at this special time in her life. I haven't been this excited about a bachelorette party since the Belles hosted one for me before I married you." Hoping fond memories might coax out his smile; she pursed her lips when he grimaced instead.

"That was just for an evening, not four days out of town."

"I promise that when I come back from the trip, we'll do something fun. Whatever you want."

"Oh, all right," he huffed. "I guess I can't change your mind."

Absolutely not. "The time will fly. You'll see."

He shuffled past her toward the kitchen table.

"I'll sit with you while you finish breakfast," she offered, tailing him. "And I'll wash the dishes before I leave."

5

Joe parked the cruiser in Laci's driveway and hung over the steering wheel, drained and exhausted to the marrow. Chills coursed through him as he remembered the parents' bottomless grief with heartrending clarity after another incomprehensible murder of a child. His frustration with the unsolved case and loathing of the serial killer churned a fire in his gut and had his blood roaring through his veins.

After he dropped Laci at O'Hare, he intended to work out with free weights like a madman to sweat the dispiriting impotence that haunted him straight out of his pores.

Achy and depressed, he left the car and climbed in slow motion the slate steps leading to the front door of his fiancée's brick townhouse. Testing the brass doorknob, he huffed an aggravated grunt when it turned and the door unlatched.

"Lace!" he hollered as he trudged inside, his voice echoing in the two-story hallway. "How many times do I have to tell you to lock the door?"

Laci appeared on the second-floor landing above

him, fresh-faced and grinning. "I knew you were coming, so I left it open," she said offhandedly.

He froze in his tracks and gaped up at her, more overpowered than usual by the mere sight of her.

"Come on up here and give me a hug," she invited.

Clad in white capri pants and a feminine, rose-colored blouse, she had to be the most beautiful woman in the world. His heart skipped a beat at her warm smile which blanked out his irritation with her for trusting her fellow man too much to lock them out of her house. Bounding upstairs, two steps at a time, he nearly plunged back down the staircase as her two Maltese pups scampered figure eights around his feet.

Gaze downturned, he lifted a boot at a time to avoid crushing the wriggly, fur snowballs and hooked an arm around Laci's waist. She sighed and melded her warm body against his. Her musky perfume and the brush of silky hair beneath his chin flooded his senses with familiar euphoria. With Laci in his arms, how could he be anything but happy?

The dogs tag-teamed, batting against their ankles, and she acknowledged them laughing. "Belle, Mary, give it a rest. Go lie down," she commanded.

Obeying their mistress, the puppies tottered away, wiggling hindquarters and clicking nails on the hardwood flooring.

Laci turned her attention to him, widening her moss-green eyes, and giving him a welcome kiss.

Overwhelmed with love for her, he couldn't breathe, didn't need to. Laci was all the air that he had ever needed.

She beamed him a smile and said, "Good morning, Joe."

"Great   morning."   He   smiled   at   that

understatement. Waiting until their wedding night required a will of iron.

Smiling, she slipped out of his grasp and then clasped his hand. "Come talk to me while I finish packing."

He nodded in response. The woman undid him and had cast the same brain-scrambling spell over him since they were kids in school together. She was the radiant, blonde beauty, and leader of the pack of the popular Belles of St. Mary's. Sweet and innocent, she had trained worshipful, green eyes on him at the freshman dance, and from that moment on, neither one had looked at another member of the opposite sex with any interest. He still couldn't believe that the girl of his dreams, having morphed into the woman of his dreams, wanted him as much as he wanted her.

Tethered to her hand, he trailed her down the hall. At the threshold to her room, she stumbled and nearly missed trampling the dogs that lay like a white Persian rug in front of the door. "Ow," she grumbled, standing on one leg and rubbing her foot.

"We have to train these two to sleep downstairs by the time we're married," he said. "They drive me nuts."

She stooped and dealt out loving strokes to the pair. "Don't listen to grumpy old daddy. He really loves his girls."

"Yeah, right," he remarked, rolling his eyes. "I'm more of a retriever or setter man myself."

He stepped over the dogs and entered her room. "What's all this?" he asked, incredulous at the heap of clothes covering every square inch of the bedcovers.

"The things I'm bringing with me this weekend," she replied with a cheery lilt in her voice. "Just shove some of them aside."

Joe noticed the sales tags attached to just about every item. He picked up a tank top and read the tag. "Wow, Lace, you spent a hundred and six dollars for this?"

"Well, it's from Switzerland..." She scurried over to him and snatched the top out of his hand. "It's silk and cotton." She flew into action gathering the clothes.

"Hold on," he said, placing his hand on her arm.

Confused when he detected her trembling beneath his touch, he scrutinized her face. The guilty expression in her eyes confirmed his suspicions that the rest of the prices for all that new stuff would stagger him, too.

"Holy cow," he said reading the tags in succession.

Five or six of those Swiss shirts, two fifty for just one pair of jeans, another two hundred for a bathing suit with as much material as underwear...

He paused and faced her, dangling a sequined dress by the tag that he clutched in his now sweaty palm. "A thousand bucks for one dress?" he bellowed.

A flurry of nail clicks sounded as the dogs raced under the bed.

"Oh, stop," she scolded, whipping the dress out of his grasp. She smoothed it lovingly on the bed. "I needed new things for this weekend. Besides, everything is so practical. I can use them all on our honeymoon, too."

"Honeymoon? I thought we were driving to my brother's cabin in Wisconsin. You don't need to wear silk to hike around in the woods."

With a shrug of her shoulders, she beamed him a dazzling smile. "Well...maybe I'll surprise you with the wedding gift I have planned for you."

"What?"

Her eyes danced, and she clapped her hands, delighted. "I found an all-inclusive deal in the Bahamas."

"When were you planning to explode this bombshell? Are you out of your mind?"

"I wanted to surprise you." She pouted. "I'm an accountant. I know how to manage money."

He sat on the edge of her bed in a state of disbelief, wobbling his hands on his knees.

She folded and packed the clothes in the suitcase on the floor. Her graceful movements blurred as all he could see were mounting dollar signs.

Apparently satisfied with the lack of noise in the room, the dogs reemerged from beneath the rose-colored bed skirt. Taking up their posts at the door, they yawned widely and then nodded off.

He hadn't asked how much she had blown on the pedigreed Belle and Mary a couple months ago.

Now he had to know. "How much did they set you back?" Frowning, he flicked his gaze at the fur-balls.

"What?" Her look darted, following his gaze. "Oh. Only two thousand each. The breeder gave me a thousand off since I bought two from the same litter. But, Joe. They're show dogs."

His stomach sank as the numbers multiplied in his head. He'd never support her like this no matter how many shifts he pulled. And there weren't enough rungs on the force's pay-scale ladder to climb either, no matter how stellar his performance on the job.

Stellar? I have a high-profile serial killer to apprehend with no leads that's spinning me in circles. Have I been so buried in the case that I haven't paid attention to Laci? Is she compensating with spending sprees?

"Are you running up all this...?" He waved his hand in a circle. "On credit cards?"

****

Her chest constricted and her hands trembled as she placed the last folded article of clothing in her suitcase. "Of course not," she replied, her gaze downcast as she breathed deeply to regain her composure. Determined to win him over, she met his look and declared, "I pay my bills in full every month."

He narrowed his eyes and then gazed around the room as if taking inventory.

She held in increasing discomfort and prayed that he wasn't tallying the astronomical cost of her custom furniture and window dressings in his head. "Joe," she said, trying to divert his attention.

He continued his visual inspection and muttered, "What?"

"Joe, look at me."

He swung his face in her direction, and she gave him a winning smile. He didn't smile back at her. Instead, his penetrating gaze spoke of the expert investigator that he was, and she shivered under his scrutiny. But she had planned carefully, and if she could hold her own during the critical conversation that she always knew would come, then she'd be home free. "I have saved my whole life so that we could start our marriage exactly how I dreamed, sweetheart," she said softly. "This is once in a lifetime."

"I've known you for half your life, Lace," he

retorted, the ominous, probing expression on his face unchanging. "You don't make this kind of money, and I don't want to start our marriage in debt. Your house pets cost nearly a month of your take-home salary."

Flustered, she regrouped. "I told you I'm not in debt."

She stooped and zipped her suitcase, seeking relief from the unnerving heat of interrogation. "Anyway, the dogs were engagement presents," she improvised.

"That's news," he said. "From whom?"

"Um." She stood erect in front of him. "Daddy."

"Daddy?" His eyes narrowed to slits. "Since when are you talking to Daddy? He knows we're getting married?"

"No."

He ran a hand through his thick, brown hair. His blue eyes darkened, and he cast an unblinking gaze at her that bored into her soul. "I want the whole truth, Lace. You aren't making a single bit of sense."

She sat next to him on the bed, bumping hips, cozy, to dodge the searchlight of his built-in lie detector.

"Mom made him set up a fund for me as part of the divorce proceedings. She used it for college expenses and then turned the rest over to me for...whatever," she fibbed. As if the evil jerk would give Mom a penny that she hadn't begged for every month.

"Let me get this straight," he insisted, his breath hot on her shoulders. "You're taking money for our dream wedding from the man you refer to as the evil sperm donor? You wouldn't even let me contact him to ask for your hand."

"I know. He doesn't deserve the courtesy, and I

don't even know where he is," she spat out. "But I don't feel guilty at all draining that fund for the wedding. It's the least the louse can do for his only child."

Genuine tears stung the corners of her eyes as Joe's muscular arm circled her back. He rubbed the side of her arm, tender, soothing strokes. She sighed, relieved that she'd apparently convinced him.

Although she was terrified to flirt with having to embellish her tale further, she had to know for sure. "Do you understand now, Joe? Are you OK with this?" she dared.

He huffed a breath. "I guess so. If you are. But don't you want to slow down some? Save a little for our kids' futures?"

She wagged her head. "No. I won't let him near our family, even symbolically."

"All right, then. Whatever makes you happy," he conceded.

Thank You, God, for this. I promise that after the honeymoon, I'll scrimp and save and somehow put every penny back that I've taken. I'll go to confession and clear my conscience, and then I'll set things straight. Joe will never have to know the truth. She sniffled and gave Joe a half-smile. "You make me very happy."

6

Anna's thundering heartbeat jolted her awake. Peering apprehensively into the shadows cast on the walls of the unfamiliar room, she tried to connect to her surroundings. Matt's even breathing in the bed next to her offered little comfort. Instinctively, she twined her fingers around his warm arm, seeking his soothing companionship in her alienated state.

His eyes flickered open. "What is it, darling? Are you all right?" he mumbled.

"Where are we?" she asked, her voice hoarse and tremulous.

He wrapped his arms around her, drawing her close to his chest. "Safe in St. Mary's rectory." He gave her shoulders a comforting squeeze.

"Ah, of course." Her displacement eased, but what lay ahead still fueled her racing pulse.

She gazed at the crib at the foot of the bed. Her Ruža's dear face appeared striped through the bars of the crib. The child slept deeply, her favorite bunny blanket tucked under her chin.

"What time is it?" she whispered.

"Only 1:00 AM. Your body clock is probably still on Croatian time," he responded, his voice a low rumble her ear.

She furrowed her brow. "My what clock?"

He grinned and then softly kissed her forehead. "It's an expression. It means your body thinks it's time to start the day because if you were home in Valselo, you'd got up now."

"I'm so glad the baby's body clock is on Chicago time." She smiled at him. "I'm sorry I woke you." Brushing her fingertips along the side of his face, she added. "Go back to sleep, love. We have a few hours before we need to leave."

Anna shifted within his embrace, but Matt held her tighter and prevented her from turning toward her side of the bed.

"I'm wide awake, Anna. My mind is spinning. I can only imagine what must be racing through your mind. Would you like to talk about anything?"

"I'm so nervous." Resting her head down on his pillow, she faced him and continued the whispered exchange. "How can I be worthy to do Our Lady's will? What if I fail?"

"You know that won't happen. Your faith is too strong," he reassured her. "Our Lady has picked you out of all the people on this planet because she trusts you alone to convey her messages of salvation to the world."

"All the people on this planet..." Anna repeated, shivering despite the warm, summer night. "How do I speak so people understand? I'm not special. I'm just a country pumpkin."

Matt clamped a hand over his mouth, muffling a burst of laugher.

She narrowed her eyes. "What?" she probed.

His eyes dancing, he replied, "I think you mean bumpkin."

"Ugh, see? I can't say anything right," she retorted, shaking her head.

"You are a humble, but very special, woman from a tiny village who has had a personal relationship with the mother of God since you were a kid. Nobody on the planet can say that."

"Elizabeta and Josip can," Anna reminded him.

"True." His eyes gleamed. "But Our Lady chose you. And dear God…me. I still can't believe it. She has total faith in you, and so do I."

"You have no idea how huge this is." She shivered again.

"I think I do. Judging from the stunned expression on Father Mark's face after your meeting with him, I figure we're talking earthshattering. Am I right?"

"Yes."

Father Mark McKenzie had ushered Anna into the St. Mary Faith Center yesterday afternoon, shocked and delighted that one of Our Lady of the Roses' visionaries had made an unannounced, coincidental appearance at his doorstep as he hosted a reunion of Valselo pilgrims.

After the introductions were made, Anna, Matt, and Ruža had joined the festivities. Anna had enjoyed catching up with some of the dear people she had met through Father Mark's frequent trips to the village, leading pilgrim groups. With each conversation, Anna had marveled at Our Lady's wisdom in calling the wide assortment of people to Valselo over the years.

When she had asked for some private time with Father Mark to disclose his role in the forthcoming miraculous events, she had no longer questioned the priest's selection as the Most High's chosen shepherd.

Reverent and awestruck, he had received the parchment and instructions relating to his testimony that Gospa had foretold coming events. After she concluded the meeting, he had asked Jack Dunne to step into his study. Behind closed doors, he had solicited Jack's agreement to finance the rarest pilgrimage that Father Mark planned leading—no questions asked. Our Lady had called Jack to Valselo as part of her master plan several years ago.

And Our Lady had called Matt to Valselo, too. She had chosen Matt for Anna. Stroking the side of Matt's face lovingly, Anna whispered, "I am so blessed to have you."

"The feeling is mutual, my love." He clasped her hand and kissed the palm.

"Father Mark has wonderful friends, doesn't he? Beth and Jack Dunne seem so happy. Katarina told me that when they came on pilgrimage to Valselo they were separated and grieving the loss of their baby. Now look at them. They're expecting another child, and it's clear that they're so much in love."

She gazed again at her precious daughter, her heart overflowing with gratitude for the blessings of a happy marriage and a beautiful child.

"Such generous people, too. We have Jack to thank for all of our first-class arrangements. He's paying for everyone to make the trip to the desert," Matt said rounding his eyes.

"It will cost a fortune."

"Yes. A remarkable man. He considers spending a fortune under the circumstances a privilege and a repayment to Our Lady for the goodness She's brought him. Beth and Jack will follow us to the desert with Father Mark and some of the parishioners after Jack coordinates everyone's arrangements. My mom and dad will travel with their group, too."

"There is so much to organize and to do." Anna sat up in the bed as adrenaline coursed through her.

Matt propped up against the headboard behind her and massaged gentle circles on her back.

"Don't worry about all that. Father Mark and Jack will handle the logistics perfectly. I think that we were all born to do our own parts in this. Heaven decided for us…"

Anna nodded agreement. "I wonder if Father Mark has read the entire parchment yet. I don't think he'll have problems translating. He's fluent in my language."

"He's so astounded by all this that I'll bet he's read the secrets over and over all night long. And I'm sure he's praying around the clock, too." He gazed at her. "Any chance you might tell me exactly what's written in that parchment?"

Anna frowned as her heart skipped a beat. "I can't. I'm not permitted."

Matt gave her a sheepish grin. "That's OK, darling. I thought as much."

Ruža sucked her thumb with a few loud smacks, bringing another smile to Matt's face. "Our little cherub will be up soon. You can use the shower first."

He kissed her cheek, and she grinned at him, now fortified to embark on her critical mission.

****

Anna concluded that O'Hare International Airport in Chicago would intimidate even the most seasoned traveler. Long corridors forked and veered this way and that, filled with people bumping into each other as if they competed in a race. Little motorized carts beeped behind her without warning and made her jump. Gaping at the restaurants and shops lining both sides of the traffic pattern had Anna dizzy.

A huge globe hung overhead between two rows of countries' flags. The noise level was deafening.

Matt toted Ruža and, thankfully, clasped Anna's hand securely. Ruža's wide eyes darted, fascinated by this strange, stimulating place. Matt, apparently unfazed by the chaos, cheerfully pointed out some of his favorite shops and restaurants, stopping when Ruža squealed in delight, noticing a display of stuffed animals. He selected a purple, furry monkey wearing an "I heart Chicago" T-shirt. The baby grasped the stuffed animal greedily in her chubby hands and gifted the saleswoman with a dazzling smile.

"*Hvala vam*," she chirped.

"In English, please, Ruža," Matt instructed.

"Tank you." Shyly, she buried her head in Matt's shoulder.

"You are welcome, princess."

Anna chuckled. "You spoil her."

Matt stopped again at another store, this one filled with exotic chocolates. He bought a box of chocolates and presented it to Anna.

"Oh, you spoil me, too?"

"I can't resist. You have me wrapped around your little finger."

He grinned as Anna gazed at her pinky finger, leaned toward her, and kissed the tip of Anna's nose. "Just like our daughter."

Entering their designated gate area, Anna selected seats near a window that afforded a view of the fuselage and tail fin of their plane.

Ruža pressed her nose against the glass, seemingly mesmerized by the baggage handlers' labors below. With the monkey tucked under her arm, she stared at the conveyer belt moving multi-colored luggage into the belly of the aircraft.

Feigning relaxation, Anna thumbed through a magazine she had selected in one of the shops. Wowed by the fashionable American stars, Anna thought the simple white blouse and a below-the-knees, cotton, navy skirt she wore seemed dowdy.

Four stunning women entered the gate lounge and sat to her right. Absorbed in reading his book, Matt didn't glance up. Good thing. Anna felt every bit the country mouse compared to those beautiful women.

Intrigued, she peered at them over her magazine. *They must be famous.* Three of the women chatted and laughed, cell phones in hand. But one lady, the prettiest of the four and surely a movie star, gazed fixedly at Ruža, her lips pursed.

Maybe she thinks my Ruža will be a pest on the plane. Not my little angel. She will behave.

"Earth to Marlo," one of the women called out, and she turned her attention to her friends. But Anna observed the frequent glances she cast in Ruža's direction, a sad, melancholy expression on her flawless face.

Boarding began as the attendant behind the desk called forward the first-class passengers. Anna gathered her things and Matt scooped Ruža up into his arms, dealing with the child's mild protest by explaining that she would now ride on the big plane.

The four women jumped up, bustled over to the boarding area, and queued in line behind Anna. Seated on the third flight in her life, Anna observed the women taking seats a few rows in front of her.

They obviously celebrated something because they ordered champagne before the plane left the gate and stretched their arms out into the aisle to clink their tiny, flute glasses together. The pretty one who watched her Ruža toasted with her three friends, but never put the flute to her lips. Once airborne, the attendant brought them more champagne and the ladies' laughter and conversations grew increasingly louder. But their merriment was amusing, and none of the other passengers seemed to mind.

Undisturbed by the noise, Ruža slept through most of the flight, curled up in Matt's lap.

Anna leaned her head against Matt's shoulder, her thoughts drifting. She couldn't wait to land and reunite with her friends from her village. Increasingly homesick, Anna intended never to leave Valselo again once she had completed her mission...unless Our Lady bid her otherwise.

The answer to Anna's prayers waited outside the jet bridge after the flight. She beamed a smile at Katarina Lidovic, who waved both arms gleefully as Anna and Matt disembarked at McCarran Airport in Las Vegas.

Anna rushed into Katarina's outstretched arms. "Oh, Katarina, it is so good to see you."

"And you, Anna. I've tingled with excitement the whole time waiting for your plane to come."

Katarina hugged Anna tightly, gazed at Ruža in Matt's embrace, and then opened her arms, her eyes locked on the baby. Matt placed the little girl down on the carpet, and she ran on chubby legs into the welcoming embrace. Katarina lifted her up and twirled her around, cooing.

"*Diijete*, I have missed you," Katarina exclaimed.

Ruža wore a serious expression on her innocent face as she gazed at Matt. "Rina call Ruža little one, Papa. I big girl."

"Yes, you are, sweetheart." Matt chuckled. He scanned the gate area. "Where is Mikhail?"

"He was worried about our luggage. He did not want to leave it on the carousel so long. He will wait for us at baggage."

"A carousel? Can I ride, Papa?"

"It's not like the carousel in your book, sweetheart. It's different. Come. I'll show you." Matt lifted his daughter out of Katarina's arms. "My mother sent her a magic pony carousel book. We read it every night," he informed Katarina.

Ruža's disappointed pout had the adults chuckling.

Anna linked her arm through Katarina's, and they ambled toward the moving walkway. Anna grinned at Ruža's delighted fascination as she and her friend preceded Matt and hopped on the conveyer slidewalk. Following baggage claim signs, the foursome waited outside the tram doors. Anna gazed out the window and watched for the approach of the tram. The monorail track connecting to the terminal gleamed bright white beneath the desert sun.

"Are my sisters with Mikhail?" Anna inquired, eager to see Katarina's daughters whom she regarded as siblings.

An only child after the loss of her parents in the Croatian War, her loving grandmother raised Anna into her early teens. When her grandmother entered eternal life, Anna had been left alone. The villagers treated their orphaned visionary as family. Katarina and Mikhail all but adopted her. Their daughters, Sinka, Nadia, and Maya, were closer to Anna than blood sisters; they were sisters of the soul.

"My girls haven't arrived yet. We all stayed overnight at Maya's condo in New York. The girls are still there. They love the craziness of the city. Mikhail and I could not leave soon enough. Everything is so loud." Katarina covered her ears and shook her head. "They will follow as soon as Colin rearranges his shooting schedule for the soap opera."

"I can't wait to see Maya and Colin again. I miss them."

The tram clattered into the "station," and the double doors in front of Anna swished open. After a short, tilting ride, Anna and her family entered the crowded baggage claim area.

Mikhail Lidovic stood next to a gentleman who held a sign bearing the name, ANNA ROBBINS.

Mikhail caught sight of her and rushed forward to dole out hugs. He gave a hearty shake to Matt's hand and then gazed at Ruža as if she alone held the key to his happiness.

His face lit when she wrapped her arms around his neck and said, "Poppop, Ruža miss you."

Perpetually outnumbered by women at home, Mikhail treated each female as if she were a priceless treasure. Ruža adored the man who exuded nothing but kindness since Anna let him hold her minutes-old newborn. In Mikhail's heart, Ruža was just as much his granddaughter as his precious Emma, Maya's little daughter.

Herding into the baggage claim area that posted their flight, Matt directed the limo driver as each of their bags lumbered along on the conveyor belt. Then they were led to the parking garage where an opulent coach awaited.

The driver provided instructions to watch the television, showed them the cooler filled with beverages, and opened a couple of cabinets loaded with snacks. Jack Dunne had anticipated every need, including a fancy car seat for Ruža that Anna certainly had never seen in a store in her home country.

The drive to their motel on the outskirts of the desert would take about an hour and a half.

Anna tried to relax, but she alone knew what the days ahead would bring.

Katarina and Mikhail chatted quietly as Ruža slept, her chin on her chest.

Matt concentrated on reading messages on his cell phone.

Her treasured loved ones trusted her so much that they didn't question why they needed to follow her across the world to the desert in America. Her heart swelled.

"I have an email from Elizabeta," Matt stated, leaning toward Anna to show her the cell phone's screen. "She and Father Josip have arrived and are waiting at the motel. She's hoping that we will arrive in time for her visit with Our Lady."

****

Twenty folding chairs were arranged in rows, church-like, behind a small table-altar covered with a plastic cloth. A dusty air conditioner poked out of the wall at eye level, sputtering while it spewed out lukewarm air.

Elizabeta, clad in a white blouse and dark skirt, similar to Anna's outfit, sat next to Josip in the first row of chairs. Their heads bowed, rosary beads dangling from their hands, they led the recitation of the rosary.

Elizabeta's husband and children sat in the second row.

Father Josip, the single Valselo visionary who had entered religious life, had no living family members.

A few other Valselo villagers occupied scattered seats.

Anna and her group slipped into the back row and joined in the recitation of the rosary.

Elizabeta rose, stepped forward, and knelt on the linoleum floor in front of the makeshift altar table.

The assembly hushed and knelt on the floor in unison.

Elizabeta's upturned gaze fixated on a spot above the altar. She often nodded her head and smiled for several minutes. Then she covered her face with her hands and sat back on her haunches, immobile and silent.

No one uttered a sound.

Josip hurried forward and helped Elizabeta stand.

"Our Lady came joyful, smiling today," Elizabeta said. "She is happy that we have answered her call and that we are all together in this foreign place. She conveyed this message:

'Dear children! Today I desire to tell you that I love you. I love you with my maternal love, and I invite you to open yourselves completely to me, so that through each one of you, I can convert and save this world which is full of sin and bad things. That is why, my dear little children, you should open yourselves completely to me so that I may carry you always farther toward the marvelous love of God the Creator who reveals Himself to you from day to day. I am with you, and I wish to reveal to you and show you the God who loves you. Thank you for having responded to my call.'"

Anna rose, tiptoed to the front of the room, and joined Elizabeta and Father Josip in the front of the room. She would not leave Elizabeta and Josip's side from that point forward until the Lord had revealed all.

Her friends and fellow visionaries had some idea about the events that would unfold in the barren desert, so different than Valselo's verdant hills and pastures rimmed by the Adriatic Sea. Only Anna knew the details of the coming of the new Easter. The world could and should change forever.

7

Scuffing in flip-flops, the Belles at her side, Bernadette entered the mammoth, jaw-dropping, conch shell doorway marked on top with a shimmering, purple, neon exit sign. She plunged into velvety shadows within the tunnel-like walkway where the walls gleamed pearlescent, and the sound of an artificial, distant ocean echoed. Ahead, brilliant light radiated as if she approached the gates of heaven rather than the pool deck of Decadence Hotel.

Emerging out of the "conch," she blinked as her dilated pupils shrank to pinpoints in the glare. Her eyes adjusted to the bright sunlight as she and her friends strolled behind Laci toward what she had described as their private cabana.

Stunned into silence by the staged excess of the hotel's aquatic paradise, Bernadette focused on her surroundings. Water sounds muted ambient conversations. Rushing, tinkling spray-sputters emanated from waterfalls, fountains, and sprinkler arms misting water that evaporated like smoke in the arid air. At three o'clock in the afternoon, the temperature hovered near one hundred and five degrees. Despite the attempts to saturate the atmosphere with cooling moisture, the sun prevailed. Bernadette's skin felt oven-baked and swollen as if she might erupt like a hot dog on a grill.

Every square inch of the pool deck furniture's arms, legs, and posts were encrusted with seashells. Huge, fabricated shell umbrellas atop shell-barnacled poles shaded the multitude of chaises that lined three gigantic, various shaped pools. Similar shell umbrellas overhung the tables situated on the luminescent deck and upon patches of unnaturally green lawn. Even the composition of the expansive decking imprisoned seemingly millions of tiny shells beneath its surface, like fossils. Surely every beach in the world was denuded of shells due to the construction of Decadence.

An army of servers bustled about toting frothy drinks and quart-sized martinis on trays or hovered on the fringes at the beck and call of sun worshippers. The message seemed clear. No need to lift a finger in this manufactured paradise.

"Do you believe this place?" Tina said, her tone awestruck.

"Uh uh," Bernadette responded. "It's mind-boggling."

Laci halted in front of a tent-like structure, partitioned from neighboring cabanas by silky white material, suggesting a row of mini desert oases. She ushered them inside. Overhead, a paddle fan stirred the arid air. Two cushioned love seats and armchairs were grouped around a glass coffee table laden with plates of fresh-cut fruit, pound cake, and a fondue pot of aromatic chocolate.

"Yum," Laci exclaimed. She twirled a strawberry in the fondue and popped it in her mouth, leaving a track of chocolate drippings on the palm of the hand that she cupped beneath her chin. She closed her eyes and chewed. "Oh...absolutely delicious. Eat, girls."

Laci's command still triggered her cohorts' unquestioning obedience as when they were in high school.

Bernadette, Tina, and Marlo nabbed morsels and sank them into the fondue pot.

Laughing, Bernadette downed a chocolate-sodden square of pound cake, sugary enough to make her molars ache.

"I'm never taking this cover up off," Tina said, rolling her eyes as Laci untied her sarong, revealing her slim silhouette in a white, crocheted lace bikini. "I haven't stopped eating and drinking since we boarded the plane. And you make me feel like a cow, Lace."

"I second that," Bernadette chimed in. "I look like a very pale cow...like the underbelly of a humungous frog compared to all of you." She grinned as her three friends burst out laughing. "With freckles," she added.

"Oh, that's silly." Frowning, Laci stretched out on one of the four thickly cushioned chaises outside the cabana. "You guys are gorgeous. Get your skinny bodies over here and relax."

Marlo untied the sarong she wore at armpit level, draped it on a love seat in the cabana, and sashayed over to the deck chair next to Laci. Marlo wore the daylights out of a black, knit one-piece suit.

"Mar, you look amazing." Laci's strident tone caught Bernadette's attention. "I've never seen a suit like that. If I had, I would have snapped it up in a second. Who's the designer?"

"Um..." Marlo glanced downward as if to refresh her memory. "This one is Ashley Paige."

"Doesn't she design exclusively for celebrities?"

There was that discordant ring in Laci's voice again, which Bernadette interpreted as envy.

"I don't know, honestly. She always outfits the models' *Sports* shoot. I have dresser drawers full of her suits."

"I have three or four, too," Bernadette mentioned. "Glen likes to buy them for me as gifts ever since I had to wear one on air during that Spring break-gone-wild puff piece."

"You girls have all the luck," Laci groused. "Joe is clueless about designer pieces."

Marlo narrowed her eyes and gazed at Tina. "You are seriously overdressed for this heat, sweetie."

"Come on, Tina. Let's not let those two body beautifuls intimidate us," Bernadette coaxed, tugging her cotton tunic over her head and tossing it atop Marlo's sarong. "When we're with those two, no one will notice us, anyway." She kicked off her sandals and scampered the short, sole-scalding distance to a vacant chaise next to Marlo on the end of the row. Sinking into the cushions, she had the disquieting sensation that the chair would swallow her. She cast an anxious glance at Laci. "Memory foam," she said, interpreting her distress.

Bernadette acknowledged the explanation with a nod.

Tina perched on the edge of the chair to Laci's right, stubbornly still swathed in her tropical print muumuu.

Laci squinted at Tina. "You'll roast in that thing."

One of the servers approached at the foot of the

lounge chairs with an antique perfume bottle in his hand. He squeezed the rubber bulb at the end of the hose attached to the perfume chamber, releasing a lavender-scented water spray over Bernadette's freckled legs.

"Don't worry about the heat, ladies," he chirped. "I'll mist you every ten minutes."

Marlo giggled as he baptized her with the mist and then zipped down the line christening Laci and Tina before retreating to a spot a discreet distance away from the cabana. Laci playfully tugged on the sleeve of Tina's dress and stretched out the elastic at the neckline, down over her shoulder to the elbow.

A chorus of gasps sounded as Tina yanked the material back up, concealing the angry, purplish ring around her bicep.

"What is that?" Laci exclaimed as she shot out of the chair and hung over Tina. Hands on her hips, Laci demanded, "Please take off your cover-up, Teen?"

Cowed, Tina wiggled the edge of the dress out from under her rump, pulled it up over her head, and dumped it on the deck. "It's nothing. Just a little bruise."

Glaring at the black-and-blue circle marring Tina's olive skin, Laci's eyes traveled the length of Tina's body. Marlo and Bernadette followed suit.

"Did Ramon do that to you?" Laci probed through clenched teeth.

Tina's gaze landed on each of her friends' faces in succession. "Please quit staring at me. It's nothing. Ramon held onto me a little too hard. That's all."

Laci touched the bruise lightly. "It feels swollen to me," she said. "If Ramon is abusing you, I swear I'll beg Joe to throw him in jail."

Tina swatted away Laci's hand. "Oh, my goodness. He's a total pain, but I'm not afraid of him," Tina spat out.

Laci's gaze softened. "Are you sure, honey? You wouldn't lie to protect him?"

Tina narrowed her eyes to slits. "I'm sure. Don't worry about it, OK?"

"OK, then." Apparently convinced, Laci backtracked and plopped down into her chair.

Bernadette wasn't so easily appeased. Furious with Ramon, her protective instincts flew into overdrive. She sat upright and folded her legs under her lotus style. Leaning forward to gaze past the intervening deck chairs and directly at Tina she said, "How often does he hold onto you a little too hard?"

Tina pursed her lips and glared over the top of her sunglasses at her inquisitor. "Drop it, Bern. I mean it. My husband is a good man at heart."

Breaking the stare, Tina lay back in the chair and stretched out her legs. "I think it's time for that gentleman to re-mist us."

The cabana man instantly reacted to the prompt, setting droplets of water gleaming on their bodies.

Laci declared, "It's also time for a drink. What's your specialty, sir?"

"A fabulous appletini here in the Garden of Eden," he stated, dead serious.

Bernadette snorted, amused. "The poor apple… always accused of being the fruit." She rolled her eyes. "We'd like a round, please. On me," she said on a bead for the cabana where she had left her beach bag.

"A sparkling water for me, please," Marlo tossed out.

Bernadette fished a hand inside the tote for her

credit card and pointedly ignored Laci's protest, "No way. I'm paying for everything this weekend."

Presenting her credit card to the server, who accepted it with one instantaneous swipe of the hand, Bernadette responded, "Nope. All drinks are on me. Period."

"No..." Laci sputtered, screwing up her face in that petulant expression that had broached no opposition from any Belle since the formation of their friendship. "And what's with you, Marlo? Sparkling water?"

"My stomach is queasy all of a sudden. Must be something I ate." Marlo said, seemingly unperturbed by Laci's snit. "I think Bern and I will split everything. Including whatever crazy thing you have cooked up for the party tomorrow night. I can afford it now that I landed the television show."

"I can't get over how awesome that is, Mar," Tina remarked. "You're going to be..."

"What are you all talking about?" Laci stormed. "This is my party, and you're ruining it."

Bernadette automatically assumed her historic role as group diplomat. "We wouldn't think of spoiling your plans, Lace. This is your special weekend, and it's wonderful to share it with you. But—we're your bridesmaids and best friends, and you have to understand that we want to give this party for you, not the other way around."

"I do appreciate that," Laci grumbled. "But you know I've planned this for ages. And I never expected any of you to pay for my fairy-tale bachelorette party."

"I know," Bernadette replied. "But since the day you told us what you arranged, we planned to surprise you by sharing some of the expense. Don't spoil our fun? Please?"

"Come on, Laci," Marlo urged. "Let us do this little thing. You deserve it."

Good one, Mar. Laci can't resist acknowledgement of how deserving she is to be spoiled.

"How can I say no? Thank you." Her tone all sweetness and light, Laci's lovely face lost the disapproving glare and radiated self-love and undisputed entitlement.

The waiter's expedient return with a tray of drinks halted further conversation.

"To my waning single days," Laci proposed.

Throbbing pain jabbed Bernadette's temples. She assumed the reason was the combination of cheap airplane champagne early in the day and hot sun overdose. She placed her glass on the lounge's built-in side table. "I think I'll slow down on the alcohol."

"I'm with you," Marlo said. "All those calories."

"Are you going anorexic on me?" Laci asked in an accusing tone.

"Don't be ridiculous..."

"Well, good," Laci huffed out. "Drink up. We will have fun starting right this minute."

Eyeing Laci over the rim of her glass, Tina took a sip. "I'm drinking, Lace. See?"

8

Father Mark sat stiffly in his chair behind the altar and gazed at the perplexed faces in the congregation as his deacon approached the pulpit for the Gospel reading. Numb and burdened, it seemed that the weight of the world rested squarely on Father Mark's shoulders. In truth, it did.

"Then a voice came from heaven, 'I have glorified it and will glorify it again.' The crowd there heard it and said it was thunder; but others said, 'An angel has spoken to him.' Jesus answered and said, 'This voice did not come for my sake but for yours. Now is the time of judgment on this world...'"

Deacon Mike finished reading the Gospel passage that departed from the prescribed, worldwide liturgy for that day in ordinary time.

Father Mark had insisted upon the use of this particular Gospel passage, John 12:20-33, at all the weekend Masses—surely the reason for the furrowed brows of parishioners who had attempted in vain to follow the reading in their missals.

Reaching under his robe, the pastor turned on his

mic as the deacon occupied the chair next to his. *Guide me, Holy Spirit. I am unworthy to fulfill Your wishes.*

The priest's irrepressible exuberance in preaching dampened under the mantle of responsibility he now bore. He had answered God's call to the religious life eagerly as a youth, never once doubting his decision. As a young cleric, he had been assigned to the Church of St. Mary—fitting because of his lifelong devotion to the Blessed Virgin, the intercessor to the throne of the Most High. Rotating to various positions in churches within the Chicago suburban archdiocese, he'd delighted in his return to St. Mary's later in his career as pastor. He didn't aspire to loftier positions in the church hierarchy, although his superiors had urged him to consider upward mobility. He loved this parish community, and if he had a choice, he'd never leave. Now, his plans and aspirations—the plans of all mankind—were about to be rendered...ridiculous.

Rising slowly, he rejected hiding behind the lectern, preferring to deliver his homily informally, closer to the congregation. Anything but lighthearted, he'd nevertheless continue his practice of beginning sermons with a joke or humorous anecdote.

He descended three steps off the altar, faced his flock, and said, "Little Danny was in one of his moods. The rambunctious five-year-old wanted to be anywhere other than stuck in church at one of Father O'Malley's long, drawn-out Masses. He kicked the pew repeatedly and tore pages out of the hymnal. His sainted mother tried to harness the little boy's energy, diverting him with dry cereal and little toy cars. His father's patience stretched to the limit as his son continued to misbehave. The final straw was drawn when Danny bounced a bit of his cereal off poor Mrs.

Cook's head. Mumbling an apology to the lady seated in the pew in front of his family, Danny's dad scooped him up into his arms, surged out of the pew, and stomped toward the back of the church. Visibly frightened, Danny shouted out to the congregation at large, 'Pray for me!'"

Laughter erupted, and Father Mark paused, smiling.

"When Danny was old enough, he actually became an altar boy," Mark continued. "I honestly believe that he alone explained why Father O'Malley took his extended sabbatical."

Peals of laughter rocked the church. Mark waited until the merriment subsided before he repeated, "Pray for me....such powerful words," he added. "How many times in your life have you uttered those words or had someone ask for your prayers? People stop me on the street when I wear my clerical collar to ask me to pray for them or their loved ones. So many people need my prayers these days with the economy in a downward spiral, the loss of jobs, escalating crime, social and political injustice, denied health insurance claims...I could go on and on. And I will continue to pray. But..." He heaved a sigh and leveled his gaze on the congregation. "Today I sorely need your prayers." His heart constricted, viewing the multitude of concerned expressions on his dear parishioners' faces.

"Is Father Mark sick? Have you heard anything?" the organist blurted out to the lector.

"Let me put your fears to rest. I'm not sick. Praise God. Then why do I need your prayers so desperately? I have been chosen as Our Lady's shepherd. Unparalleled world events will begin tomorrow. Our Lord's words in the Gospel reading that I chose today could not be more appropriate or urgent. 'This voice did not come for my sake but for yours. Now is the time of judgment on this world.'"

Silent, Mark stood before the assembly, gazing at the wonderstruck expressions, furrowed brows, and open mouths in the audience as the powerful words sank in. His knees knocked, contemplating the implications of his role.

"I'll bet some of you are thinking Father Mark is completely nuts, and I can't wait to get out of this church." He chuckled. "Maybe some of you will continue to listen with open minds but still conclude that I'm crazy. Many of you are disciples of the Virgin Mary, and you know that I speak the truth. All I ask is that you listen to my story with an open mind and heart."

The church was eerily silent. The assembly sat statue-like, all eyes glued on him.

A trickle of sweat started a slow crawl down his back. *Holy Spirit gift me with the words I need.* "Many of you have heard me talk about the Adriatic village, Valselo, my dedication to the orphanage there. I have preached on the messages Our Lady imparts for the benefit of the world and the conversion of hearts to her Son." He paused briefly gathering his thoughts. *How much do I reveal? Perhaps a little context first.*

"To understand my devotion, I'll give you a bit of the history of miraculous events in Valselo. On April 7, 1992, near a hill, it rained rose petals. A deluge that lasted several minutes." He paused again as the fantastical words echoed.

Those who had accompanied him on pilgrimages to the remote village smiled, their faces glowing, familiar with the myriad of blessings that Our Lady of the Roses had showered on her followers—and had continued to do so every day thereafter.

"Three parish children walked along a road at the base of that hill. They quickened their pace when it began to rain but halted in amazement when they realized fragrant, white rose petals, not rain, showered down from the sky. They stooped to gather handfuls of the petals and threw them up in the air, joyful, romping and giggling like the innocent children they were. When the deluge stopped, mounds of petals had collected around their feet. Ready to run home and report their awesome experience, they gazed up the hill and stopped dead in their tracks. A beautiful young woman with a child in her arms stood at the top of the hill smiling down at them. She didn't speak but gestured for the children to come join her.

"Utterly terrified, the kids raced home instead—and hid. Those three children were Anna, Elizabeta, and Josip, now an ordained priest. In the weeks that followed, the children started to experience daily apparitions with Our Lady. Let's fast forward to the present. The children are now adults. The two women have children of their own. Father Josip and Elizabeta still receive daily Marian apparitions.

"Anna's daily visitations stopped on her wedding day. She has yearly visits on her anniversary. Her daily visitations stopped because she received seven secrets from Mary. Let me explain a little bit about the secrets. Mary informed the three visionaries that she would entrust secrets to them concerning future world events.

"Not much was known about these secrets except that they have to do with chastisements for mankind if hearts remain hardened to God's merciful offer of salvation.

"All the messages associated with the Valselo apparitions have essentially been bids to open our hearts to God's love, to embrace His light, and reject the darkness of sin—before it's too late.

"We also learned through the visionaries that the last secret foretells a visible lasting sign that will manifest somewhere in the world. It will be permanent, indestructible, beautiful, and inexplicable in earthly terms.

"Our Lady gave Anna the responsibility to reveal the secrets at God's discretion. She further instructed Anna that when the time came to disclose the secrets, she must choose a priest who would bear witness to these revelations. He must attest that Our Lady foretold these events as the messenger for the Most High. Anna must present that priest with a parchment containing the secrets and the timeline for unfolding events. He will accept the mission understanding that his role represents God's sacred will."

Trembling, Mark's eyes closed involuntarily. "Anna visited me yesterday afternoon. Last evening, she gave me the parchment I just described. Pray for me."

The crowd gasped as Father Mark turned around and ascended the altar's steps. He sagged into his chair behind the altar, his body quaking with emotion. God was with him on that altar. His presence was tangible among them as never before.

Perhaps that's why the Mass continued without anyone voicing questions about his shock-and-awe homily.

The remaining order of the Mass passed in a blur, the memorized prayers and motions flowing automatically for Mark. After the lector read the weekly announcements, Father Mark rose to bestow the final blessing.

"Before I send you forth to spread the good news, I have one more announcement. There will be a meeting in the parish hall immediately following Mass and after all Sunday Masses tomorrow. I will lead a pilgrimage to the site where the permanent sign will appear. Anyone interested in accompanying me is welcome. Now please bow your heads and ask for God's blessing."

Father Mark refused to comment any further on the Valselo secrets or his role in their unveiling as he shook parishioners' hands in the church narthex. Instead, he asked for patience and urged them to come to the meeting.

****

Father Mark hadn't notified anyone except Jack and Beth Dunne concerning the impromptu meeting. Apparently, the ladies of the parish Rosary Guild had launched into action as soon as Mark's announcement left his lips, judging from the scene he encountered upon entering the parish center.

A banquet table covered with an immaculate linen cloth was set with plates of cookies, brownies, and cupcakes. The huge coffee urn percolated on a pass-through shelf between the parish center hall and the adjoining kitchenette. Paper cups, plates, and plastic utensils were placed on the table's corner. Full pitchers of ice water sweated rings on the cloth. Folding chairs were set up in rows in the center of the room.

"Gloria, Terry, Nan, I can't thank you enough," Father Mark greeted the breathless volunteers as he strode into the room. "I don't know what I would do without you."

The ladies beamed under his affectionate gaze.

Folks streamed into the basement level room nonstop.

Jack Dunne had dragged a desk from one of the offices into the corner of the meeting room. He booted a computer while he stacked pads of paper on the desk. "I'm set, Father," Jack reported. "Beth will be along soon. She was just waiting for her coffee cake to cool. Looks like the Rosary Guild ladies have this under control without Beth's cake."

Mark returned Jack's grin. "Thanks for all this, Jack," he said. "I can't imagine how I'd do this without your help."

"I'm beyond honored to help in any way I can, Mark."

The local cable channel's cameraman in tow with the anchorman, Ron Edison, made a grand entrance into the room. Edison's attention darted until his gaze zeroed in on Father Mark.

"Uh-oh," Mark remarked, feeling distinctly on the verge of ambush.

The reporter wasted no time on preliminaries as he planted himself in front of the priest and probed, "Father Mark, is it true that you spoke with the Virgin Mary?"

"Ah, the telephone game at work, huh, Ron? News travels fast in this parish, but I'm afraid facts distort some from mouth to ear. No, I did not speak with the Virgin Mary."

"What's going on here, Father?" the newsman persisted as the camera lens loomed in front of Father Mark.

The priest squelched the impulse to shield his face with a hand and suggested, "Grab a cup of coffee and come sit with me, Ron. I'll tell you everything I can."

"Can Harry film your statements?" Ron pointed to his cameraman.

"Of course, he can," Mark responded despite his reluctance. If he were to fulfill his role to the best of his ability, he had to capture a broader audience than the faithful of St. Mary's.

Ron filled two to-go cups with piping hot coffee and handed one to Father Mark. He raised his eyebrows as he extended a cup in Harry's direction, and the cameraman wagged his head, declining the offer.

Mark and Ron pulled two chairs close together in the back of the room, and Harry unfolded a tripod and mounted the camera. Peering into the viewfinder, Harry signaled the go-ahead to Ron and began taping.

"I attended Mass today, Father, and I heard your unusual sermon."

Mark gave a nod and said, "Good, Ron. Thank you for visiting the congregation."

"Would you care to summarize for our audience, Father?"

"Certainly. A Marian visionary, Anna Babic Robbins, and two fellow villagers from Croatia have communicated daily with the Blessed Virgin Mary since the early nineties. Yesterday, Anna delivered a parchment to me, documenting seven secrets given to her by Our Lady that concern God's plan to rivet the attention of mankind. I am to testify that coming events were foretold…Among them a universal sign given by God Almighty and a permanent sign to follow this universal phenomenon that cannot be explained by earthly means. The events are upon us. I'm organizing a pilgrimage group that will depart in the near future to the intended site of the permanent sign. This meeting is an opportunity for folks to join the pilgrimage and travel with me."

"Frankly, that's utterly incredible," Ron stated. "Where are you going?"

"I'm not permitted to reveal that quite yet," Mark replied. "But I assure you, it is my deepest belief that these statements are totally credible. And the Lord God is the Author."

Ron's eyes widened as he leaned towards the priest. "So, you intend to ask the people at this meeting to follow you without fully explaining why, or even where you're going?"

"Yes."

"And you think they will follow you?" Ron's brow furrowed as he wagged his head.

"I do."

Mark pinched his temple and gazed around the room. Almost every chair was occupied, and judging from the number of people milling about, they were over capacity already.

"Why, Father?" Ron continued.

"One word, Ron. Faith." He gazed deeply into the anchorman's eyes. Mark frowned as he read the pure skepticism in Ron's expression. "Now if you will excuse me, I have a discussion to lead."

"Any problem with our staying until the meeting is over?"

"Not at all." Mark rose from his seat and gestured

toward the banquet table. "Help yourself."

Rosa Castillo bustled into the parish hall juggling a platter of fragrant cookies, intercepting Mark's forward progress. His stomach growled as he relieved her of the tray and placed it on the banquet table. He had prayed continuously and hadn't stopped to eat since the parchment had come into his keeping.

"Sorry I'm late, Father. I rushed home right after Mass so I'd have something to bring to your meeting." Rosa hitched the strap of her bulging purse over her shoulder. Beads of perspiration dotted her upper lip.

"These treats smell wonderful. Thank you." He poured ice water into a plastic red cup, handed it to her, and then broke off a piece of cookie to pop in his mouth out of politeness. "Delicious, as usual," he said, although he didn't taste the morsel in his preoccupied state. Scanning the room, he searched for Rosa's son-in-law. "Where's Ramon? Working?"

"No. He's home alone. I called and asked him to meet me at Mass, but he refused. He won't go out without Tina since..." She rolled her eyes. "Well, you know..."

"I'm sorry, dear. Have you heard from Tina? Are the Belles having a wonderful time?" He chuckled, remembering Tina's excited anticipation of the girls' bachelorette party weekend.

"She called when they got to the hotel and said everything was out of this world. She promised to take pictures."

"I look forward to seeing them. Have a seat, Rosa, before the meeting is standing room only." He glanced at his watch. "I'd better make my announcements, so everyone can get home to dinner." Mark strode to the front of the room and addressed the attendees. "I want to thank you all for coming on such short notice. Let's start with a prayer and a Bible reading."

He led the Our Father and Hail Mary prayers, opened his Bible, cleared his throat, and read, "As Jesus was walking beside the Sea of Galilee, he saw two brothers; Simon called Peter and his brother Andrew. They were casting a net into the lake, for they were fishermen. 'Come, follow Me,' Jesus said, 'And I will send you out to fish for people.' At once they left their nets and followed Him. Going on from there, He saw two other brothers, James, son of Zebedee and his brother, John. They were in a boat with their father, Zebedee, preparing their nets. Jesus called them, and immediately they left the boat and their father and followed Him."

Closing the holy book, he smiled before reiterating, "And they immediately left the boat and their father and followed him.

"They dropped what they were doing and relied on faith and followed without question. I want you to follow me. And I ask you to trust me. I can't tell you where I'll lead you. I can tell you that Our Lady is calling, and I am answering her call. I invite you to come answer her call with me. I promise you that you won't regret it.

"Many of you know Jack and Beth Dunne," Mark continued. "Their generosity will make this trip possible. They will cover all your expenses. All you need to do is sign up with Jack, pack one suitcase with light clothing, and wait for me to contact you with departure information. We'll leave in the next few days—no later than next Friday. How quickly we can make group arrangements will determine exactly when we leave and how long we'll be away. I will tell you that we will travel by bus and by air, and we should return within a week after we leave. This invitation is not exclusive to our parish family or even members of the Catholic religion. All are welcome to join us. If you feel that you're called to follow, see Jack and sign up no later than after the noon Mass tomorrow."

Jack stood and waved from behind the desk in the corner. Seated in a chair next to him, Beth smiled.

"Faith is defined in the dictionary as strong or unshakeable belief in something...without proof or evidence. Whether you choose to travel with me to witness the bestowing of the permanent sign firsthand or not, I pray you remember my homily comments today as the events of the next week or so unfold. God intends to bless us with proof and irrefutable evidence that the faithful are right in believing in Him. Thank you for listening to me and for considering—"

A thunder crash sounded, and the lights blinked off and on in rapid succession.

"Whoa." Father Mark chuckled. "I'll let you all interpret that in your own way. Please drive home safely in the storm."

9

Ink-black thunderheads extinguished sunset hues on the horizon. The wind whipped through overhead branches, and the leaves flapped silvery white, riding the gusts. He smelled the earthy dampness of the impending deluge before the first fat drops splattered the crown of his head. Unprepared for the rapid advancement and escalation of the storm, his clothes were drenched in seconds.

Jogging the path with his head bent, he blinked away the water that streamed down his face. A bolt of lightning sizzled down from the sky, striking a tree a few yards to his right. The hair on his arms and legs stood on end from the blast of static electricity. The acrid smell of ozone pinched his nostrils, and a resounding thunderclap plugged his ears.

He dashed into a clearing, now worse off, lacking the better than nothing shelter of over-hanging branches. Racing out across the open road that intersected the path, he sloshed through ankle deep water. Uncomfortable and irritable, he cursed the opening heavens, hating the saturated sensations as his suit stuck to him and his hair plastered to his face and oozed water. He equated his suffering to a metaphor for his very existence. Everybody, including God, dumped on him every miserable day.

Back on the path on the other side, the sodden earth seemed to suck at his feet like claws tugging him down to hell while heaven hammered him downward for good measure. His gait clumsy, he turned his ankle on the slippery ground. Another thunderclap roared, and the sky flashed white as a sharp pain jolted his ankle and had him hopping in place on one foot.

"Ow!" he bellowed.

"Need some help?" came a high-pitched voice.

He snapped his head to the left and spied the speaker, a figure under a giant umbrella, descending the concrete steps off the community library's parking lot. The open, golf umbrella concealed the female from the shoulders up. She wore red Bermuda shorts, and her knees and calves glistened wet from the driving rain. Bare arms wrapped around a bunch of books and the umbrella handle.

"No. Mind your own business," he retorted belligerently as he eased the sore foot downward and tentatively shifted his weight, praying the ankle wouldn't buckle. Relieved that he hadn't suffered serious damage, he instinctively scanned the area as she approached. The parking lot was empty, and the library windows were as dark as the sky.

The striped umbrella bobbled toward him propelled by two tennis shoe-clad feet and shiny, skinny legs. She angled the umbrella backward and revealed a pixie-like face contorted with seeming revulsion. "You're so mean," she mumbled.

He'd been called worse and probably deserved her

opinion of him. But…*Do I know her?* "Sorry," he said, sincere in the apology—if she were innocent. "I hurt my foot." He studied her features as she closed the distance between them. Her unsmiling face hit him as all too familiar, but still he wasn't certain.

When she moved abreast of him, he ducked his head under her umbrella for a closer look and brief respite from the rain. "Share your umbrella for a minute? Just until the worst passes?"

Close-up, she didn't look like her. She smelled like fruit gum and baby powder. Maybe he was mistaken, and she was just any kid.

"Get away from me!" she protested, as she dumped her books and yanked the umbrella away, poking the back of his head with one of the spokes.

His eyes slit, he jutted his hand into the cuff of the glove in his right pocket. Jerking his arm up and out, he clasped the umbrella handle and snatched it out of her grasp. He took a broad hop backward and scrutinized her from beneath the umbrella as the downpour drummed relentlessly on the canopy.

The rain doused her and molded her summer clothes to her body like a second skin. She dipped her chin, glanced downward, registered how revealing her wet blouse had become, and then scowled at him, droplets of water dripping off her ear lobes.

"You perv!" she cried, clearly confirming her identity and sealing her fate.

His chest heaved as blind rage seethed into every pore. Slipping his left hand into his pocket, he shimmied his fingers into the other glove, closed the umbrella, and took a swing. The "bat" smacked her square in her face, and another thunder-boomer sounded, punctuating the crack of her nose. Blood gushed out of her nostrils as she toppled backward and sprawled flat on her back on the ground.

Moaning and gurgling, rain filled her open mouth.

It might be interesting to let the rain shut her mouth permanently.

Rejecting the novel idea as too time consuming, he let the umbrella slip out of his hands, pounced on her lax form, and rolled her over in the mud. Jutting his knee into her spine, he pinned her to the ground. And then he clasped the back of her scrawny neck with his left hand and used his other hand to press her face flush into a puddle of water. He tensed every muscle and pinioned her while she bucked, jerked, convulsed…and then stilled.

Leaning back, he felt the side of her neck for a pulse. "Nope," he concluded.

He dragged himself to his feet; his soggy clothes weighing him down like twenty extra pounds of glop. Gazing longingly at the umbrella on the ground, he resigned to the necessity to slog along in the merciless rainstorm without it.

"Do me a favor. Stay dead," he uttered to the corpse.

Head bowed, he waded through the rising water along the path, no longer as desperate to find shelter from the storm.

10

Joe twisted the wipers' knob to the highest setting as the downpour increased. The overworked windshield wipers squeaked and shuddered as if gasping for a final breath. Squinting through the streaked glass, Joe blurted out in exasperation, "Couldn't we just call this ridiculous thing off? The whole bachelor party tradition is a waste of time."

From the passenger seat, Charlie Hartman chuckled, and then he remarked, "It's a rite of passage, man. Come on, Joey, you're the guest of honor tonight."

Only his mother and Charlie, his best friend since grammar school, referred to him as "Joey."

"Rite of passage, I doubt it," Joe retorted. "You all are just using my wedding as an excuse to drink too much, and act like adolescents."

"Maybe if you down a few beers, you might actually enjoy yourself," Charlie predicted.

The cloudburst released torrents, and the road ahead disappeared behind a curtain of water.

Charlie clutched the door handle. "Hey, Joey. Why

don't you spring for a new pair of wipers?"

"I can see just fine," Joe replied through clenched teeth, fiercely concentrating on driving while essentially blind, as sheets of water overwhelmed the wipers. Although he hated the thought, he would have to spring for the new wipers soon, and maybe a general overhaul for the car. The doors stuck and the tires were nearly threadbare, judging from the hydroplaning wheels.

As Joe had discovered the extent of Laci's recent spending, he had become proportionately more frugal. The wedding coordinator had left a message on the answering machine last evening, cheerfully reminding Laci that the second payment of ten thousand dollars was due by August fifteenth. Ten thousand dollars? Wedding coordinator?

Nothing could diminish his devotion to Laci, but once they were husband and wife, Joe would insist on participating in financial decisions.

He parallel parked between two trucks on the crowded street in front of the bar with the precision of a racecar driver, squeezing the car into the space with only inches' leeway front and back.

Charlie forcibly opened the passenger door with one solid kick of the heel of his boot. The hinges on Joe's door groaned like the front door of a movie set haunted house as he swung it shut.

"Nice car, Corello," one of the guys quipped as Joe ducked under the bright pink awning at the entrance of the Kitty Cat Bar and Grill where the bachelor party revelers gathered.

Joe wagged his head and sent raindrops flying off his jet-black, curly hair. He frowned when he recognized Barry Jacobs reaching for the knob on the bar's front door.

"You had to invite that guy?" Joe asked Charlie under his breath. "Never liked him."

Charlie snorted in reply and then claimed, "Hey, don't blame me. I called Laci for the list."

He circled an arm around Joe's shoulder. "Let's party."

Inside the place, murky bar lighting failed to obscure the substandard sanitary conditions. The sticky floor sucked at the soles of Joe's shoes. The stench of stale beer and locker room-like odors assaulted his nostrils. "What a dump," he muttered.

His friends pointedly ignored the comment.

Charlie walked up to the bar. The bartender pointed to a large, apparently reserved table in the corner.

Waving Joe and the guys forward, Charlie led the men to the table.

A voluptuous waitress clad in the cat-theme uniform bustled over to their table, beaming as if counting up the forthcoming fat tip. She tilted her cat-eared, crowned head coquettishly. "What can I get you, boys? Taking a break from big business for while?"

"We're mostly cops," Joe said.

The avaricious gleam extinguished in her narrowed eyes. "Oh...well, what can I get you fine officers?"

Charlie ordered the first round of beers and shots, the waitress sashayed away, and then he addressed the group, "You guys all know each other?"

Next to Joe, Dr. Glen Foster nodded. "I think we all met at Joe and Laci's barbeque last year."

"Have you heard from Bern?" Joe asked Glen.

The waitress plopped a tray of sweating beer

bottles on the table. "Be right back with the shots."

"No. I told Bernadette she didn't have to call. I'm sure she's having a wonderful time with her friends." Glen paused and took a swig of beer. "Have you heard from Laci?"

Yeah, and your wife, too. He viewed Bern's husband as a bit of a stiff and an academic snob. Joe had known Bern since grammar school, and although she had been the smartest kid in all his classes, she was a riot who brimmed with personality.

He'd never understood the attraction between the idealistic, Catholic at heart, Bernadette O'Neal, and her serious, atheistic, bookworm husband. But hey, who was he to question what brought people together—or what kept them together through life's twists and turns? Apparently, Bernadette was crazy about the guy. Funny that she could take a vacation from her spouse but not her job. She had followed up with Joe on the Strangler case three times since she had left.

He discreetly omitted mentioning his conversations with Glen's wife and replied, "Laci called a few times. Mostly to make sure that I haven't starved Belle and Mary."

Glen furrowed his brow.

"Belle and Mary are her new Maltese puppies," Joe explained. "I took the little rats to my place, but they tag-teamed me and chewed up half my rug. So now I'm staying at Laci's townhouse where they can dine on designer rugs." Joe huffed, displeased with the bitter tone that rang in his own voice.

Money worries had overshadowed his eagerness to begin married life with his soul mate, investigation of the serial killer case went nowhere, and his mood was foul, in general. He contemplated his untouched beer, and for the umpteenth time since Charlie had informed him about his bachelor party, he wondered who had thought up this idiotic tradition. He couldn't wait until the wedding was over, his angel was his wife, the scumbag Strangler was behind bars, and he and Laci could resume enjoying each other. He missed just plain Joe and Laci.

Charlie stood and raised a shot glass. "I want to say a few words to my best friend who is like a brother to me."

One drink and Charlie's already emotional. This will be a very long night.

"Let's toast the good things in life—freedom, irresponsibility, dating lovely ladies…these are just a few things that you'll have to give up as a married man, my friend. But…I'm sure—we're all sure—that you'll receive much more in return." A smile played at the corner of Charlie's lips. "When you find out exactly what that is, be sure to let us know. Cheers." He knocked back the shot and thumped the empty glass down on the table.

Joe lifted his glass in Charlie's direction. "Thanks, I think, Hartman," he commented.

Grinning, the other guys at the table rose from their seats in turn and each proposed obviously coordinated toasts.

"Marriage is an institution but who wants to live in an institution?"

"Marriage is the process of finding out what kind of person your wife would have preferred."

"Marriage is like a hot bath. Once you get used to it, it's not so hot."

"Marriage is a three-ring circus: engagement ring, wedding ring, and suffering."

"Marriage is the only war in which you sleep with the enemy."

"Marriage means commitment. Of course, so does insanity." Glen, the last man in the act, smirked and sat back down.

This torture apparently over, Joe rose and wiped a fake tear from the corner of his eye. "Ah shucks, you guys. Why'd you have to go and get all sentimental on me? I'm touched." Giving in to the spirit of the thing, Joe paused dramatically as if overcome with emotion. "Really, thank you all." He waited a beat before adding, "For saving me so much money. You are all uninvited to the wedding." Glaring at the group, he sat down abruptly.

His behavior was met with stunned expressions and silence.

Joe hooted a laugh. "I'm kidding. I love you guys. Thank you."

The waitress was surprisingly discreet and efficient in continuously replacing empty beer bottles with cold brews. Joe nursed his first beer and left the full shot glass on the table. As the beer flowed, the volume of the guys' banter increased.

Joe's cell phone vibrated in his jeans' pocket. He fished it out and viewed the caller ID displayed on the screen. "I hate to bust up the party." He shoved his chair back from the table and stood. "I have to go."

"No way." Charlie stood, swaying a bit. "You're not on the duty roster. That's why I scheduled this for tonight."

Joe clapped a hand on Charlie's shoulder. "Can't be helped, buddy. Thank you for going to the trouble. Don't leave on my account, guys," Joe remarked to the table at large. "Have some fun on my behalf. And make sure you call a cab to get home."

Joe strode away from the merriment, eager to respond to the captain's call. He jumped into the car, plopped a flashing beacon atop his roof, and headed toward the reported crime scene, thankful that the rain had reduced to a steady drizzle that didn't impede visibility. The lights cleared traffic in front of him.

He screeched into the library parking lot, noting the gaping open doors on the coroner's van. Slamming his creaky car door shut, he sloshed through the puddles, descended four steps onto the muddy Prairie Path, and ducked under the yellow tape strung at the bottom of the stairs.

Fellow detective, Phil Consuegra strode over to Joe. "Sorry I ruined the bachelor party, Corello, but the Cap and I figured you'd would want to be here."

"Yeah, thanks. You figured right. Tell me we have something new to catch this sick lunatic."

"The pattern isn't identical, and the victim is only fifteen, so we may have a different perp. My gut says it's the same sick lunatic, though. Forensics is doing their thing, but it doesn't look like we have prints or DNA here, either. Even if this guy got careless and left us something concrete, more than likely the torrential rain tonight would have sent it down the sewer."

Consuegra yanked a soggy, spiral-topped notebook out of his back pocket, opened the top flap, and consulted his notes. "Vic's name is Jordan Mills, according to a library card and state ID in her wallet. We're waiting for next of kin to confirm. ID card shows DOB fifteen years ago." He paused and huffed a breath. "My kid is probably in the same grade as the vic."

"Body was found by a jogger who got caught in

the storm. He's in my squad car, major shook up and soaked to the skin. I called the librarian, Geraldine McIntyre, for timeline. She remembers checking Jordan's books out around five to six. The library closes at six, and Jordan said that she wished they were open later because she was almost finished researching her report. She was the last to leave the building other than the librarian. Jordan exited the front door and McIntyre used the back exit. She stated that Jordan is a regular, never a problem. Also, she didn't observe anyone suspicious hanging around the library tonight."

"OK," Joe said. "I want a closer look."

The detectives plodded through the muck to the coroner who knelt in the mud next to the body while his assistant shot photos.

"Hey, Joe," the ME said, gazing up at him. Exhaustion lines creased his face and dark circles ringed his eyes.

"Hey, Ed. What do you have so far?"

"TOD estimated at 6:00 PM. Victim's nose and right cheekbone are fractured. She put up a struggle. All the fingernails on her right hand are broken to the quick."

"Was she strangled like the rest?" Joe asked, as Ed clumsily stood. The knees of his chino pants oozed mud.

"No. She drowned."

"What?" Joe did a double take. "Not the serial killer, then?"

"The bruising on the back of her neck is extensive, so she didn't fall on her face and accidentally drown. Considerable force was applied to hold her face down in a puddle until she asphyxiated. Could be the same perp. For what it's worth, I think it is. And it's getting late." He patted Joe on the shoulder. "I'll take her to the morgue." Ed kneaded his neck. "She's number four tonight. Ugly weather brings out the uglies. I have to go home and put on some dry clothes."

The coroner preempted Joe's protest, promising, "She'll get my full attention first thing in the morning. I'll expedite my report and have it to you by 9:00 AM. We have the suspects in custody for the other three."

"Don't rush it, Ed. It's more important that you find some trace evidence."

"I know. Go home, Joe, and get some sleep. You look beat."

Whether his bachelor party had fizzled out yet or not, Joe drove straight to Laci's place. His cell phone rang as he switched off the ignition in front of the townhouse. Glancing at the caller ID he barked into the phone, "How did you hear so soon?"

"Hi, Joe. Yes, I am having a wonderful time. Thanks for asking," Bern replied.

Her sugary sarcasm amused Joe enough to tease out a smile. "Can it, Bern. It's late. I'm furious, and even if I had inside info—which I don't—I wouldn't give it to you now. Aren't you supposed to be swilling drinks and relaxing or whatever?"

"I'm not sure I know how."

He snorted a laugh. "I'll say."

"I can't be away from my desk for more than twenty-four hours, or I get the shakes. I called into the station. Is it the Sweet Sixteen Strangler?"

"If you use that tag again, you'll never get another news lead from me."

"All right, all right. Detective Corello, in your professional opinion, do you believe that the same perpetrator to whom the press maddeningly refers to as the Sweet Sixteen Strangler is responsible for this crime?"

"Yeah, Miz O'Neal. I believe that this was the same perp. MO is different on this one, though." He yawned audibly. "Sorry, it's been a long day. I won't have the ME's report until morning. I'll call if there's anything I'll let you report."

"Thanks. I better go prevent Laci from doing something she'll regret." She hung up on a chuckle.

"Great. Give me another reason to be aggravated," he said to the dead connection.

Joe opened the front door cautiously and prevented the rollicking puppies from escaping outside and adding to his headache. He bent down and permitted the quivering animals to jump on him unimpeded. Relieved after inspecting the house and finding rugs and upholstery intact, he hooked up the dogs' leashes, walked them, and then fed them bits of his hastily made ham and cheese sandwich.

Joe lazed on the couch and surfed the channels until he landed on a sports' channel. The dogs leapt onto the sofa, cozied up next to his thighs, buried their snouts in their forelegs, and snoozed.

In her home, surrounded by her beloved pets and fancy things, he missed Laci more than ever. He dialed her number and left the message, "I miss you, Lace. I can't wait to marry you. Have fun—but not too much."

He leaned his head back, closed his eyes, and drifted to sleep, grateful that at least his bachelor party was behind him.

11

Marlo sipped her soda water with lime, amused at her friends' antics.

Laci tapped her fingertips lightly on her cheek. "I can't feel my face," she announced and erupted in giggles. "Isn't it great?"

A movie star handsome bartender served the keep-them-coming supply of cocktails. The merriment did wonders for Marlo's disposition. She almost forgot her pregnancy as she lazed regally on a heavenly comfortable chaise in the opulent, apartment-sized hotel room.

Laci's accommodations were a notch above her trio of friends' rooms. The breathtaking spectacle of Las Vegas by night viewed through the massive floor to ceiling windows in the corner suite would illuminate the room without switching on a single light. But Laci had created an interior, Vegas-style spectacle for her party in the glittering hotel room. Flashing fairy lights strung around the room glowed like fireflies, and tiered tapers in the ornate candelabra on the grand piano near the windows flickered starry reflections in the gleaming glass. The pianist's extensive classical music repertoire added another dreamlike dimension to the bachelorette party. At that moment, he played *Pachelbel Canon in D.*

Content and grateful for the respite from nausea, Marlo gazed at the neon vista below. A realistic Tour d'Eiffel tilted toward a neighboring hot air balloon. The golden Palazzo Hotel, bathed in up-tilted light, presided in the background like a shimmering palace. A displaced L'Arc de Triomphe strayed from the Champs Élysées and capped the scene. The surreal panorama coupled with the sight of Tina, looking ten years younger as she chatted happily with Laci on the far side of the room, wrapped the moment in a fantastical aura.

Bernadette, however, dependably provided the sole hints of reality each time she excused herself and left the room to call in to the station.

Marlo heard her faint phone conversation beyond the suite's closed doors. When she had contemplated this weekend, Marlo had assumed that the party would be lavish. So far, Laci had wildly exceeded that expectation. Just the poolside cabana alone was over the top. Marlo closed her eyes, savored her loose, mindless state, and instantly regretted it. Her head swam.

Desperate to stem the whirling sensation, she opened her eyes, but the dizziness didn't subside. The glittering world spun faster and bile rose in her throat with alarming speed. She swung her legs off the chaise, slapping her bare feet down on the marble floor. Clapping a hand over her mouth, she fled to the bathroom, intent on reaching the toilet bowl before she humiliated herself and puked all over Laci's classy cocktail hour.

Achieving her goal, she slammed shut the bathroom door, flung up the toilet seat, and purged her stomach of the few tidbits of food she had consumed that evening. Her inflamed esophagus burned as if she had swallowed acid, and she hung over the bowl, dry heaving, and quaking. Her hand at her midriff, she straightened up. Chilled and trembling, she unfurled a ribbon of toilet paper, dabbed her mouth clean with a shaky hand, and then scrubbed splatter off the porcelain.

Her system normalized gradually. Pregnancy vomiting was a rare kind of torture. Stepping over to the sink, Marlo examined her clothes in the mirror. Happy that she hadn't stained her black, sequined dress during the episode, she gargled some cold water. The nauseating, sour taste in her mouth persisted.

Cracking open the door, she shouted, "Lace, do you have any mouthwash?"

"What?"

Ducking out into the hallway, she spied Laci standing near the piano and repeated, "Mouthwash?"

"Oh, sure. In that red paisley cosmetic bag."

"Thanks."

She found a travel size bottle in Laci's bag, swigged a mouthful, and swished the minty stuff from cheek to cheek until the antiseptic taste overlaid the rank residue in her mouth. Twisting the cap back on the bottle, she spat into the sink, slipped the bottle into the kit, ran the water, and cleaned the basin with her hand.

Fairly poised, she returned to the party and headed toward the chaise, circumventing the bar. Obviously, even soda water didn't sit right in her stomach.

Bernadette had rejoined the festivities, and her gaze heated Marlo's back as she passed in front of the TV journalist and scurried across the room.

As if she were a deer appearing in a glade, her "hunter" friends descended on her, apparently prepared to unload their ammunition.

"What's going on with you, Marlo? You keep barfing every five minutes," Bern said.

"What makes you think I barfed?" she hedged. "I just wanted to get rid of a bad taste in my mouth."

"As if," Laci countered. "Don't be embarrassed, but we could hear you in there. And we've noticed how frequently you run to the ladies' room. You don't look well, and you're way too thin, even for you. Are you sick?"

"Of course not," Marlo replied. "You know I have Milan coming up. And then there's filming for the show in the near future. I have to watch what I eat. And alcoholic beverages are caloric mine fields."

"OK, I'll ask," Bern said as she cast pointed glances at each of her inquisitors. "I know you're all thinking it. Mar, are you bulimic?"

"What...?" Marlo said.

Bernadette held up her hand and continued, "Because if you are, we need to get you help. We all know bulimia is a casualty in your industry. This is serious, and we love you."

She sat silent, guilty, as the trio pinned her with penetrating gazes. Her conscience waged battle as she considered the tradeoff between confirming her friends' seemingly unanimous and completely off the mark conclusion, or revealing the equally problematic truth. Except to avoid hurt feelings, she had never lied to these women. *Mama's gone, and they're all that I have.*

The compulsion to confide in her sisters of the heart swamped her. Maybe she didn't have to remain so achingly alone with the knowledge of the baby in her womb. *I can't think about the baby. It's not a baby. It's a cluster of cells, nothing more.*

Her heart wrenched. She couldn't rationalize her decision with the pro-choice stance. Despite her desire to end the pregnancy, she believed that the tiny fetus inside her was a baby—her baby—already the unique soul that God had created. She couldn't risk brain damage to her baby by drinking. Completely at odds with her protectiveness, abortion would end her child's life. Tortured, she wanted to howl out the truth and lean on her friends. *They'll try to convince me to keep the baby. Or worse case, give it up for adoption. I can't...*

Donning the placid mask that she effortlessly wore on the runways of the world, she chose evasion. She smiled serenely. "I'm the last person on earth who would force myself to throw up. I hate vomiting. I don't think I even know how to induce it. Sticking my finger down my throat never worked when I was a kid trying to get out of going to school. Relax, girls. I must have picked up a stomach bug. Airplanes are germ factories."

"That's true," Laci said, swaying slightly on her skyscraper heels. "Want me to order you some coffee?"

"No, really, I'm good. I think an empty stomach might work best."

Despite the declined offer, Laci strolled over to the bar. "Can you please give Marlo a cup of coffee? She takes it black." Laci's tone rang with regal authority. Maybe the cheesy, crystal tiara she wore dubbed her royalty for the night.

"Sure thing," the bartender replied. "I'll call down for a pot."

"Thanks."

There was no missing the bartender's appreciative regard for their hostess. Laci looked sensational in a scarlet off the shoulder cocktail dress right up to the silly tiara with a wisp of wedding veil that crowned her long, golden tresses.

"You know what, Lace?" Marlo said. "You could be a model, too."

Laci blushed and flashed a grin. "That's the nicest thing you've ever said to me. I'm just a frumpy old accountant."

Bern snorted. "Yeah, that's why handsome Joe is nuts about you. Because you're so frumpy."

"Seriously," Marlo pressed, "you could be a contestant on the show."

Beaming, Laci responded, "Maybe I'll give that some thought. Drink up, girls. The night is just beginning."

The bachelorette waltzed over to the piano and laid a hand on the musician's shoulder. "Thank you, John, for making beautiful music for us," she dismissed him.

"Well, then," Marlo said as the pianist exited the room, "time to give the bride to be a little memento of her bachelorette party. Right, Teen and Bern?"

"Uh huh," Tina concurred. "I tucked it in the coat closet."

Tina strode to the closet, removed the gift, and brought the shoebox-size package to Laci, who wriggled in her seat on the sofa, beaming a radiant smile. Nobody loved the spotlight more than Laci. *She'll work that walk down the aisle more than I ever worked a fashion show.* Tina handed Laci the package.

Smiling, she picked off the tape carefully, unwrapped the gift, folded the paper, and set it aside. She removed the lid and peered inside the box while her friends exchanged knowing smiles. "Holy cow!" she shouted. "Is this what I think it is?"

Laci held up the knit, virginal-white swimsuit and flapped it back and forth at arm's length, seemingly thrilled with the gift, as Marlo had predicted.

"Yep, an Ashley Paige, custom-made swimsuit. It's one of a kind and should be a perfect fit. I called the bridal shop for your measurements," Marlo said.

"Pretty ingenious, if you ask me," Bern opined.

"And isn't it beautiful?" Tina said.

"Absolutely," Laci agreed. "Thank you, thank you, Marlo."

"Oh, we all pitched in," Marlo explained. "I just knew how to go about it."

"Well, thank you all. Hang on," Laci said. "I think I have enough time before the performance."

Speeding past the bar, Laci tossed out, "Thanks so much, Derrick," before she disappeared into the powder room.

"You're welcome, ma'am," the bartender replied in a snappy, military tone. He grinned at the women as he finished packing a cart and then wheeled it out of the suite.

Laci reappeared a few minutes later and struck a pose. "What do you think, girls?"

"Perfect."

"Beautiful."

"Ditto."

"I can't wait for Joe to see it. I'll wear it every day on our honeymoon."

"I thought you were driving to the cabin after the wedding. Is there swimming at the lake?" Bernadette asked.

"Change of plans," Laci replied lightly. "I found a good deal on a tropical island." She scooted back into the powder room and closed the door before anyone voiced further comment.

After a quick change back into her evening dress, Laci sauntered into the suite's living room. "Ready to continue partying?" She wiggled her eyebrows and beamed a smile.

"What do you have up your sleeve now?" Tina asked.

Laci draped an arm over Tina's shoulder. "We're going to a show. In a stretch limo. Down the Strip with the moon roof open."

"You know, Lace, we are perfectly capable of walking," Bern said.

"Not in these heels," Laci retorted. "Besides, we don't want to be late for the show."

"We're going to a show?" Tina's widened eyes lit with her smile. "Oh, boy."

"Front row seats," Laci exclaimed, naming the singer they'd be seeing.

"Good grief, those tickets are ridiculously expensive. I can't accept this, Lace. I just can't." Bernadette wagged her head.

"Me, either," Marlo chimed in.

"You guys are such party-poopers," Laci groused. "I'll ignore all of you and go by myself."

Bernadette burst out laughing as she sidled over to Laci and gave her a warm hug. "You just can't stand that the Belles don't take orders from you anymore."

"That's so untrue," Laci declared, garnering a rash

of hoots from the women. "All right, all right," she conceded. "Let's not bicker." She huffed a sigh. "I already bought tickets, people. And prepaid the limo and everything. Why do you want to spoil this for me? Come on!" Laci stepped toward the door.

"I think we have to do whatever the little bride wants," Marlo said, biting back a grin.

Laci beamed as her friends fell into step behind her. She flung open the door.

Tina bustled around the room, snuffing candles, and switching off lights. "What?" she said as all eyes focused on her.

"Love you, Teen," Marlo pronounced.

"Me, too," Laci echoed.

"And my vote makes three," Bernadette said.

"Aw, thanks. Love you back," Tina said with a smile.

12

Anticipating her ailing friend's comfort, Tina gathered up the crumpled shawl that had slid off Marlo's chaise onto the floor. The temperature difference between the evening air, still in triple digits, and the air-conditioned hotel corridors, surely would heighten Marlo's misery without Tina's thoughtfulness. *I don't want her to feel worse than she already does.* She folded the delicate, probably expensive wrap, and then tucked it into the crook of her arm.

Bernadette's voice drifted through the suite's open door. "The elevator's here. Hurry up, Teen."

Her eyes swept the hotel room like a discerning housekeeping inspector. Pleased with the pristine condition of the suite, Tina switched off the lights, zipped out into the hall, and closed the doors behind her. By reflex, she checked the door handle for assurance that the lock had engaged.

Bernadette barred the sandwiching elevator doors with an outstretched arm.

Tina rushed inside the elevator and edged toward the back behind the other Belles. The doors swooshed closed and the mirror-walled compartment launched into a stomach-sinking plunge. She couldn't avoid looking at herself surrounded by reflective surfaces unless she stared at her feet or closed her eyes. Self-conscious and forever self-critical, she furtively glimpsed at her image in the glass, fluffed her hair, and sucked in her stomach muscles for the remainder of the descent. The girls smiled and made faces at each other's reflections in the gilt-edged mirrors. Inferiority gripped her, and she longed, as usual, to possess half their confidence.

Despite her insecurity, the limo ride and the V.I.P. treatment afforded them at the event venue bolstered her self-esteem. She had never felt more important. And empowered. When a waitress approached them for drink orders before the show started, she decided to substitute the ginger ale she had sipped all night with a Tequila Sunrise.

"Are you sure, Teen?" Bernadette asked when the waitress left. "Remember the last time you downed tequila?"

"Vaguely."

Bernadette snorted out a laugh. "Let me refresh your memory. It was at my wedding, and you had stubbornly refused to eat solid food for a week before then."

Tina sat back down next to Bernadette. "It wasn't my fault that you picked skin tight, bridesmaids' dresses, and I had to compete with these skinny women wearing spaghetti straps." She smiled as she waggled a finger at Marlo and Laci. I starved and wore that dress with pride. And boy, those sunrises were delicious."

"My Uncle Jack still asks me about my 'little hot tamale friend'—his exact words, meant as avid appreciation not an ethnic slur, I promise," Bern said. "Ninety-three years old and one of his favorite memories is your dancing with Ramon."

"The details are blurry, but I do remember that Ramon and I had the best time at your wedding, Bern.

I miss those days. We were so in love then."

"But not so much now?" she probed.

Chagrined, Tina replied, "I didn't mean to imply..." She paused as the familiar black cloud enveloped her at each thought of her husband. Avoiding further discussion with her friend, Tina said, "You know, I think I'll call him before I have that drink. I promised I'd check in before the night was over when I called him earlier."

Marlo huffed a breath. "Oh, for Pete's sake. He's a man, not your child. Surely, he can survive a couple nights without your feeding his depressing dependency."

"Are you eavesdropping on our conversation?" Tina countered.

"Of course, I am. Don't you ever just want to tell him to take a jump, Teen? You deserve better."

"Oh, Mar—"

"You still are a hot tamale. Ramon should appreciate you more," Marlo insisted.

Tina's loyalty to her marriage vows prevented her from surrendering to the compulsion to howl out complaints about Ramon to sympathetic ears. "I promised to call him," Tina uttered as she grabbed the cell phone out of her purse and left her seat.

She pressed the listing for her home number while she trudged up the aisle. Slipping out into the lobby, she held the phone to her ear and headed toward a wall at the farthest edge of the crowd milling into the theater. Not much improvement minimizing background noise. She stuck a finger in her free ear as the connection clicked. "Hi, honey, how are you?"

"How do you think I am? Awful. Even worse than this morning. I told you not to go. You know how unhappy I am without you. Come home now."

His whiny, needling demand triggered an intense desire to fling the phone on the floor and crush it underfoot. Instead, she dutifully reassured him, "*Amor,* you know I'll be home in two days. The time will fly until I'm back. Just think about that and you'll be fine."

"Easy for you to say. I'm stuck here all alone. What's all that noise I hear? Are those men's voices?"

Closing her eyes, Tina leaned heavily against a wall. "I'm in a lobby. It's really crowded here."

"Right," he growled. "Tina the socialite out in a crowd. You're so selfish."

He can't help himself. It's the depression talking, not him. "I'm sorry you feel that way. You're obviously having one of your bad nights. I didn't call to make you feel worse. I'll speak with you again in the morning after you rest."

"Don't bother." He hung up.

Bumping her head lightly on the wall's unyielding plane, weariness enveloped her, and tears rimmed her closed eyelids. *I can't do this anymore.*

"Everything OK?"

Tina gave a start as Bernadette spoke from behind her. Ready to respond with her pat, everything-is-fine-thanks-for-asking mantra, Tina turned to face her. The soft expression in Bernadette's eyes had Tina biting back the lie. Total honesty seemed the first crucial step toward change.

"Things really aren't OK. I don't know what I'll do yet. But I have to change my life." Afraid that Bern's investigative skills would ferret out every last miserable detail, Tina broke eye contact with her friend. "Now's not the time to go into it. I have some thinking to do."

"I'm here if you ever need me." Bernadette hugged her, a soothing reassurance. "Anytime, anywhere."

Relief and affection coursed through Tina. "Thanks, Bern. I know."

Bernadette's phone jangled, and she focused on the caller display. With a shrug of her shoulders and a sheepish grin, she said, "My boss again. I have to take this."

"Make it fast. You wouldn't want to miss anything considering how much Laci has put into this evening. Besides, you deserve some time off. I'll see you back inside." Tina bussed a kiss on Bernadette's cheek. Itching for respite from her boring, imperfect home life, Tina hastened to her seat where her cocktail awaited. Tina guzzled the drink, the condensation on the stemware slippery in her hand. Hoisting the empty glass skyward, she beckoned the waitress back

Marlo widened her eyes and gazed at her. "Whoa. Since when do you drink booze?"

"This is sin city. I'm allowed." Tina greedily reordered from the accommodating waitress. "I am so ready to have a good time. We used to have so much fun." Tina wagged her head, spurring a whirling light-headedness. "Now look at us." She sneered.

"What's wrong with us now?" Laci slurred. "We're all having fun."

"Really?" Tina said. "Be honest. None of us has fun anymore." She squinted her eyes and peered at the girls one by one, starting with Laci, as she rattled off her tactless opinions. "You're taking money from your father—whom you detest. Marlo, you're sticking your finger down your throat so you stay stick thin."

Pointing her finger at Bernadette slipping into the

seat next to her, Tina accused, "You can't take a minute off from work, even though you're hiding your talents in that local show."

"For the last time, I am not bulimic…"

"I do hate my father. She's right about that…"

Tina's posture stiffened as if staving off a blow. "And I let my husband hit me…"

The Belles gaped at her in open-mouthed silence. The wounded expressions on their faces cut deep, and she floundered to find the means to retract her accusations. And her involuntary confession. *I should stop drinking. Or drink myself unconscious.*

"Oh, Tina…"

"Let me handle this, Lace," Bernadette demanded.

The intense sober expression on Bernadette's face sent a chill through Tina.

"He hits you?"

Tears welled. "I'm sorry," Tina blubbered. "I should never drink..."

Marlo slipped her arm around Tina's shoulder. "You have to leave him, Teen. Period."

"Maybe. I don't know. It isn't so bad. He's slapped me a few times. Nothing I can't handle…"

"One time is too many, and you're moving in with me," Marlo asserted. "You'll have the whole place to yourself most of the time when I'm traveling."

"No, I can't leave my job, my family…" Tina wrung her hands. "I'll work it out."

"You can move in with Glen and me. We have plenty of room. The commute to St. Mary's from the city isn't too awful."

"Joe works crazy hours. Come live with me now and stay after we're married and keep me company. The school is only a couple blocks away from my house." Laci didn't slur a word. Apparently, Tina's spontaneous admission had been figuratively and literally sobering.

"Oh, I'm so sorry," Tina lamented as tears streamed. "You're all wonderful to me, and I don't deserve it after I said those things. The tequila...I didn't mean anything I said. Please forgive me. I'm fine. Ramon is not. And I will do something about it "

Marlo stroked her back in soothing circles. "Promise?"

Tina sniffled as she nodded her head, bereft at airing her frustrations during Laci's party of a lifetime. "I've ruined your evening, Lace. I'm so very sorry."

"You haven't ruined a thing." Laci beamed a winsome smile. "This songstress is about to sing to us. What could be more perfect?"

As if on cue, the house lights dimmed. "And don't forget tomorrow," Laci stage whispered. "A whole day at the spa."

Forgetting her troubles was easy as the singer's heavenly voice raised goosebumps on Tina's arms. She'd think about solutions tomorrow...or maybe the next day.

****

Tina freshened up in her suite after the amazing concert before meeting the girls in Laci's suite for a nostalgic pajama party. Life didn't have to involve depression, anxiety, and hopelessness. Laci had given Tina a precious gift this weekend—the certainty that

Tina hadn't fundamentally changed since she had married Ramon. She hadn't done anything to deserve her husband's shoddy treatment. When she returned home, she'd either fix or finish her marriage. Swishing water in her mouth, she heard her cell phone's ringtone sound. *I'll let it go to voicemail. I am too happy to let Ramon spoil this for me now.*

She spat toothpaste into the sink and dried her mouth with the face cloth. Folding the towel lengthwise, she draped it on the towel bar. Her voicemail indicator chimed.

Humming, she strolled out of the bathroom over to her bed. Removing the phone from her purse, she checked missed calls, expecting the call identifier to read, Home. *Mamá's number? So late? Something's wrong.* Her heart racing, she didn't bother to listen to the voicemail before redialing her mother's phone number. The second the connection clicked, Tina blurted out, "Mamá, are you all right?"

"I'm perfect. How are you? Having fun at your party?"

Baffled, Tina frowned as she perched on the edge of the bed. "You called me in the middle of the night to chat? What are you doing up so late?"

"Oh, Tina, I can't sleep. I have such exciting news. It's happening."

The odd tone her mother used in emphasizing the mysterious subject of the last sentence rang alarm bells in Tina's head. "What do mean?"

"The prophecies of Valselo!"

Tina sighed as she identified the zealous timber of religious fervor in her mother's voice. She didn't share her mother's devotion to the Marian visionaries. In fact, she didn't believe a word about supposed visions of Mary, prophetic messages, or miracles of the sun, or whatever else had inspired her mother to waste time and money traveling across the globe on her many pilgrimages to Croatia.

"Don't sigh, Tina," came her mom's predictable admonition. "You may not have believed it before, but now, Anna, Elizabeta, and Father Josip will reveal the secrets that they have received for years. And...our Father Mark is Our Lady's chosen shepherd. He has been given the secrets of Valselo." Rosa's voice trembled. "The permanent sign is coming. I can't believe how blessed we are to be a part of this."

Her mother's voice caught on a sob.

"Mamá, don't cry."

"They are happy tears, my angel. You have to come home. Father Mark is leading a pilgrimage to the sight of the permanent sign. I want you with me. I don't know what to expect."

Her personal life in shambles, Tina wanted to accept her mother's incredible tales of the unconditionally loving, impossibly beautiful, virgin shimmering on a cloud, visible only to her chosen three, as truth. Just like the child who had listened to her mother read fairy tales, at heart, Tina longed to believe in magic.

"Where is this permanent sign appearing? And will it really appear? I can't believe I'm even entertaining the possibility that this is real. Mamá, don't leave until I return home, and we can talk about this."

"Oh, I can't wait! Father Mark said to be ready to board the buses Monday morning first thing. Arrangements are moving even faster than he expected when he told us about this at Mass this evening."

"Bound for where? You honestly don't know where he's taking you?"

"Honey, of course I know where I'm going— wherever Our Lady leads me. You have to come with me. Papá doesn't want to come. You can't miss this," she pleaded.

Her mother's escalating blind faith alarmed her. But logic tempered her foreboding. Father Mark, although a Marian disciple and Valselo pilgrimage leader for years, had never struck Tina as fanatical in any way. In fact, he was affable, articulate, and extremely intelligent. He was a dream boss—the most humble, honest person she had ever met. *At least Mamá will be safe with him.*

Deferring a confrontation with her mom, she would solicit Bernadette's help in investigating the situation first. "I'll give this some serious thought. I'll call you in the morning."

"Wonderful. Maybe I'll know more then, and we can plan where you'll meet me."

"Sure. Sleep well."

"Good night, my angel."

13

Bernadette hadn't bothered to switch on the lights when she entered her room. She peered at her iPhone as she thumbed the home button to awaken the device's display. The screen's illumination flared in the darkened hotel room. Her blackout drapes blotted out the incandescence of the Vegas strip outside her windows.

Seated on the foot of her bed, she might have been holed up in any room on any assignment in her past when she had lived out of the sparse contents of a duffel bag: a fresh shirt, a comb, a toothbrush and paste, a stick of deodorant, and some detergent to rinse out her underwear in the sink every night.

The motion of her index finger stalled over the telephone icon at the memory of Tina's outburst. *You can't take a minute off from work, even though you're hiding your talents in that local show.*

The candid pronouncement spurred Bernadette's self-questioning.

After graduating from the School of Journalism with minors in foreign language, Bernadette had moved to New York City for a grunt job in a major television network's newsroom. Brimming with ambition and empowered by her stellar performance as a college student, she had traded her Spartan, one-bedroom apartment on the university campus for the closer quarters, cubbyhole loft in Manhattan's East Village that she had shared with an aspiring, broadcast meteorologist.

Because she "never took a minute off work," she had gained the notice of her superiors who threw occasional crime beat reporting assignments her way. Pretty, articulate, and unflappable, the camera loved her and vice versa. Within months from her first day on the job, her on-camera blips had increased to longer spots. Before she had completed a full year of employment, she had vied for a posted, international correspondent's position since she was fluent in four languages, including Russian and Mandarin Chinese. She beat out three candidates with considerably more experience.

Nothing stood in her way. She'd go anywhere at a moment's notice—war zones, third world refugee camps crawling with disease and poverty, the Vatican, Tibet, World Summits. No assignment was refused, and her reporting was flawless.

Destined, it seemed, to scale the skyscraping, career summit of prime time, world news broadcasting, Bernadette was home in New York and headed for the television studio when the first plane hit the World Trade Center North Tower. Like all Americans and humanitarian citizens around the world, the series of terrorist attacks struck horror into Bernadette and her colleagues' hearts. But like a much smaller percentage of Americans, Bernadette experienced the intimate, personal terror of the violent loss of a loved one firsthand.

In the chaos of the newsroom, Bernadette watched the network feed with wild eyes as the third plane crashed into the west side of the Pentagon. Before the infamous eleventh day of September had ended, it was confirmed that Chief of Naval Operations, Admiral Michael O'Neal, counted among the fatalities. Her loving, funny, brave, accomplished, beloved father was murdered by those who viewed the mass murder of innocent Americans on a sunny workday as a world-cleansing act of heroism.

Her grief and outrage manifested into vehement bigotry. There was no place for Bernadette's secret intolerance in the post-9/11 world news scene. At odds with her training, she had instantaneously lost objectivity concerning a religious group that comprised almost a quarter of the global population. Rather than take the leave of absence that her confused boss had begged her to consider, she had resigned without honest explanation and moved back to her family home in Chicago. Her kid brother—her only sibling—had quit his junior year at university and had enlisted in the Army on the same day Bernadette left New York.

Still reeling with generalized loathing for the terrorists, Bernadette had had to contend with her mom's despondency and relentless panic attacks triggered by her only son's headlong leap into harm's way after the cruel loss of her cherished husband. Bern might have forgiven her brother's abandonment as he unleashed his grief and rage by blowing up caves in Afghanistan if he had shared her condemnation of terrorists, too.

Instead, he married an Afghani woman, brought her to the U.S. after his honorable discharge, and fathered three kids. Maybe he had even embraced her religion in raising his children.

Bern had received second-hand through her mother, the meager, personally unsubstantiated updates on her brother's life over the past seven years. Each time her mother took another stab at ending her children's estrangement, Bernadette promptly diverted further comment by voicing the repetitive dictum "I don't want to hear about this, Ma."

Time healed, terrors abated, and Bernadette's family adjusted in their own ways, she supposed. Joining the morning show's team—understaffed and then slipping in the ratings—had seemed the ideal job for a workaholic newshound like Bernadette. She could investigate the local crime scene, effortlessly churn out the show's mostly puff, feature pieces, and wake up before dawn charged with energy to smile pretty for the camera next to her virile male co-host, starting at 5:30 AM every weekday. Bernadette, gal Friday, had become the show's golden girl who garnered devoted viewers and popularity awards.

Had her inside track on Joe's homicide investigations lulled her into believing that she was a real reporter? Did Tina's assessment hit the mark? *Am I hiding my talents? No, more like hiding my prejudices.*

Despite Tina's valid criticism, nothing changed. The job remained all-important to Bernadette for an exhaustive list of personal reasons regardless if others considered it fluff or viewed it as hiding. She couldn't change the circumstances that brought her to a local show any more than she could rewrite history so that she had no reason to hate.

The phone rang in her hand, and she jerked as if shocked.

The caller ID read T. Hernandez. She huffed out a laugh at the consistency of the Belles' uncanny, group mental telepathy.

"I was just thinking about you, Teen," she answered the call.

"I wanted to ask you a favor before I go to Laci's room. I'm afraid she'd kill me for talking shop while we're supposed to party. I'm coming right over, OK?"

"Sure." Bernadette disconnected the call and hopped off the mammoth bed. On second thought, the lavish suite had nothing in common with the dingy hotel rooms in Bern's former life. She flipped on the light switch, opened the door, poked her head out into the hallway, and smiled in greeting at Tina as she emerged from the neighboring suite.

"Come on in," Bern said as Tina reached her doorway. "God knows there's enough seating in this room."

"Thanks." Tina bustled past her, trailing a gardenia-scented breeze in her wake.

Bernadette sat on a loveseat upholstered in garden-print chintz, facing Tina, who perched on a fire engine red ottoman shaped like a Gulliver-sized, halved apple. "Whose shop do you want to talk about?" Bernadette inquired. "Something going on with your teaching job?"

"No. I just had a strange conversation with my mother, and I need a favor." Tina cast her a sheepish grin. "Even though I'm breaking the rules by adding to your workload this weekend."

"I thought you didn't approve of my work-every-minute lifestyle," Bernadette quipped, arching her eyebrows.

Tina's face fell. "I'm so sorry I went on like that. Maybe this can wait until we return home." She rose from the garish footstool.

Bernadette waved off the idea. "No, I'm kidding. What do you need, Teen?"

Tina sat back down. "You asked me about Father Mark McKenzie yesterday from the limo. Why?"

"My boss thought I'd be interested in checking into a farfetched announcement attributed to him Friday evening before we left. I forgot to discuss it further with you beyond asking if you knew him. Frankly, I didn't take it too seriously."

"Uh huh. Well, my mom is taking it seriously, that's for sure. She's about to leave on a trip with Father Mark to some unknown destination so that she's on the spot—wherever that is—where God presents some sort of mystical, permanent sign to mankind. She wants me with her. I've never heard her sound so...caught up before. Could you investigate this for me?"

"Hmm. Sure." The electric zing that came with a challenging puzzle to unravel shot through Bernadette. "What little I know so far had to do with Father Mark's claim that God will speak to the world. Does that jibe with what your mom said?"

"Possibly. It all has to do with secrets associated with Marian apparitions in Croatia. For years, my mother has traveled with Father Mark's pilgrimage groups to a village called Valselo, and she's been present at sites where these apparitions of Our Lady of the Roses have occurred many times."

"Actually, I've been there, too," Bernadette interjected. "Two administrations ago, I spent some time with the UN Peacekeeping forces in Sarajevo. I made a side trip to Valselo and interviewed Anna Babic. It wasn't too long after she and the two other visionaries had submitted to the last of the scientific and psychological tests. World-renowned scientists couldn't disprove the visionaries' claims that they saw and communicated with the Mother of God. Fascinating, really."

"Well, you have more background than I do," Tina concluded. "Now, apparently, the Blessed Virgin has selected Father Mark to play a role in the revelation of some secrets imparted to the visionaries. And Mom is getting on the bus to go wherever Father Mark goes, no questions asked. Can you please ask the right questions for me? I honestly don't know how to go about this... And I'm really uncomfortable with my mother's involvement. Together, we might be able to talk her out of taking the trip. She respects your professionalism and loves you like a daughter."

"I love her, too. Of course, I'll help," Bernadette responded. "Just to confirm, though. You did say that Father Mark is stable, right?"

"I think the world of him, but he's human. Given the right circumstances, anyone's sanity is tenuous." Tina's dark brown eyes held hers, a riveting gaze that Bernadette couldn't decipher. *Is she referring to Ramon?*

A chill coursed through her at the memory of a missile crashing into the Pentagon building at five hundred miles per hour...and her consuming, probably insane, hatred of an entire world segment. *Yes, given the right circumstances, your life can change forever.* "Do you have Father Mark's contact info?" Bernadette asked.

Tina unclasped the buckle on her purse and pulled

out her cell phone. "Uh huh. I have the number for the St. Mary's rectory. The line has voicemail."

Bernadette glimpsed her wristwatch. "It's eleven thirty back home. I can leave a message."

Bringing up the add-contact screen on her phone, she moved behind Tina and read the St. Mary's rectory phone number over her shoulder. She tapped the ten digits into the phone and saved the information. "I'll call right now, and then I'll join you girls in Laci's room."

Returning Bernadette's smile, Tina rose off her seat and faced her. "Want me to stay until you're finished making the call?"

Bern shook her head. "No, I'll just be a minute. I want to call my boss, too. See if he knows anything more than he did on Friday. Go keep Laci happy until I free up?"

"OK. Thanks, Bern."

"No problem."

As Tina left the suite, Bernadette placed the call to the rectory.

The connection clicked on the second ring. "Hello, Bernadette," came a baritone voice.

"Um," Bernadette stammered. "Father McKenzie?"

"This is. I've been praying for you to call me, and now your call identifier pops up. Stay safe. I recognized the phrase as your signoff on the show. I watch *Now Chicago* as often as my daily Mass schedule allows," he responded.

Surprised on several levels, she chuckled. "My boss's odd sense of humor. My cohost's caller ID on his business cell phone is Stay Well." She smiled and then continued, "Father Mark, I don't think anyone has ever prayed for me to call...especially so late at night."

"I'm not sleeping much lately," he said. "I've prayed for assistance, and it seems I have my answer. You're just the right person to help me accomplish what I'm entrusted to do."

"Huh," Bernadette said, pacing as she gathered her thoughts. "I'm extremely curious about why you think that's true."

"I need the right publicity. Your show focuses on human interest stories—shoring up the spirit rather than sensationalizing darkness like those highly rated news shows," he said.

Still smarting from Tina's earlier criticism, she retorted, "I'm not sure if I should be flattered or insulted by your opinion."

"Oh, I mean it as a high compliment. Especially in light of the recent, and future plans that I need you to publicize."

She parted the drapes and blinked at the brilliant illumination below her window, her mind racing. "I'm actually calling about your plans to lead a pilgrimage group to an unknown destination. I'm traveling with Tina Hernandez, and she's worried about her mother's intentions to join your group."

Unless the priest did the impossible and convinced her otherwise, publicizing the "mystery pilgrimage" that Tina had described would not make Bernadette's professional to-do list.

"Ah, yes. Rosa Castillo. The dear lady is a true disciple of Our Lady of the Roses."

"Why don't you give me the facts, Father," she suggested, interested to hear if he responded with anything she'd describe as remotely factual.

"I want to spread the Word..." He paused. "In this

case, I think you should capitalize the W in word. Because prophetic events are coming to fruition—per God's plan and at God's hands."

"All right," she exaggerated the pronunciation of both words as if speaking to a small child. "Can you be more specific? What does this have to do with your trip leaving Tuesday?"

"The trip will end at the site of a permanent sign given by God."

"Where?"

"I can't tell you. It's not time yet."

Bernadette tapped her foot. "OK, then when?"

"Soon."

"Father," she said, frustration evident in her clipped voice. "How can you profess that you need my brand of publicity when you don't give me any information—public or otherwise?"

A rumble of laugher sounded in her ear. "Good question. Stay with me on this, Bernadette. Tomorrow you may not understand my reasons fully, but you'll definitely have evidence that the human interest story of the modern age will begin to unfold."

She narrowed her eyes, homing in on the tidbit of information. "What will happen tomorrow?"

Another riff of laughter preceded his remarking, "If I say I can't tell you, you'll probably hang up on me."

Frowning, she tossed out, "So, should I hang up?"

"I don't know the precise answer to your question. But, please, don't hang up," he shot back at her. "A sign is promised. From God. I believe that God will keep His promise. And the whole world will recognize at the same instant that only God could create this sign."

"I..." At a loss to complete the sentence, Bernadette cast a blank stare through the window. *What? Think you're a loon? A zealot? A prophet?* "Father, if this...sign becomes apparent, then what?"

"You'll call me. I'll talk with you in the morning," he said breezily as the phone connection clicked off.

Part II.

The Universal Sign

14

The First Day

Eyelids sticky and gritty with last night's mascara, Tina blinked open her eyes with effort. Off her bearings, she squinted and darted her gaze in the darkness. She turned her head on the pillow. Someone else's soft hair brushed her cheek, and light snoring, distinctly not Ramon's, rattled in her ears.

Her world righted as she made out Marlo's shadowy silhouette next to her; her long black mane of hair spread out on Tina's pillow. Tina calmed, nesting her head in goose down-filled comfort as she gazed at the ceiling far above the bed. Last night's events replayed in her memory. The nostalgic pajama party that Laci had suggested to top off an already over-the-top evening was Tina's favorite part of the festivities. Talking half the night away and squeezing into one bed, as they had as kids, seemed the perfect ending to the *esprit de* Belles' day.

Thank goodness, the bed in Laci's hotel room was twice the size of her friend's childhood bed. Even so, lying precariously on the edge of the bed, sardine-like with her three cohorts, Tina marveled that she hadn't awakened on the floor.

Always first to rise after Belles slumber parties, the urge to use the restroom compelled Tina to roll out of bed, barely making a ripple beneath the three sleeping bodies. She tiptoed to the bathroom without detecting stirrings behind her.

Viewing her reflection in the mirror, she washed her hands. Raccoon mascara spectacles framed her brown eyes. Red lipstick smears clown-painted her mouth and streaked her chin. Squeezing a generous dollop of Laci's lavish face wash out of the tube, she lathered off the makeup, patted her face dry with a plush towel, and then brushed her hair into a ponytail, using one of Laci's elastics.

Her cheeks silky beneath her fingertips, she took a stab at guessing the cleanser's price and then chuckled. *If you have to ask how much something costs, then you can't afford it.*

Considering the couple of tequila sunrises she had imbibed when she almost never drank alcohol, she should have felt worse. Her stomach heaved a bit, and she had a mild headache. But overall, she'd emerged intact the morning after. *All I need is a brisk walk to clear my head.*

Switching off the bathroom light, she gingerly opened the door, padded out into the hallway, and crept past the bedroom to the living area. She parted the heavy brocade draperies, allowing a sliver of sunshine entry into the dimness. Her face edged between the gap in the curtains, she squinted to focus against the sun's glare. *Darn, I really wanted to walk. Too bad it's snowing.*

Taking a step backward, the drapes swung closed.

And then she ripped them open and took a second look at the fantastical tableau outside. Incredulous, she rubbed her eyes and tugged the curtains fully open. Lacy snowflakes descended, a surreal faux blizzard that sparkled crystalline in the desert sun.

Is this some Christmas in July stunt? Amazed at the awesome, special effects capabilities of Sin City, Tina gaped at the scene like a delighted child awaking on a snow day.

This wasn't just a Decadence Hotel spectacle. *How in the world had this been coordinated? They must have machines on every roof!*

Traffic below from one end of the Strip to the other was at a standstill—a virtual four-lane parking lot. Car doors ajar, drivers and passengers stood in the road, gaping upward. Heads craned out of car windows in suspended animation, the cascading snowfall the only visible movement.

Unsure how long the magical show would last, Tina bolted out of the room. "Wake up! Get up!" she yelled as she tore down the hallway into the bedroom. Racing to the windows, she grasped the slender, vertical pull-rods in each hand, stretched wide her arms and thrust open the drapes.

Reacting to the sudden contrast of brilliant sunlight, Marlo yanked the pillow out from under her head and plopped it over her face. "Turn off the lights!" she squawked. "I'm trying to sleep!"

"I swear, Tina, this hotel better be on fire, or I'm going to kill you." Laci's raspy voice sounded from under the sheet where she had escaped the glare of daylight.

"Get up!" Tina trilled. "I promise you'll thank me. You've got to see this!"

No one moved.

"It's snowing!" she exclaimed.

Bernadette groaned as she propped up on an elbow. "Have you been drinking already, Teen?"

"Just come over here and look outside."

Bernadette drooped out of the bed and limped towards Tina. Squinting, she leveled her gaze at the window. "Unreal, it really is snowing."

Fat, brilliant white flakes continued to stream in front of the tinted gold glass panes.

"This is unbelievable," Marlo said as she and Laci approached.

"Told ya so." Tina grinned.

Minutes passed as the foursome stood rooted to the spot, viewing the confetti's unremitting downpour.

"What do you think the effect is for? Is there a Christmas in July thing going on? Or maybe a new Cirque de Soleil show?" Tina posed.

"I don't have a clue. I haven't seen any special event advertisements. Why didn't the concierge tell me about this?" Laci grumbled.

"Who cares?" Marlo asserted. "Let's go outside before they turn it off!"

Tina abandoned the window bank in a flurry of excitement as her roommates scattered, whipping pajama tops off over their heads and searching for their clothes.

"Where's my dress?" Marlo said.

"I changed in my room before I came over here," Tina said.

"Right," Laci replied, her voice scratchy. "Hurry. Just put on the hotel robes."

Giddy, Tina laughed and joked with her bathrobe-clad friends during the elevator ride to the lobby, happy that she had awakened early enough to sound the alert. What a shame if they had missed this unique extravaganza.

Once on ground level, she scurried toward the main entry, the Belles keeping pace, and spun through the revolving doors out onto the wide sidewalk lining the Strip.

A sizable crowd had gathered along the sidewalks and among the idling cars in the street. Like the steady streaming snow, people poured out of the Decadence Hotel and neighboring buildings. It was eerily quiet. Conversations reduced to whispers, as if newcomers to the scene entered a church already populated with worshipers. So peaceful.

Tina raised her eyes heavenward and smiled.

Marlo flung open her arms and twirled around, jostling the tight-knit group.

Laci giggled and spun in circles with her.

"I expected it to feel cold," Bern remarked, cupping her hands beneath the falling snow. Bernadette knit her brows as she stared at her upturned palms. "I can't explain this weird sensation."

Her questioning gaze lit on Tina.

"The flakes feel soft, like feathers," Tina suggested. "But look… They disappear entirely as soon as they touch my skin. And look at the ground. Nothing. I wonder how long this stuff has been coming down?" Tina grinned. "The pavement isn't even wet. This is just amazing."

Craning her neck, Bernadette gazed skyward. "I don't see any machines, do you?"

Tina turned her attention to the tops of the surrounding, multi-story buildings. Squinting as she lifted a hand over her brow to shade her eyes, she scanned the gleaming façades and detected no evidence of artificial snow manufacturers. "Uh uh. I can't find the machines, either."

"This seems like an impossible feat. I have to find out who pulled this off." Planting her hands in the center of her back, Bernadette arched her spine and swiveled her torso back and forth, her scanning gaze like a persistent searchlight.

Bern's jutting elbow poked Marlo's arm.

"Ouch," Marlo groused, massaging the apparent offended spot on her upper arm. "For once, can't you just let loose and enjoy the moment? I'm sick to death of Bernadette, the dogged reporter. Stop questioning everything and just enjoy yourself." Marlo pointedly paced away from Bern's side and positioned on the fringes of the group.

Bernadette's fair skin flamed crimson.

Tina hung her arm over Bern's shoulder.

"I can't help it, Teen. I have to know the answers," Bern said.

"Don't apologize. It's what makes you so good at what you do. Anyway," Tina reduced her voice to a whisper, "I think Marlo is jealous of you."

Bernadette snorted. "As if. Name one thing I have that Miss Absolute Perfection lacks."

"A handsome husband who adores you...I could go on and on." Tina hugged her best friend. "Don't let Marlo upset you."

"If you say so..." Bern's attention riveted on a point to Tina's left.

Tina followed her gaze, noticing that the crowd's numbers had multiplied. Some stood statue-like, nearly shoulder-to-shoulder now, and basked in the wonder of a desert blizzard with no need of snowplows. Some folks threaded their way along the walkways, apparently going about the business of having seen it all in Vegas.

"Look at that guy's face," Bern directed her.

A young man trained saucer eyes on his cell phone. "No way!" he blurted out, still staring at the phone. "It's snowing in the Dominican Republic."

Bernadette clasped Tina's arm and edged closer to the man. "What did you say?"

He didn't respond.

Bern tapped him on the shoulder.

Tugging an earphone out, his hazel gaze darted and focused on Bernadette.

"What did you just say?" she repeated.

Refocusing on his cell phone display, he replied, "I just read this news update that it's snowing in the Dominican Republic, too. The reporter said it has never snowed there. Like never ever. How cool is this?" He freed the other earphone to dangle around his neck.

"You mean this isn't a Vegas special effect?"

"No way. Lady, haven't you seen the news? It's snowing in crazy places all over the world." With a doesn't-that-beat-all shake of his head, he refitted the plugs in his ears and sauntered away.

"How is that possible? How is it snowing all over the world?" Bernadette jammed her hands in her bathrobe pocket. "Shoot, my phone's in my room. I have to get it." Bernadette trained wild eyes on Tina.

Unsettled, Tina urged, "You go. I'll get the girls." She scurried over to Laci and Marlo as Bern raced into the hotel.

"Where's she going? Another call to the TV station, I suppose?" Marlo sniped, glancing at the revolving door.

"Come on. We have to go inside." Tina tugged on Laci's sleeve.

"Why? I want to stay until they turn off the snow. I love the way it feels on my skin." Laci closed her eyes, and an angelic smile beamed on her upturned face.

"They're not turning it off," Tina said in a hushed voice. "It's snowing everywhere. The kid…"

"What?" Marlo interjected.

"Everywhere? How could that be remotely possible? This isn't even real snow," Laci contended, swooping a scooped hand at the descending, disappearing snowflakes.

"That kid we just talked to said that news outlets are reporting this phenomenon all over the world. Bernie is investigating on our behalf, Marlo." Tina couldn't resist the implied jibe. "She'll know what this means."

Tina led the three-woman race into the lobby seconds before a siren blared outside, followed by a bleating horn that sounded like the tornedo alert system back home. An amplified male voice sounded, "Return to your vehicles immediately and proceed safely to your destination. Pedestrians, move now…"

The doors closed on an upward bound elevator before the potential mob surge.

Rushing into Laci's room, Tina encountered Bernadette, operating in full business mode. Flat-toned news announcers' voices issued from blaring, multiple televisions in the suite; she had her e-tablet propped in an easel-like case on the desk and cradled her cell phone to her ear with an up-shrugged shoulder.

Laci slid her sunglasses up to band back her hair, stomped to the desk, and seized the portable hotel phone off its stand.

She jabbed her finger on one of the buttons, and then pressed the device to her ear. "I need coffee," she said. "Don't worry, I'll share…Hello. Yes, please. Two pots of coffee…uh huh. That's right. Thanks."

Bernadette rose from the desk as if she had erupted out of the heart of a volcano, sending the chair clattering against the wall. "I know now!" she yelled into the phone.

"What's going on?" Marlo whispered as Bernadette plopped onto the over-stuffed couch and sat trembling as she stared at the television.

Aggravation? Frustration? Fright?

"I'm not sure…" Tina told Marlo as her heart flip-flopped.

She turned her attention to the TV and witnessed the on-screen, winter scape montage, captioned, "Real Time: The hot deserts of the world."

Snow falling in the Arabian Peninsula, the Kalahari, the Sahara, Chihuahua…

She ventured a glance through the windows, hopeful that at least the snow had ceased in the outreaches of the Mojave Desert area. Maybe her trepidation had mounted since she had learned that it was snowing in the Caribbean, but now the snow seemed thicker than before.

"What do you want from me, Chuck? I said I'm sorry," Bern said at full volume, topping the televised newscasts' drone. "I'm entitled to vacation time. We partied last night, and I slept in my friend's suite. I left my phone in my room." Bernadette took a breath.

The loudness of her boss's voice through the phone publicized his end of the conversation to all present in the suite.

"I agree it's the story of the century..." Bern clamped her mouth shut. And then she fired out, "Don't you dare assign this to someone else, Chuck..."

SPECIAL REPORT flashed on the TV screen.

Bern snatched the remote control off the end table, vamped up the volume to deafening, and said, "Hold on, Chuck. Listen."

She held the phone up toward the TV.

"The FAA has imposed a temporary all-airport ban on takeoffs, pending conclusions from the emergency video conference of members of the World Meteorological Organization. Officials stress that this is merely a safety precaution until the worldwide phenomenon is explained. No incidents have been reported of pilot navigation difficulties since it started snowing. On the contrary—the weather hasn't seemed to interfere with any mode of transportation with the exception of numerous traffic clogs. State police are out nationwide, directing traffic flow. Stay tuned for updates."

Open mouthed, Tina slumped into a chair.

Bernadette lowered the volume, surfed away from the big news channel, and dropped the remote on the couch cushion when a mainstream media show played on screen. "You heard?" Bernadette said into her phone. She nodded. "I may not be able to fly, but maybe I can work something out using my cell phone video calling. Give me a few minutes to get organized. I'll call you back with my plans." She disconnected the call and then paced around the room, jiggling the phone in her hand, one eye on the falling snow outside the floor to ceiling windows.

"Al, what can you tell us about this freakish July snowfall?" the anchor's voice blared through the speakers.

The camera panned to the weather forecaster. Brows knit, his lips in a solemn line, he stood in front of the weather map. "Doppler radar shows no storm systems across the entire continent. I've never seen such a high-pressure system in my life..." He broke eye contact with the camera, seemingly faltering. Somber, his eyes met the lens again. "I...don't know what to say. There isn't a cloud in the sky anywhere. But something that looks a whole lot like snow is falling. I don't know how. It's not measurable precipitation. It just seems to...evaporate. I'm stumped."

Bernadette strode to the couch, scooped up the remote, and jabbed the channel button. Pausing a couple seconds on each channel, disjointed fragments of the same inexplicable facts repeated, and images of cascading snow in impossible locales flickered on the monitor.

Laci responded to the doorbell chime, ushered the room service attendant into the suite, directed him where to leave the cart, and then closed the door behind him. Surprisingly subdued, Laci quietly filled a coffee cup and presented it to Bernadette without a word.

"Did your boss know what's going on?" Tina asked as she rose to help herself to a jolt of caffeine.

"He's as clueless as the rest of the world," Bern replied, depositing her cup on the desk on one of her to and fro passes.

"Marlo, do you want coffee?" Tina asked.

"No..." Marlo clamped a hand over her mouth. "I feel..." She dashed down the hall, and the bathroom door slammed closed.

"Sick," the Belles said in unison.

Tina shook her head. "My stomach isn't steady today, either." She sipped the delicious, reviving brew, eyeing over the rim of the cup Bern's caged animal pacing. "One good thing about this crazy weather, Bern. Maybe my mother won't go on her mystery trip with Father Mark."

Bernadette stopped dead in her tracks and whirled to face Tina. "That's it. That's what's happening." She ran to the desk, flew to a landing on the chair, and dragged the e-tablet closer to her. "I took some notes during my conversation with Father Mark last night to talk over with you, Teen."

Tina left her seat and positioned behind Bernadette.

"Um…here." She pointed to the screen and gazed upward over her shoulder. "Read this part."

"A sign is promised. From God. I believe that God will keep His promise. And the whole world will recognize at the same instant that only God could create this sign," Tina read aloud.

"Snow everywhere is the sign from God that he's referencing here. Father Mark says he has the secrets of Valselo. And they're about to be revealed," Bern rattled off in a rush.

"Now you sound as crazy as my mother," Tina said as she returned to her seat.

All fired up, Bernadette added, "Father Mark told me last night that something would happen this morning."

"You knew all along that it would snow, and you didn't tell us?" Laci accused.

"Of course not. I would have told you all and then dragged Chuck Barton out of bed to broadcast that prediction immediately had I known. But the priest said that I'd understand in the morning. And then I'd call him. I have to call him. I have to get to Chicago somehow."

"You believe that this is a sign from God?" Tina probed.

"Yeah." Bernadette launched to her feet, her head bent over her cell phone. "What other explanation makes sense?"

"Um," Laci sputtered. "I can't think of one, but there must be…"

"Good morning, Father," Bern mouthed into the phone. "OK. You have my attention."

15

Father Mark's hearty laughter boomed in Bernadette's ear. "I'm not the one capturing the world's attention this glorious day, Bernadette. Praise the Lord our God! Isn't this absolutely marvelous?"

Off balance at the jubilant timbre in the priest's voice, Bernadette fought to calm her nerves. Her head throbbed, and she couldn't determine if the adrenaline gushing through her bloodstream stoked the killer hangover or vice versa. The news commentators' background noise irritated her, and the flickering TV images' psychedelic effect disturbed her—not to mention, the claustrophobia she began to experience, occupying the unearthly snow globe Laci's hotel suite had become. "Forgive me, Father…" She stopped speaking as her preamble rang a confessional gong in her head. *Should I be on my knees begging forgiveness?* Ignoring the Catholic school guilt, she pressed on, "I'm not sure I share your, uh, enthusiasm. It seems to me this is more chaotic than marvelous."

"I expected a kind of stop-the-world reaction when I learned of the universal sign. But this? Leave it to God on high to electrify us and still love us enough not to harm a hair on our heads."

"Huh," she responded as his take on the situation appealed to her. "You know...I like that assessment."

"I can't wait to publicly bear witness that Our Lady foretold these and other events. It makes everything that's to come so much more...I don't know...magnificent versus ominous. And your call last evening was so opportune. As I told you, you're just the person to help me proclaim these truths. How do you want to do this?"

OK, Chuck. I have a bead on your story of the century. An extensive list of questions streamed rapidly in her mind, overlapping and out of sequence like chain reaction collisions. "Father, I don't know where to begin to attack this objectively," she admitted, glancing at the TV monitor and absorbing the stop-the-world effects in progress.

"If you provide the forum, I'll take it from there," he said.

"All right," she agreed, her mind reeling to develop the means to conduct the interview of her life. "I can't fly to you, so I have to make arrangements to set up a remote feed from my end. Perhaps we could film you in the Chicago studio. How are the roads there?"

He chuckled. "A jam of mammoth proportion. But it will clear," he said lightly. "And you will be able to fly to me. The FAA will lift the ban."

"How do you know that?" She surfed channels again for corroboration that conditions were moving in that direction.

"Two reasons. Number one, I'm leaving from O'Hare with my group the day after tomorrow, and

I'm certain that nothing will interfere with those plans. Number two, a dear friend and parishioner is a commercial pilot. His flight was at 35,000 feet when the universal sign began, and he claims he experienced the most ideal flying conditions and smoothest descent to landing in his long career. Hundreds of other pilots operating aircraft at the same time echo that experience. I'm told that the FAA will lift the ban within the hour. I'll pick you up at the airport whenever you arrive. Just text my cell number with your flight information. Thank you, Bernadette. I'll see you later."

Bernadette checked the digital clock on her cellphone: 11:30 AM. Tapping furiously on the keypad, she searched scheduled commercial flights bound for Chicago. Rejecting available options due to late evening arrival times, she opted to arrange a charter flight and really work the expense account. As she searched contacts for a charter company, she became aware for the first time since she had begun the conversation with Father Mark that her friends were in the same room.

"Oh," she said as she met Laci's gaze, and then Tina's, Marlo's. "I'm sorry, guys. Give me a second to do this last thing, and we'll talk." After she placed the call to charter the plane, assuring the reservationist that she had information that the takeoff ban would be lifted by the time she arrived at the departure lounge, she faced the Belles. "OK," she said as she sat next to Laci on the couch. "I'm leaving for Chicago on a charter flight to conduct an interview as soon as I can throw clothes on and make my way to the airport."

Standing near the windows, Marlo peered downward. "Looks as though they have traffic moving again down there. It's crawling, but at least maybe you can hire a taxi."

"Use the hotel limo, Bern. I'll call the concierge for you," Laci promised. "Should we come with you?"

"I plan on coming back. I'll leave Chicago first thing tomorrow morning. If I learn anything that makes me think you all should check out before Tuesday as planned, I'll alert you," Bernadette said. "I just spoke with the pastor of St. Mary's, Father Mark McKenzie. Tina asked me to contact him last night because Mrs. C planned to travel with the priest to an unknown destination because of miraculous events afoot. I was supposed to help Tina convince her mom to stay home. Well..." Bernadette pursed her lips and shook her head. "Instead, I'm going back to interview Father Mark on camera as fast as I can manage. Because he says that the snow is the universal sign from God that heralds imminent, prophesied miraculous occurrence."

Laci gave an exaggerated eye blink and sputtered, "What?"

"Is it the end of the world?" Tina whispered, frowning.

"I don't think so," Bern replied. "How did he phrase it? He said that since the snow is benign, what will come will be more magnificent than ominous. His attitude gave me the impression that he views this crazy snow as a gift from God."

Marlo perched on the chair across from Bernadette, wringing her hands. "And you believe him?"

Bernadette rolled her eyes and then cast Marlo a sheepish grin. "I'll interview him; that's for sure." She launched off the sofa. "If I can figure out what in the world to ask him between here and Chicago."

"What do you want us to do?" Tina asked as Bernadette sped past her toward the door.

"Just stay put. Um…" Bern looked askance at the cascading snow. "Soak up the sun?"

Laci hooted a laugh. "I guess I'd better call Joe."

"Gee, I completely forgot to call my mom and Ramon," Tina said. "I'll walk with you, Bern. My phone is in my room."

Bernie grinned at her friend. *Glen must be having a heyday with the science of all this. I'll call him from the car.*

****

When Bernadette reached Glen by phone while riding in the limo bearing DECADENCE1 license plates, Glen remained steadfast and borderline fanatical in his pursuit of a scientific explanation of the phenomenon.

In fact, he had sounded as jubilant about the weird weather as had Father Mark for utterly contradictory reasons. He had derided the mysterious godly topic of Bern's upcoming interview with Father Mark as lunacy of the first degree. The gulf that separated their diametrically opposed beliefs concerning a Supreme Being widened a mile.

Bernadette still respected Glen's high intellect and absolute right to believe what he wanted. But as she had fixated on the falling snow through the jet's porthole, her head angled as far back as possible gazing upward, and she had discovered no conceivable source of the deluge in the highest perceivable heavens, Bernadette had feared that her atheist husband might be the "lunatic in the first degree."

"I'm not going to identify our location for security reasons," Bernadette explained from the passenger seat in Father Mark's car. "I think that's a prudent safeguard. I'll simply introduce you as Father Mark, an ordained Roman Catholic priest."

"That's clever," he responded. "I knew I could count on you. Thank you again."

He eyed the curb along the busy city street fronting the studio. "Where do you want me to park?"

"Just pull up right there," Bernadette pointed a few yards ahead, disoriented yet again by the curtain of snow spotting her vision.

"See those men standing outside?" she asked as she spied Chuck and one of the studio grips standing on the impossibly dry sidewalk. "They'll take care of the car."

Chuck ushered Bernadette and her charge into the studio, exhibiting a stunning servile demeanor as if hosting royalty's visit to his humble workplace. His behavior pressed home the indescribable state of world affairs and Bernadette's de facto role in history in the making.

She waved off the suggestion of makeup and hair styling before the live shoot and requested a solid, sky-blue background behind two stools to compose the set. Once the sound crew had threaded wires and secured body mics in place, Bernadette perched on the stool angled to face Father Mark and then gazed at the priest. "Ready?"

He nodded, and a half smile lit his navy eyes. The

tall, strikingly handsome man would appeal to a broad audience. As she gave the nod to go on-air, Bern was struck by his commanding presence.

Chimes sounded signaling the break-in SPECIAL REPORT: THE WORLDWIDE SNOW screen that interrupted all network broadcasting.

Her heart racing, Bernadette gazed into the camera lens as if encountering the face of a cherished friend. The director signaled from the booth, and she said, "I'm Bernadette O'Neal, broadcasting from a remote location to bring you information about the snow that began falling simultaneously around the world today. Joining me is Father Mark, an ordained Roman Catholic priest who claims special insight into the unexplained weather conditions. Father Mark..." she said, giving him the floor.

Father Mark crossed himself reciting, "In the name of the Father, and of the Son, and of the Holy Spirit, amen." Smiling, he continued, "My church frequently refers to priests like me as shepherds, a reference to Christ, The Good Shepherd of mankind. Friday evening, I was told that I have been selected by Our Lady of the Roses to fulfill the role of shepherd far beyond any training I have received in a seminary or through my ministries during Catholic parish assignments. I am to bear witness that the Mother of Christ, as the emissary of the Most High, foretold the Almighty's execution of world events as they unfold. "The first prophesied event has unfolded as predicted...the snow has begun."

"God has sent this snow, is that what you claim, Father?"

"Yes, I proclaim it, Bernadette."

"You knew it would snow before today?"

"No. I knew that God would provide a universal sign, simultaneous upon the earth at precisely sunset at Mount Sinai and irreversible by earthly means."

Bernadette shifted her gaze to the control booth. "Can someone please confirm that time Father Mark just quoted for our viewers' benefit?" She gazed at Father Mark. "Excuse the interruption, Father. To continue, how did you know about this future event, whether described as God-given or not?"

"I received a parchment from Anna Babic Robbins, one of three Marian visionaries residing in the village…"

As Father Mark provided a brief history of the decades-long Valselo apparitions, Bernadette perched on the stool. She wore a charcoal gray suit and beige, knit tank top, her ankles crossed demurely to keep her knees together and her hands nested in her lap. Although she gazed at the priest, composed and patiently impartial, her impressions of his explanations and the unreal position she had assumed in telecasting his statements as "news" weighed heavily on her conscience.

Despite her show's softer approach to television journalism and focus on human interest stories, she had insisted that staff researchers thoroughly vet any individual she had interviewed on-air. Now, when the world's attention potentially riveted on her professional ability to ferret out the truth, she permitted a man whom she knew virtually nothing about to ramble about roses raining from the sky and Mary of Nazareth's secrets entrusted to three uneducated kids.

True, she knew something about Anna and the other two visionaries, examined by a panel of stellar medical and technical experts during trances while they claimed to speak to the Mother of God. No one had succeeded in debunking the trio's assertions via scientific testing.

A motion off-camera caught her attention.

Shifting her gaze away from Father Mark, she spied Chuck waving his hands and pointing to the teleprompter. HE'S RIGHT ABOUT MT. SINAI TIME.

"...The parchment contains seven secrets concerning the fate of the world," Father Mark stated.

"And worldwide snow is the first secret, Father?"

"Yes, expressed in the parchment as the 'appearance of the universal sign.'"

"I can confirm that Father Mark's earlier statement that it began snowing precisely at recorded sunset in the Mt. Sinai region. Father, what are the remaining six secrets?"

"I can allude to them, but I can't bear witness until after they have occurred."

Bernadette leaned toward him. "Under the circumstances, isn't withholding this information inappropriate, Father? You mentioned that the secrets concern the fate of the world. Shouldn't the world prepare to meet this...mysterious fate? Does this parchment refer to the Apocalypse?"

He hesitated a millisecond before responding, "No, to all three questions. Just like the first secret's fruition that we are experiencing today, the sequential secrets are more general than specific. I'm truly being as forthcoming as possible."

"So, you're asking the world to trust you?"

"I wouldn't presume..." He leveled his gaze at the camera.

On the monitor, his image robbed her breath. His

features appeared illuminated, haloed. His eyes blazed with what she perceived as intense kindness and tenderness.

"Please trust that what's happening and what will happen constitute God's plan for His people. The universal sign—the snow, will remain a total of seven days. Next Sunday, God will provide us with a permanent sign. God intends to grow close to us as never before. It is imperative that everyone on earth acknowledges this."

"What is the permanent sign?" Bernadette pressed.

"I don't know other than it will be beautiful, indestructible, and not of this earth."

"Like the snow?"

He beamed a beatific smile. "Like the snow," he reiterated. "Except never-ending."

"Where will this magical sign appear? Will it be a worldwide phenomenon?"

"No. It will appear at a predetermined place on earth."

"Where?"

"I can't tell you today."

"You'll tell me at some point? When? Before or after it happens?"

"I'll tell you before Sunday, Miss O'Neal, so that you can show it to the world as it happens."

Stunned, Bernadette forgot for several somersaulting heartbeats that she was on camera. Stifling her conflicting emotions that seesawed between terror and joy, she soldiered on with the interview and pursued another line of questioning, "Do the secrets allude to what Christians would call the New Testament, second coming...or

Judaism...might embrace as the first coming, so to speak?"

"No, absolutely not," he fired back. "God, the Father Creator is the giver of these gifts. During this next week, the world will hear the One true and only God speak. I have revealed the contents of the parchment to my pontiff, and he has or will notify the leaders of all the world's religions that they might travel to the future site of the permanent sign if they choose. I emphasize that God will speak to every living soul who needs to hear His voice regardless of who you are, what you believe, or where you are in the world at the time of delivery of the permanent sign."

Bernadette clenched her hands in her lap to arrest their trembling. "You believe this, Father?"

"I know it. I also believe that no one on earth has anything to fear...if you're willing to listen."

At a loss to lead the interview further, Bernadette posed, "Is there anything else you wish to add in conclusion?"

"Yes. In the name of the Father from whom this miraculous, universal sign comes, please live your lives this week while turning your hearts and minds toward your Lord. Let the snow remind you of Him and enjoy this awesome present that He's sent us. How marvelous, magnificent, majestic that He has chosen to first speak to us in a snowfall's whisper."

Chuck signaled the cameramen for the wrap-up. "And we're out," he said as the kliegs switched off.

"So, the world returns to regular programming," Bernadette said, leveling her gaze on the priest. "Which will continue to be mostly snow watching, I'll wager."

"Right," he agreed. "But stay tuned for a special

report coming soon."

"Did you mean it when you said you'd let me know about specifics before Sunday?"

"Yes." He unfurled his long legs and rose off the stool as two techs bustled around him, detaching the microphone.

"And you're leaving with a group in two days. I have a charter flight back to Vegas tomorrow. Should I cancel it and join your group instead?" she asked, raising her arm, so the tech could thread the mic wire out from under her shirt.

Flashing her an enigmatic smile, he burst out laughing.

"What's so funny?"

"It's just..." He caught his breath. "I think it's best that you continue with your plans. Go back to your party. You'll be where you need to be when the time comes." He beamed her an ear-to-ear grin.

Narrowing her eyes, she itched to clue in to whatever he found so humorous. "All right," she conceded. "So, I'm supposed to trust you."

"I'm a trustworthy sort," he said nonchalantly on the move toward the door.

She kept pace with him. "It'll be weird, baking in Vegas while snow keeps falling. I wonder what God thinks about Sin City and bachelorette parties?"

He held the door open for her, and she passed in front of him. "We'll soon find out."

16

The Second Day

Laci paced the length of the suite and spun each time she encountered an opposing wall. The freakish snowfall continued to drift lazily past the expansive windows, stoking her anxiety. *God is whispering? Confronting? Punishing?* A chill coursed through her.

She punched Joe's speed dial number for the tenth time, tempted to respond to God's supposed whispers with a banshee scream. "Please, Joe, call me back," she implored to his voicemail. Shaken by her squeaky voice and the tears that brimmed in her eyes, she clicked off the connection and slid the phone into the back pocket of her jeans. Halting her back and forth marching at the cluttered coffee table in front of the couch, she collapsed onto the cushions. Overwhelmed, tears tracked her cheeks. *Joe, I need you. Where are you?*

She swiped under her eyes with the back of her hand, detesting her inability to function independently. Exerting control over everyone and everything had always provided her highest source of pride. Venting her frustration on the remote control, she furiously jabbed the buttons and cued up Bernadette's recorded interview with Father Mark. Gazing at the monitor, she viewed the landmark telecast for the third time and remained suspended in disbelief. *How could any of this be real?* Antsy and unsettled, Laci launched off the sofa.

Through the windows, the soft blizzard continued while the swirling flakes reflected brilliant starbursts of orange and red from the setting sun.

"The first prophesied event has unfolded as predicted. The snow has begun," Father Mark murmured.

Laci yanked her phone out of her back pocket and reread Bernadette's text.

Taking later flight back. Hung up in studio all morning. Call Jack Dunne to reserve rooms before they're gone. We'll join Father Mark's group this week. Call home. Everyone needs to be together. Should be there about 8...blessings.

Blessings? Bernadette always signed off written correspondence with simply "B."

Marlo followed Tina into the living room. Both tiptoed, furtive and hesitant as if sneaking late into class. Despite her roiling agitation, Laci belted out a laugh at the girls' demeanor and downright comical attire.

"Just look at us," she sneered, tugging at her tunic top under which she sported two layers of tank tops. "We're all dressed for winter, and it must be over a hundred degrees outside."

Totally out of character, Marlo self-consciously plucked at the material of the full-length skirt she wore. Topped by a multi-colored assortment of camisoles and a long-sleeve cardigan, her get-up fell just short of bag lady.

Tina, clad in jeans and a hooded sweatshirt, chuckled as she gazed downward and then at each woman in turn. "Great minds…"

Their laughter echoed hollow within the walls polka-dotted by shadows of streaming flakes.

"You have to bundle up for the first snow of the season. This is the best I could do with what I packed for a Vegas vacation in July…" Tina paused and her eyebrows shot up. "It's *July* in Nevada," she exclaimed. I feel like I'm losing my mind."

The sun continued descending toward the horizon, and the daylight in the room glowed rosy maroon.

"Have you ever seen such a magnificent sunset? The colors seem brighter today than ever before." Marlo wagged her head as she took a seat on the couch next to Tina. "What do you think, Laci? Do you believe that God is making all this happen?"

"I don't know what to believe. I'll wait to hear what Bernadette says off-camera when she returns." Laci checked the diamond-rimmed face of her slim, vintage platinum watch. "She should be here soon. What's your opinion, Tina? You know Father Mark better than any of us."

"Well, he's a wonderful boss—unwaveringly fair. And he has always seemed totally honest. Normal, you know? Funny. Humble. My mother loves him and hangs on his every word. I think that if he says God is talking to us, then we should believe him." Her broad smile illuminated her features. "How awesome is that?"

Laci averted Tina's wonderstruck gaze. She

couldn't begin to embrace the possibility that God hovered near, boring all-knowing eyes into her blemished soul. "Bern texted me the name and phone number of the man in charge of travel arrangements for Father Mark's group so that we can join them. Jack Dunne."

"I know Jack," Tina said. "I'll bet you all have heard of him. Remember the man who sold his software business a few years back for a billion dollars or something? He and his wife Beth are expecting a child now. Talk about God working in our lives.

"They lost a baby to SIDS, and grief split them up. Then they went with Father Mark to Valselo. As my mom tells the story, miracles and an angel brought them back together. Anyway, they're happier than ever now. A real love story."

"He seemed very capable on the phone," Laci stated, unconcerned with the man's personal life, miraculous or whatever. "The rooms are filling up fast at the mystery motel he booked. I was only able to reserve two rooms. I thought we could take one room, and the guys could have the other room. Just to be together. Hope this is OK with everyone. Have you talked with Ramon yet about travel plans?"

"No, he's at work, so I left a message. I'm sure he'll want to come. It's free if he tags along with Mamá. How about Joe…is he coming?"

"I haven't been able to reach him since yesterday just after Bern left. After I received her text last night, I've clogged up his voicemail box with frantic messages to tell him he needs to come here." Laci resumed pacing, desperately needing Joe's levelheadedness to help her cope with bizarre circumstances. She had reserved lodging in an unknown destination to…What? Meet God?

"Leo is grabbing the next flight out," Marlo added quietly. "He checked while we were on the phone and confirmed that the commercial flight restrictions were lifted. If the plane left on time, he should be in the air already."

"Really?" Laci halted in front of Marlo, her interest piqued. "You haven't mentioned him once this trip. I didn't know you were that close. Are you two a couple?"

"It's complicated." Marlo shrugged. "He was the first person I thought about after watching Bern's interview, so I went with the impulse. He said he immediately thought of me when he watched the broadcast. Maybe that means something.

"I think that's wonderful, honey." Tina hugged her. "Maybe your own love story in the making. I always thought you and Leo belonged together."

Laci scrutinized Marlo's face for her reaction to Tina's pronouncement. Marlo trained a wide-eyed gaze at Tina as she beamed a radiant smile. Something was different about her icy, supermodel friend that she couldn't define.

"Why haven't you said anything, Teen?" Marlo asked, her voice ringing hopeful.

"You had to figure it out for yourself. The way he looks at you? I think he's always been in love with you. I'm happy for you." She patted Marlo's knee.

The main door of the suite flew open.

"It's hot as Hades out there. I need a drink. And I mean booze," Bernadette quipped as she barreled through the entry and clunked her bulging briefcase on the floor.

"Me, too," Laci asserted in open-armed motion

toward Bern. She hugged her friend and clung to her as if she were long lost and the only possible sanity in a tilting world.

Chuckling, Bern slipped out of her grasp. "I'm glad to see you, too, Lace."

Bern doled out hugs to Tina and Marlo while Laci dialed room service to order dinner and a supply of wine.

Heaving a sigh, Bernadette plopped down into the vacant seat on the couch.

"I've watched your interview over and over. What's happening, Bern? Do you buy the priest's explanation?" Laci probed, easing into the barrel chair next to the couch.

"Speaking professionally, I can't fathom that God is directing the climate like this. Call me doubting Thomas, but Bernadette O'Neal for *Now Chicago* needs proof, some form of concrete evidence to convince me. Certainly, my husband is convinced that he and his colleagues will search out a scientific..."

The doorbell chimed, the bell choir tones echoing within the suite.

Laci rose and hurried to answer. She flung open the door and supervised delivery of the dinner cart.

"Wow," Bern said as the door closed behind the attendants. "Do they have a room service staff hanging outside in the hall just in case?"

Laci grinned as she poured four glasses of wine. "I only ordered a bunch of sandwiches...and wine, thank goodness," she said as she handed out full goblets. Laci returned to her seat. "You were saying, Bern?"

"Um...yeah. I have a pretty accurate fiction detector on the job. As a reporter, I'm positive that Father Mark absolutely believes that he speaks the truth, even though there's no objective way to determine if it is the truth." Bern took a sip of wine as she gazed out the window. "But," she said, setting the glass down on the coffee table. "As a woman who sat across from the charismatic priest with the honest eyes, I believe with my whole heart that he did tell the truth. These events are part of God's plan. And it's a defining moment in human history." She expelled a breath and then fell silent.

No one spoke.

Laci's heartbeat drummed in her ears as Bern's assessment sank in to her embattled conscience. Breathless, she gulped some wine, hoping the alcohol might tranquilize her frayed nerves.

"So…" Bern drawled. "What have you guys been doing all day? What did I miss?"

Laci snorted. "Oh, we've been having a blast," she said, rolling her eyes.

Marlo and Tina tittered.

"Yeah?" Bern questioned, her eyes gleaming. "I'm so jealous. I've been manning phones at the station. And hiding out from the competition. Every newscaster in the country wants a scoop on Father Mark."

Laci crossed her arms over her chest. "We've been glued to the television. I speak for the Belles—the worst cabin fever since the blizzard of '99. We tried a stint at the pool. God knows it's hot enough out there. But it totally freaked us out, lying there in bathing suits with this supernatural snow coming down on us."

Marlo nodded. "It was like being tickled or something. We lasted about five minutes, and then we hustled inside and sat next to each other at slot machines."

"But then," Tina added, "we felt guilty since all this is supposed to be biblical. God's outside and we're gambling? It didn't sit right. So, we fled up here and ordered room service all day. I swear I've gained five pounds."

"Not exactly the decadence bachelorette party of your dreams, right, Lace?"

Laci snorted again. "One thing for sure. We'll never forget my bachelorette party."

The Belles burst out laughing. But in seconds, the tone shifted, the hilarity petered out, and the women gazed out the windows, mute and unsmiling.

"Let's get down to business," came Bernadette's crisp directive, mercifully right at the point when Laci couldn't bear another second of somber silence.

Heading toward her briefcase, Bern retrieved a notebook out of the side pocket and rejoined the group seated around the coffee table. "Were you able to contact Jack Dunne, Lace?"

"Yes," she replied. "I spoke with him and booked two rooms. That's all he would allot to us. We have to share. Guys in one room, Belles in the other, or whatever works out for everyone. Have you been able to talk to Glen? Is he coming?" Laci lifted a pad of paper and pen off the coffee table, ready to update the notes she had compiled.

"I talked to him a couple of times before and after the broadcast. He thinks I'm crazy. Maybe I am. But for the first time since meeting my husband, the esteemed doctor, I think he's totally off the mark." She barked a laugh. "Guess we'll find out at the end of the week who's nuts."

"How can he still be an atheist with the snow falling?" Tina asked. "If anything, I think this is a major wake-up call from God."

"Exactly. I tried to explain that to Glen. You can't ignore that something this huge and inexplicable has to validate God's existence. He doesn't buy it, but he's taking the next available flight here. He said he wouldn't miss the opportunity to prove me wrong for the world. We'll see about that."

"OK," Laci said as she added names to her list. "So far, we have Leo and Glen."

Bernadette arched her eyebrows as she pinned Marlo with a piercing gaze. "Leo? Something you haven't told me, Marlo?"

Marlo blurted out, "I feel like he should be here with me. Do you have a problem with his coming?" She winced as if anticipating Bern's verbal blow.

Marlo's unusual behavior had Laci more off-center. If Mar's quiet approach to life crumbled where would that leave a secretive, control freak like her?

"No problem, Mar. I like Leo," Bern sang out cheerfully. "How about Joe…is he on his way here?"

"I haven't gotten in touch with Joe yet, and Tina is still waiting for Ramon to return her call. But I'm counting on both of them."

Reading from her notes, Laci said, "I reserved two four-wheel-drive vehicles, equipped with GPS, for delivery to the hotel, in case we have to drive wherever we're going. The four-wheel drive might come in handy if the snow pattern changes and it starts to accumulate on the roads. Do we know where we're going yet?" She raised her eyes and cast a quizzical glance at Bern.

"Nope. Father Mark will call me from the airport tomorrow before he boards his plane and let me know where we should meet him." Bernadette rubbed her eyes with her knuckles and rested her head back on the couch cushion.

"With the navigation systems in the cars, we'll be all right no matter where he sends us." Laci wrote a check next to the word cars on her list and then continued reading, "I ordered two cases of water, four backpacks, a case of protein bars..."

Tina's phone chirped. She jolted in her seat and gazed at the caller ID. "It's Ramon." She stood and drifted toward Laci's bedroom. "Hi, *mi amor*..." Her conversation muted as she closed the door.

Carrying her pad, Laci left her seat, switched on lights in the darkening suite, and rattled off the remaining provisions she had ordered, "I also bought flashlights, batteries, rain ponchos, candles, matches, binoculars, blankets, and a couple of Swiss army knives." She paused as she took a breath. "Everything will be delivered to the concierge desk tomorrow morning before nine o'clock. So far, that's all I have. Can you think of anything else?"

"You're amazing. I can't think of a thing."

"Aw, thanks..." Laci grinned, pleased with the compliment. "I shop."

Bernadette giggled and straightened in her seat. "I'm beat. How about we get some sleep, and then we can meet for breakfast in the morning."

Tina, her eyes red rimmed, shuffled back into the room and slumped against the arm of the couch.

"You've been crying. What happened?" Marlo leaned over and rubbed Tina's back.

"Ramon won't come. I begged him to call Mamá and make arrangements to leave with her tomorrow. He said no. He wants me to come home tonight."

"You're not even considering that, are you?"

Bernadette boomed.

Tina clenched her jaw and said, "I will not miss what God has planned for us. Ramon's selfish demands mean nothing."

"Good for you." Laci smiled. "Bern just suggested that we try to rest in our individual rooms now and then meet for breakfast in the morning."

"Great idea. What time?" Marlo said.

"Does six work for everybody?" Laci threw out.

"Sounds perfect."

"Fine with me."

"It's unanimous," Bern concluded. "If I hear from Father Mark before then, I'll call. Otherwise, we meet here at six."

Laci stood at the door and gave out hugs as each woman left the suite. Mired in unreality, she sagged against the closed door. After she switched off lights, she stood at the window, gaping at snowflakes turned into glitter by the illumination of the Vegas strip. She tugged her phone out of her pocket and redialed Joe as she ambled into her bedroom.

"Hey, baby," came his beloved voice.

"Oh, Joe. It is so good to hear your voice. I've been going crazy trying to reach you all day." Finally able to breathe easily, she sank down on the pillow-soft mattress. She stretched out on the massive, round bed, her legs dangling over the curved edge, and clasped the phone to her ear as if grasping his hand for dear life.

"I'm so sorry. I left my personal cell at home this morning. As you can imagine, things around here have been crazier than during a full moon." He chuckled.

Her heart warmed, comforted at the sound of his deep voice.

"The dogs were nuts this morning, too. Belle refused to go out in the snow at all and left a very substantial dump in the middle of the kitchen while I showered. Geez, Lace, it's still snowing. What's going on? I saw Bernadette's special report. Does she really believe this is the work of God?"

"It has to be God, Joe. What other explanation is there? When are you getting here?"

"What are you talking about? I'm not coming to Vegas." His refusal stung like a physical slap.

"It's snowing here, there, and like everywhere, Joe. I told you in all my messages that Bernadette is connected with a priest who knows what'll happen in the next few days. And that we're all going to wherever this is supposed to occur. How can you leave me alone to face…? You have to come. Even that twerp Leo is on his way. And Glen, too. He doesn't even believe in God," she shrieked. "You should be here already."

"Calm down, Lace, OK? People have gone rogue since it started snowing. I've been hauling in wagons of looters. I have a job to do, baby. And the job gets bigger the longer it snows."

"We all have jobs," she fired back. "Do you think God cares about our jobs?"

"Actually, I do," he replied in an even voice. "I'm on the side of the good guys. I'm a cop, for Pete's sake."

"How can you abandon me for a paycheck? I can't believe any of this is happening," she whimpered. "I thought you loved me."

"I love you fiercely, sweetheart. I can't take off on some wild goose chase after heavenly signs when I'm desperately needed here. Please understand…"

"I don't understand," she interjected. "You should want to be with me when…who knows?" She sat up straight on the edge of the bed, her chest heaving. "I can't talk about this anymore. I'm too upset."

"I love you so much. Please don't be mad," Joe pleaded.

Too late. Laci disconnected and then powered down her phone. She delayed letting loose the soul-aching, crying jag until she had completed her nightly routine and dove under the bedcovers.

17

The Third Day

Anna balanced the umbrella handle against her left shoulder as she sat cross-legged on the smooth sandstone ledge. The parasol shielded her from the emerging sun. But the rock beneath her heated the seat of her shorts. The fiery hues of dawn seemed to set the towering formations in the distance ablaze. Wonderment swelled in her soul, contemplating this extraordinary place fashioned from the desert dust by her beloved Lord who now sprinkled the land with magical snow dust.

Since it began snowing, Anna had experienced profound peace, the same glorious ecstasy that she had relished during Gospa's short visitations: jubilance in Our Lady's presence, and then the shattering plunge back into reality. But this rare peace bestowed by the manifestation of the universal sign, permeated her soul, soothed her heart, and blanketed her with serenity, much like the lingering snowfall.

Ruža had rejoiced at the snow spectacle in the strange, torrid landscape surrounding their motel.

Like their child, Anna and Matt romped about outside, the flakes first kissing their skin before disappearing. Still more heavenly kisses descended upon the shade-lacking landscape.

The magnitude of her mission oppressed Anna despite her delighted relief at the loving blessing imparted by the predicted sign. She had feared catastrophe at the prophecy's fruition. Instead, the Lord had given the world beauty, mystery, joy, frolic, and love—a tangible sign that the Most High is love. But much would yet occur...

Immersed in prayer, Anna didn't notice the pair's approach until she heard the tinkle of Elizabeta's laugher. Tilting the umbrella backward, she observed Elizabeta and Josip trekking along the cracked earth below her perch.

"Dobar dan," she greeted them in full voice.

"Da, Anna," Josip called out. He lowered his head when he reached the base of the outcropping and concentrated on his footing as he hiked up to her position, halting periodically to offer a handhold down to Elizabeta. He and Elizabeta climbed surefooted, accustomed to navigating the craggy slopes of Salvation Mountain and the lower, but still treacherous rocky inclines of Gospa Hill at home.

Like Anna, Elizabeta used an umbrella to screen herself from sunburn. Her friends neared, Josip clad in beige shorts and a cotton T-shirt, and Elizabeta who appeared as a bobbing, lemon-yellow canopy over shorts, creamy-skinned legs, and sneakers.

"Da, yes, dear Anna, it is an exceedingly good day," Josip said, squatting down to peck a kiss on her cheek.

She patted the smooth stone on both sides of her

seat on the rock. "Sit with me. It's so beautiful here, is it not?"

"Absolutely gorgeous," Elizabeta agreed. She plopped down to Anna's right, emitting a grunt. "Phew. *Vruće je.* It's so hot, though. So strange to sit out in a snowstorm and sweat—how does Maya say? Lemon balls." Her hearty laughter boomeranged echoes off the canyon walls.

As Josip took a seat on her left side, Anna's contentment swelled. Only these two people understood her to the core, having experienced the identical, supernatural phenomena since childhood. She had no need to explain anything to them, or to assume any duty in conveying heavenly messages. They heard Our Lady speak and received her counsel, too. Despite their toe in paradise existence, the trio had lived normal lives residing in their humble village in the interim between apparitions. Well, except for fulfilling the roles Our Lady defined for them as emissary of the Most High.

Josip had interpreted his role by entering the priesthood, dedicating his life to spreading God's Word and protecting orphans, the most fragile among the world.

Elizabeta's role entailed praying for non-believers that their hearts might open to receive God's love: a very difficult, sometimes tortured mission that had her crying rivers of tears. Elizabeta proclaimed the annual message for the world that she received from Our Lady's lips.

Anna tended Our Lady's supernatural rose garden in her Adriatic village, always knowing that a greater mission loomed. She was charged with the singular role of certifying the secrets, helping a troubled world interpret the signs, and somehow convincing people that whole-hearted acceptance of God's will constituted the only means to avert catastrophe.

Snuggling between her compatriots and co-visionaries, Anna marveled that three unremarkable people had received abounding insights into Our Lady's heart, and through her, had basked in the infinite love of the Lord. Anna scanned the terrain, an abundance of color rising mountainous in the far distance from the valley of desert sand—more spectacular dotted by preternatural snowfall.

"How lovely is our Lord," Elizabeta commented, voicing Anna's thoughts. "He's so clever!"

Anna burst out laughing and Josip threw back his head and hooted. Yodeling reverberations sang in the air.

Catching her breath, Anna joked, "You're clever, my friend. Perhaps our Lord is better described as cleverest?"

She hung a warm arm over Anna's shoulder. "Your English is so much better these days, Anna. Cleverest...good one."

Smiling, Anna said, "How did you know where to find me this morning?"

"She led me," Elizabeta responded.

"Ah," Anna said, requiring no clarification of Elizabeta's use of the third person singular pronoun in their exclusive Marian society. "For some purpose?"

"Yes," she replied.

"She will come," Josip added.

"And you didn't gather the others?" Anna questioned, accustomed to permitting, even encouraging, witnesses to their shared visitations.

"She called us alone. Very clearly," Elizabeta

casually responded. "Just before I awakened, her voice came."

"I see," Anna said. "Were Matt and the baby up when you left the motel?"

Elizabeta's face glowed with affection as her broad smile illuminated her features. "That little darling sang a song to me in between spooning up porridge. I'm not sure about the words except for snow and star."

Anna grinned, visualizing Ruža's cherubic face and hearing her baby's soft singing voice in her mind. "I am so blessed."

Elizabeta chuckled. "Yes. We certainly are."

Josip asked, "Have you heard from Father McKenzie since the TV show?"

"I have, yes," Anna replied. "His flight leaves Chicago tomorrow morning. The group will nearly fill the entire plane! He is quite clever, too." Anna beamed a smile at Elizabeta. "He changed the meeting site from St. Mary's Church to Jack and Beth Dunne's house. But Jack has a huge bus with dark windows leaving from the church and driving to Midway Airport while the real bus leaves from his house and takes the group to O'Hare airport. You know, to confuse other reporters? Father Mark has chosen that lady who interviewed him on TV, and he doesn't want to speak to other reporters. So smart. It is obvious why he's the chosen shepherd."

"I'm so grateful to him and to Mister Dunne," Elizabeta said. "The hotel he switched us to is so cheerful. The air conditioning is heavenly, and Ruža loves the swimming pool."

"I know..." The aromatic smell of roses pervaded Anna's senses.

"She comes," Anna, Elizabeta, and Josip whispered in unison. "Hail Mary, full of grace..."

Mary of Nazareth's exquisite visage transcended Anna's physical universe. Unburdening her heart in silent interlocution, Anna's fears evaporated like the snow raining down from heaven. "Mother, my heart rejoices at the majesty of the universal sign."

"My child, you are so dear to me and to your Father. You are ready for the moment at hand."

Her chest constricted and even Our Lady's comforting presence didn't slow her racing pulse. Anna quaked, fully aware of the manifestations she would steward. "The permanent sign, Mother?"

"It shall bestow greater joy."

"What will you have me do?" Her mind blanked to receive instruction as if Our Lady inscribed words, employing her brain as a tablet.

"Thank you for having responded to my call."

As Gospa prepared to leave, panic seized Anna.

"Mother, wait!" Anna's soul shouted. "Please…is this the last time we'll speak?"

"I will come once more to speak through you to those who gather in the desert, my rose." Smiling, Our Lady imparted reassurances. "I will return to you on your wedding anniversary until you leave this life and dwell in eternity with me. Remember, I'm your mother. Thank you, dear child, for having responded to my call."

Gratitude surged through Anna at the sacred promise. She could withstand the dimming apparition as Our Lady left her, fortified by the Holy Mother's trust and the sure knowledge that her loving God overlooked her human imperfections. She must convey that knowledge, so that everyone on earth appreciated what riches God would give those who love Him.

Beside her, Elizabeta and Josip emerged from their

conversations with tear-glazed, blinking eyes and quivering limbs, much like Anna.

"Anything to share, 'Beta?" Anna asked.

Elizabeta nodded and replied in a tremulous voice, "Yes." She gulped from a water canteen and then passed it to Anna. "A message for the world before the appearance of the permanent sign," Elizabeta said.

Josip unfolded his legs, stood, and made the sign of the cross with his hand over their heads. Then he accepted the canteen Anna held up.

He drank. Resuming his seat on the rock ledge, he returned the flask to Elizabeta and stated, "I received the message, too."

"I'm sure what I received is identical," Anna said. "I brought a notebook and paper. Also," she said as she extracted the implements to record the message from her tote bag, "Our Lady revealed the location to expect the appearance of the permanent sign."

Anna looked up from the paper, stretched out her left arm, and pointed her index finger at the yawning expanse of barren, desert floor below. "There," she said roughly pinpointing a spot in the reddish sand dotted with creosote bushes and spiny, cholla cacti.

"All right," Elizabeta commented, training her gaze on the area where Anna gestured. "Will we kneel right there in prayer, or should we gather the pilgrims farther away?"

"We three will stand at the site." She lowered her arm and continued writing. Focusing on her notebook, Anna jotted down the message. When she finished, she asked, "Shall I read?"

Elizabeta and Josip spontaneously recited, "Dear children! On this message, which I give you today through my servant, I desire for you to reflect a long time."

Smiling, Anna silently read her passage line by line as Elizabeta and Josip voiced each word she had written on the page.

"My children, great is the love of God. Do not close your eyes, do not close your ears, while I repeat to you: Great is His love! Hear my call and my supplication, which I direct to you. Consecrate your heart and make in it the home of the Lord. May He dwell in it forever. My eyes and my heart will be here, even when I will no longer appear. Act in everything as I ask you and lead you to the Lord. Do not reject from yourself the name of God, that you may not be rejected. Accept my messages that you may be accepted. Decide, my children. It is the time of decision. Be of just and innocent heart that I may lead you to your Father, for this that I am here, is His great love. Thank you for being here!"

Josip gave Anna a crooked grin and ruffled the crown of her head with his knuckles. "So, how'd we do?"

The trio chortled like the children they were when the visitations began, and they had played the recitation game with each other. The game represented their private method of "pinching" each other to check if they were dreaming or not.

"Perfect," Anna opined. "Word for word. Of course, you knew that." She bumped her elbow against the side of his arm playfully.

Elizabeta set her umbrella upside down on the ledge, twisted, and leveraged up to stand on the rock shelf. Bending to scoop up her parasol, she said, "Shall I post the message on the Valselo website like I do the annual messages?"

Anna rose to stand beside her. "Yes, please," she responded. "But I'm to convey the message, too," Anna added.

"Good," Elizabeth said. "Through what channels?"

Following Elizabeth's descent down the path, Josip in tow, Anna responded, "I'm to advise Father Mark's *Now Chicago* reporter. Our Lady wants a wider audience."

The visionaries' light-hearted laughter rang within the sandstone walls, encompassing the Valley of Fire. And the snow cascaded.

18

The Fourth Day

Father Mark canted his head and sandwiched his cell phone between his shoulder blade and his ear. "I know, Sam, but I can't imagine going without you," he said fumbling with the latch on his suitcase. The phone jiggled out of his tenuous hold and plummeted to a soft bounce on the bed coverlet. Sam's garbled baritone emanated into space as Mark retrieved the phone. "Sorry, I dropped the phone. I'm packing and failing at multi-tasking. What did you say?"

"I said that I can't remember a single time in my life when you weren't completely honest with me. What do I tell Emma? She's frazzled enough cutting our honeymoon short."

"Cutting short? Are you on your way back to the States?" the priest asked, eager to devise a plan for Sam to join him.

Maybe he had purely selfish motives, but Sam, and now Emma, were his only living family members. On his knees in pre-dawn devotions, Father Mark had pleaded with the Almighty to supply him strength. He had understood with piercing clarity that he desperately needed someone who loved him as a person, rather than a religious professional, to stand with him in the desert.

"We're in Lisbon. They say our flight to Newark is on time," Sam said dryly, apparently mistrusting that information.

"Good, good," Father Mark rattled, "It's physically possible for you both to be with me then. I'll make all the arrangements. All you have to do is say yes."

"I suppose this has to do with...snow, right?"

"Did you see my interview on TV?"

Sam huffed a laugh. "Yes, but they dubbed you in Portuguese, no subtitles. I have the gist. But I can't describe the pandemonium of the last few days. The tour guide abandoned us in Fatima, and we've been left to our own devices. My credit card is probably maxed out, and Emma is exhausted. The prospect of more travel on top of suffering through lousy seats on an international flight and a layover in Newark before the flight to Chicago is more than we can handle. At this point, I just want to go to bed and sleep through this...miracle or whatever," he grumbled.

Mark's stomach sank, absorbing Sam's litany of legitimate complaint. *If it is Your will, my Lord, I'll do this alone.* He closed his eyes and breathed deeply, yearning for Sam to grant him the gift of banishing this clawing loneliness. His nephew breathed heavily into the phone, and Father Mark inwardly debated how best to persuade him without resorting to begging.

"OK, we'll be there." Sam snorted.

Exasperation? Should I feel guilty? Father Mark laid a hand on his heart as he grinned broadly. "Thank you, Sam. I'm deeply grateful, and I promise you won't regret the decision."

"So…um," Sam stammered. "What am I supposed to do now?"

"I'm sure whatever you packed for your honeymoon will suit. I'll ask Jack Dunne to work with you on coordinating travel details in a few minutes. How long do you have before you board?"

"An hour."

"OK. That'll work. What's your flight number?"

Sam rattled it off. "Should we continue with the connection to Chicago out of Newark?"

"I'll leave that up to Jack. See you soon, Sam. Stay strong. God is with you."

"I'll try, Uncle Mark. Who's Jack Dunne?"

"A parishioner. Amazing. He's footing the bill for everything, so don't worry about that credit card."

"Well that's a relief. Love you, Unc."

His heart warmed, and for the first time since he had received the parchment, Mark McKenzie experienced the singular encouragement that only a loved one could provide. "I love you, too, Sam." About to disconnect, Father Mark pulled up short and sputtered, "Oh, and Sam? Please don't tell anyone other than Emma about your final destination. I'm trying to contain specifics for as long as possible."

"All right. But why? Can you at least tell me that?"

"We'll witness the Valselo prophecies' fruition, and Our Lady of the Roses will cease communicating through the visionaries after this is all over. I want to hand pick those physically present at the site of the permanent sign as much as I can. I'm shooting for unified reverence regardless of religious affiliations. This is our Creator's show, Sam."

His nephew sucked in a breath. "The snow isn't

the big show?"

"Just a warm-up act."

Father Mark's heartbeat thudded in his ear. Or could he hear Sam's racing heart through the telephone connection. "I know, son. Wow, right?"

"Yeah, Uncle Mark. I don't know whether to sing Alleluia or go hide somewhere."

"You don't want to miss this. You'll have a front row seat." Mark chuckled. "Safe flight. God bless you, Sam."

The priest slipped the phone into his pants pocket. Both hands now free, he easily snapped closed the clasp on his suitcase with one flick. He slid his slim computer into his briefcase, hung its strap over one shoulder, and rolled the suitcase out of his bedroom into the rectory's second-floor hallway.

Purposely leaving the lights on in his room as Jack had instructed, he hurried down the hall, grasped the handle of the suitcase, and carried the bag down the back stairway. Through the door's glass panel, he spied Jack, hulking in the shadows. "Hey," he whispered in greeting as he joined Jack at the bottom of the brick stoop.

Jack nodded in response, typing frantically on his phone.

Over Jack's shoulder, Father Mark read the one-word text message, "Go."

Idling diesel engines roared, and the buses that had rumbled to the curb in front of the rectory a half hour earlier zoomed away, bound as planned for Midway Airport.

Matching Jack's strides down the alleyway out onto the sidewalk, Father Mark continued carrying his rolling bag to minimize noise.

"The O'Hare bound buses are loaded and waiting in front of my house," Jack related.

The subterfuge tickled Father Mark, and he beamed Jack a smile. "I'll never be able to thank you for all you have done to make this trip possible. You haven't overlooked a single detail."

"It's the least I can do to repay you," Jack said, returning the grin.

"You don't owe me a thing," Mark insisted. "Quite the opposite."

"If you hadn't forced me to go on pilgrimage with you to Valselo, Beth and I would be divorced by now."

"Force is a strong word." He patted Jack on the back, "And I will not take credit for your renewing marriage vows. What therefore God has joined together, let not man put asunder. You were meant to be with Beth. I believe you both would have figured it out without my interference. I just gave the two of you a gentle nudge." He adjusted the briefcase on his shoulder. "I just got off the phone with Sam. He and Emma will arrive this afternoon from Lisbon into Newark International. They have a connecting flight into Chicago if you want to work with that."

Jack tapped an icon on his phone. "I'll research the best way to route them to Las Vegas. I'll have to limo them to the hotel. No problem. I reserved a room for them already, and I'll send him a quick text with everything he needs once I line things up. How much time do I have?"

"I'm sorry. Less than an hour before they board in Lisbon."

"Well then, I'd better be quick about it," Jack retorted unfazed. Rounding the corner two blocks north of the rectory, Jack pointed down the street.

"Your flock awaits."

Two sleek buses, motors rumbling, were parked in front of Jack and Beth's mansion.

"I know you don't want to hear it, but thanks for the time you're devoting and the fortune you're spending on my behalf." Father Mark hugged Jack and then gave his hand a hearty shake.

"I think we're agreed that we're doing our part on Our Lady's behalf. Mine pales in comparison to yours. Now go." He waved toward the buses. "Beth and I will meet you at the hotel. Maybe I can coordinate with Sam's incoming flight. I don't foresee any problems, but if anything happens, call me."

Father Mark squinted skyward. Delicate snowflakes landed like soft caresses on his cheeks. Smiling, he remarked, "Never gets old, does it, Jack?"

"No, it certainly does not," he affirmed.

Rambling toward the lead motor coach, the priest was tempted to twirl open armed beneath the celestial, raining snow. The door swished open, the driver lumbered down the steps, rocking the bus, and the priest's suitcase exchanged hands. The refrain of his favorite hymn chorused through the open door while the driver grunted in exertion, jamming Mark's bag into the stuffed luggage compartment.

"Here I am, Lord. Is it I, Lord? I have heard you calling in the night," the passengers sang.

He closed his eyes as the poignant lyrics swamped him. *Dear God, please guide me as I lead this group. Holy Spirit, send me the words needed to serve as your shepherd.*

****

The St. Mary's pilgrims, with an additional two other member travelers, filled the club lounge. Father Mark caught his breath while ensconced in a leather massage chair. His noisy, chattering group raided the complimentary breakfast buffet.

His secrecy regarding itinerary specifics had partially ended as he handed out boarding passes for security clearance. He nearly couldn't restrain Rosa Castillo from acting on impulse when she learned that the flight's destination was McCarran Airport in Las Vegas.

"I have to call Tina this minute!" the rosy-cheeked Rosa had exclaimed, purportedly stunned at the coincidence.

"Please leave that to me," Father Mark had implored. "I'm working with Bernadette. Tina will be with you, I promise." He lazed on the chair away from the buzzing collective, a content spectator of the interaction between newly made friends. Surprisingly, no one had pressed him to disclose the final destination. Their demonstrated blind faith impressed him and motivated him to take the next instinctive step in his assigned role. Fishing inside his slacks pocket, he withdrew his cell phone and selected a contact phone number. The connection clicked mid-tone, and he smiled, envisioning the reporter snapping up her phone. "Good morning, Bernadette."

"Father McKenzie, I've been a wreck waiting for your call," she chattered. "Good morning."

"I'm sorry to have kept you in suspense, but I'm following higher orders." He paused and scanned the vicinity to ensure that no one was within earshot.

"Have you ever heard of the Valley of Fire?"

"I have. It's in Nevada."

"Yes, it is," he confirmed. He was impressed at the young woman's worldliness. He had never heard of the Mojave Desert State Park until he'd scrutinized the parchment.

"The vista of the Valley of Fire is breathtaking. I have some stills of the red rock formations that are so gorgeous that they look fake."

"I agree. I googled the location after learning that God will bestow the permanent sign there on Sunday."

She sucked in a breath. And then he listened to white air several moments before she remarked in a small voice, "What an exquisite location for the manifestation of God's plan."

He smiled at her choice of words. "Yes, it's a fitting altar for the revelation of God's infinite goodness. And I'm counting on you to report everything that happens there to the world."

"I'm overwhelmed with the privilege you're affording me, Father. Thank you."

"You're welcome. The hotel Jack Dunne has booked is in Overton about thirty miles away from the valley and sixty-five miles away from Vegas. Will you have any difficulty meeting us there?"

"Not at all. That's where I stayed when I covered a movie story. We reserved rental cars, and we're ready to leave. What do you need from me?"

"I'd like you to report that God will place a permanent sign in the United States. You need to be vague. It's too soon to release anything more."

"Do you know what the permanent sign will be?"

"No. But it will appear on Sunday concurrent with the ending of the snowfall."

"Can I report that information?"

Father Mark raised his eyes weighing possible implications. "I'm stumbling my way through this journey, Bernadette," he hedged. *I'm to bear witness that these events were foretold three days before they occur.* "Yes," he decided. "You can report the timing. I'm looking forward to seeing you and the Belles."

"One more question, Father?"

"Sure."

"Can I bring a cameraman with me?"

"Only if you trust him completely. I cannot stress enough that it is not the time for the site to be revealed."

"I promise, Father, there will be no leaks on my end. "

"I'm sorry I have to cut this short. My flight will board soon. I'll see you at the hotel."

"Why me?" Her voice quivered. "Why do I deserve the role of God's reporter?"

Wagging his head, he answered with the question, "Why me?" Father Mark rose on shaky legs. "Travel safe, Bernadette. I'm grateful for your help." He disconnected the call, pocketed the phone, and wandered among clusters of pilgrims, alerting folks that five minutes remained before they needed to leave for the boarding gate. Father Mark smothered a laugh as Rosa Castillo stuffed apples and cellophane packages of cheese into her bulging carry on. Caught up in the contagion of the group's joyful mood, Mark floated at the rear of the trundling collective toward the gate.

People halted, gaped, and whispered behind raised hands as he passed.

Do they recognize me from the Now Chicago

interview? Edgy and mildly alarmed at unexpected notoriety, Father Mark averted inquisitive gazes. He didn't take a normal breath until seated on the plane.

Rosa launched immediately into praying the rosary.

Heartened by the soothing repetition of the devotional, his soul leapt as passengers outside of the group joined his flock in the recitation. Father Mark smiled. *God awakens the world.* He leaned his head against the glass porthole and gazed at swirling snow throughout the duration of the flight.

Twin streamline buses awaited his group's exit from baggage claim at the terminal in Las Vegas. The blazing sun and hundred-plus temperature didn't alter the snow's appearance in the least.

Wonderstruck group stragglers raised their hands up to their brows to shade their eyes from the desert glare and lingered on the sidewalk adjacent to the buses, gawking upward.

Mark assumed the group was of one mind: one could accept snowfall in Chicago as possible, even in July. But white stuff in the desert? The impossible reality hit him full blast. Pensive and subdued, he boarded the bus last behind the horde of uncharacteristically silent people. *God astonishes the world.* After the hour-plus drive, he drifted off the bus, again the last man, his muscles stiff and achy.

A smiling hostess clad in khaki shorts and a crisp, white blouse, her thick raven hair cinched at the nape of her neck with a tortoise shell clasp, greeted his group as they filed into the hotel lobby.

The aggressive air-conditioning raised goose bumps on Father Mark's arms.

"Mister Dunne preregistered each of you,"

announced the cheerful hostess. "Please proceed to the reception desk, provide your last name to either of my colleagues, and obtain your keys."

Glancing at her nametag, Father Mark said, "Thank you for your assistance, Lexie. I'm Father Mark McKenzie, group leader."

Still smiling, she turned her attention to the priest and extended her hand. "A pleasure to meet you, Father." She gave his hand a light shake and said, "One more announcement for the group, and I'll show you to your room." "Ladies and gentleman," she called out. "A light dinner will be served in the Carlyle room in two hours. The meeting room is down that corridor," she instructed, pointing toward the hallway leading off the left side of the lobby. Lexie handed Father Mark a key folder. "I'll show you to your room, Father. It connects to Mr. and Mrs. Dunne's room."

Mark trailed the hostess toward the elevator, rolling his suitcase behind him, an echoing clatter along the tiled flooring.

As the doors closed on a pneumatic whoosh, Lexie faced him. "It's an honor to meet you, Father. I've had several conversations with Anna Robbins, and she thinks very highly of you."

He smiled. "Anna is an extraordinary woman…Our Lady's rose."

She trained saucer eyes on him. "Oh, I know! She's mesmerizing."

The doors slid open, and Father Mark held a suppressing hand on the mechanism's frame as Lexie stepped out of the car.

Ambling down a narrow, dimly lit, industrial-carpeted hallway lined by brass, electric candle sconces hung every ten feet along the beige walls, Lexie continued, "Ever since the snowfall started, I feel different...more alive, peaceful, happy. You probably think I'm crazy."

"Of course not," he contradicted. He halted at her side as they reached the end of the corridor. "I'd think you're crazy if you didn't accept the snow as a loving gift to delight in and marvel at," he said.

"Mister Dunne stipulated a larger room with a sitting area for you," she said as Mark slid the key card into the slot above the door handle.

A green indicator light flashed above the slot. She pushed open the door and leaned her back against it allowing him to pass in front of her. A loud click sounded as the door swung shut.

"This is huge," he remarked, unslinging his briefcase and setting it down on the sky-blue, upholstered sofa.

"Mister Dunne thought you'd need a suite, so you can meet with Anna in a private setting." She referred to a clipboard that she had carried tucked under her arm and unclipped a few pages. "Here is a tentative list of reservations Mister Dunne arranged, guests' names and their corresponding room numbers. Anna and her family, Father Josip, Elizabeta's family, and Mr. and Mrs. Dunne have rooms on this floor with you. Also, Mr. Dunne added Mr. and Mrs. McKenzie to this floor last evening."

Even before I reached Sam. Jack continues to delight me. "My nephew and his bride," he said as he shoved his hand into his pocket, withdrew a five-dollar bill, and offered the tip to her.

Lexie waved the gratuity away. "I couldn't," she said.

"All right," he conceded, pocketing the bill. "But

thank you very much for your assistance. I will definitely commend you to Mr. Dunne. You've done an excellent job."

"Father?" she asked, her voice tentative. "Can I ask you a favor?"

"Of course, anything. What can I do for you?"

"I'm Jewish, Father."

"All right," he said, curious about the nature of the favor she would ask after her declaration. "I assume Anna told you about Our Lady of the Roses."

Her widened brown eyes shone. "Oh, yes, she has. And she said that what's happening with the weather and the reason that you've come here isn't a Catholic thing. It's for everybody."

He gave her an amused smile. "Absolutely true."

She bit the corner of her lip and clasped her hands together. "She thought you might be willing to speak with my rabbi. Would you?"

In that split second, the majestic coherence of God's plan and Mark's symbolic role staggered him. "I would relish the opportunity," he barely croaked out.

"Thank you." She beamed. "If there's nothing else you need, I'll let you rest before dinner."

"I'm fine, Lexie. Thank you." He wasn't fine. He was electrified by his circumstances: the streaming snow, the huge task that lay before him, and his lack of confidence that he, of all the surely higher educated and certainly more holy religious on the planet should serve as the head shepherd of humanity.

Quaking, he flopped onto the sofa and stared vacantly at the desert winter scape. A few seconds passed before he snapped out of the temporary funk. *This is God's will. Who am I to question?* Immediately, the need to express gratitude compelled him to dial Jack.

"Father, is something wrong?" Jack answered the call.

"No, Jack. Is Beth there?"

"Yes, why?"

"Can you put me on speakerphone?"

"Sure," he said.

"Hi, Father Mark," Beth sang.

"Hi, dear. I'm calling to thank you both. I'm at the hotel, and I'm dumbfounded by your foresight and generosity. I'm in awe. There are no words to fully express my gratitude."

"We are incredibly honored to help Our Lady any way we can," Beth stated, her voice soft. "As my Uncle Karl used to say, 'You can't hook a moving truck to the back of a hearse, Beth. A blessing isn't really a blessing until it is shared.'"

Father Mark burst out laughing. "Speaking of your uncle," he said when he caught his breath, "how is your aunt doing since his passing?"

"Aunt Jeanne is doing OK. I tried to get her to come with us to Nevada, but her Parkinson's limits her movement."

"I'll keep her in my prayers."

Beth chuckled. "She said that she would keep you in her prayers."

"I appreciate all the intercession I can get. Thank you both again. When will you arrive?"

"We're on the red-eye tonight. We'll wait for Sam and Emma in Vegas," Jack replied. "We should be there by lunch tomorrow."

"Great. I look forward to seeing you."

"Enjoy a little peace and quiet. I recommend a nice bracing shower to wash the travel away," Beth suggested.

"I'll do that. Safe travels." Lacking the energy to immediately act on Beth's advice, he sat heavily on the sofa, leaned his head back, and prayed. *Dear God, I ask for Your wisdom regarding my future, knowing that You give to everyone liberally and without reproach. I ask in faith, without doubting, expecting You to give me divine direction in every area of my life. I thank You in advance for the wisdom You assure me You will give. Amen.*

19

The Fifth Day

"I swear by all that's holy, I didn't breathe a word of this to anybody," Bernadette avowed. Mopping her sweaty brow with the back of her hand, she squinted at Father Mark's profile. He wore sunglasses, so she couldn't detect whether or not burning accusation gleamed in his eyes. She considered it a positive sign that he wasn't clenching his jaw. *He looks calm. And hopefully forgiving.*

"I believe you," he tossed out casually, surveying the teaming mass of people milling within the vast span of encircling canyon walls. Tents had sprung up along the desert floor like snow mounds beneath the fantastical, descending flakes.

"I wonder how much the crowd will multiply by Sunday," he mused.

Vastly relieved that he didn't hold her responsible for drawing the couple hundred souls to the valley that afternoon, Bernadette sighed. "How do you think all these people found out about the location?"

"The visionaries have been here for days, and I

know for a fact that they've interacted with the hotel staff," he said. "When my group arrived yesterday, surely things clicked for hotel personnel after my televised interview. I know I didn't imagine that I was recognized in the O'Hare terminal and possibly McCarran, too."

Even though he didn't accuse her of wrongdoing, guilt pricked Bernadette's conscience. She had examined her murky conscience increasingly lately. Had she done enough to merit Father Mark's approval? She certainly hadn't done enough to merit God's. "I'm sorry, Father, if I've contributed to undermining your plans."

"Oh, dear, is that what you think?" He whipped off his sunglasses and gazed into her eyes, smiling. "This," he said, sweeping his arm in an arc that sliced through the linear snowfall, "is for the planet. It carries its own momentum now. I couldn't stop it any more than I could have started it. I realized the second I hopped off our group's bus here today and saw all these folks camped out in the valley that I've essentially jumped the highest hurdle in fulfilling my role. And you helped me, Bernadette. You're still helping me. Neither you nor I are in charge of witnesses anymore. Let them come." He grinned. "The more the merrier."

Wilting, Bernadette gulped down some water from the half empty liter bottle. "I'm so glad that's your attitude."

Bennie, lacking concrete direction from her, panned the area with his handheld camera in wide, sweeping passes, ostensibly taping scenery.

She drooped, melting in the relentless heat as she stood next to the priest. Struggling to keep a pulse on continuing world reactions to the snow and the incessant interrogation after her news release yesterday when she had revealed the country location of the imminent permanent sign, Bernadette neared the point of collapse. Her boss had threatened to fire her at her refusal to provide him the crucial details that she had steadfastly withheld from the world—and him—as instructed. Keeping him at bay, she had vowed that she would resign on Monday and save him the trouble if she hadn't made him the most famous news show director in the world by Sunday.

She hadn't even informed the Belles, Leo, Glen, or Bennie that they would travel to the Valley of Fire when they had embarked on their exodus from Las Vegas the afternoon before. They had met Bennie at the airport and then caravanned the two rental vehicles to Overton at Bernadette's direction. She hadn't once voiced the words *valley* or *fire*. Fearing that uttering the destination, even to her close-knit group, would somehow release the secret into the ether and set it sailing around the globe, she had stoically kept her mouth shut. While she and her friends had settled into their two rooms at the hotel, Bernadette had still evaded full disclosure.

Thankfully, everyone was apparently too strung out from the surreal weather and circumstances to say much.

The four women shared a room with two queen-sized beds.

Leo, Glen, and Bennie were relegated to identical lodging and had opted to take turns bunking on sofa cushions on the floor in macho refusal to share a bed with a man.

Her travel companions had given Bernie a wide

berth, reading her mood and undoubtedly suffering from the same over-stimulated paranoia that seesawed with jaw-dropping wonder engendered by the situation.

Good thing that her friends and husband gave her space. Teetering on the brink of unhinging, she had never muddled through her days in this tense, hyper state before—even in the aftermath of her father's death. On 9/11, at least a human-based, factual cause and effect was evident.

When Anna Babic Robbins had requested a brief meeting last evening, Bernadette had trembled in her presence as if facing punishment. Graciously, the lovely woman had soothed Bernadette's twitchy nerves by supplying a cup of herbal tea and chatty girl-talk before she had explained her reason for requesting the meeting. Gallons of herbal tea couldn't unclog the suffocating lump that had clotted Bern's throat after absorbing what Anna had asked of her.

The visionary had designated Bernadette the Mother of God's "reporter" entrusting her with a Marian message.

Bern glanced at Anna, who stood surveying the valley with Elizabeta and Josip. Peace radiated from their faces like the shimmering heat mirages in the snow-dotted desert. *How reassuring to understand human relationships with God. Isn't that what they profess? Nothing more elaborate than loving. Simple. Love God. Love one another. Anything else is unnecessary and meaningless.*

That simplicity proved inhumanly difficult for Bernadette and most of the people she knew. Her deep-seated loathing of the perpetrators of her father's and thousands of Americans' murders had irrevocably shaped her life. The colorless snowfall and its supposed significance heightened her guilt and the gnawing fear that the world would end with the snow. "How can the world keep functioning through this?" she spat out.

"Amazing. For the time being," Father Mark said. "But, kiddo, you're missing the point if you think the world will keep functioning."

"What do you mean?" she pressed. "Then this is the end of the world, and all this happy God's gift explanation we've broadcasted is a ruse?"

"No," he fired back. "The world must change. What's about to end is the notion that man is, was, or will ever be in the driver seat."

"Wow," she sputtered shaken to the core. "I'm not at all sure I'm prepared to hold steady a camera lens on…Father, Anna asked me to convey a message…I…would you do that for me?"

He frowned, but his blue eyes softened. "I'm willing. But if Anna asked you, there's a higher purpose I won't question."

"Please," she sputtered. "I am not the right person to do this. I thought I was up for it. But I'm certain now that my ambition has blinded me. I'm riddled with faults. I married an atheist, for Pete's sake. And I've never had a problem accepting his non-belief. I still don't…" she trailed off.

"Your husband's here with you," he remarked offhandedly. "I saw him at the dinner buffet last evening."

"Yes. I guess you find that…irreverent," she retorted.

He raised his eyebrows and his navy-blue eyes twinkled. "I am elated that he's here."

Bernadette rolled her eyes, disoriented at the

feathery flakes that drummed her lashes and then disappeared instantaneously. "When this is all over, if I'm still breathing, will you please explain this to me, so I can understand it?"

Slipping his sunglasses back on, he beamed her a smile. "You won't need me," he replied as he sauntered away. "I'm going rock climbing. Want to come?" he said over his shoulder.

Geez, like we're tourists on vacation. In a snowstorm. When it's a hundred and ten in the shade. She laughed at the absurdity.

He halted, spun, and faced her. "What's so funny?"

"Yeah," chimed in Bennie, sidling over to her side. "You haven't cracked a smile in like, twenty-four hours." With his index finger, he tipped the visor of the black, baseball cap he wore. The gesture drew her gaze to the lettering on the cap: WHAT SNOW? His chocolate-brown eyes danced.

Her explosion of laughter had both men gaping askance at her—which only served to trigger deeper belly laughs. She doubled over holding her midriff. "I..." she gasped in the throes of another spell of giggles. She sniffled, brushing away tears from the corners of her eyes. "Love the hat, Ben," she said.

Bennie gave her a wry smile. "The à propos *chapeau*."

Bernadette snorted a laugh. "Watch out, or I'll steal it," she vowed.

Still grinning, he tugged the cap tighter on his head. "For the right price..."

She wagged her head. "Capitalism flourishes even in the strangest of times. Come on, Bennie," she requested, placing her hand on his shoulder. "I want to tape a segment."

"Yes'm," he replied cheerfully. "Where?"

"Do you need me?" Father Mark asked.

"No, thank you, Father," she replied, smiling. "I've got this."

He returned the smile and said, "Good. See you later."

As the priest hiked away, Bernadette turned her attention to the surrounding landscape. The Valley of Fire blazed scarlet-orange ignited by the rays of afternoon sun. The distinctive elephant rock formation and acres of jagged valley floor set the area apart from other locales on earth.

"Let's tape in my hotel room, Bennie," she decided in motion towards a shuttle bus: one of four that Jack Dunne had chartered to consecutively loop the thirty miles between their hotel and the valley around the clock. "I still want our location to remain unidentifiable to the public. Outdoors is far from that mark," she explained.

"Sure," he agreed, loping beside her. "You know, I haven't asked you much about this whole deal, Bernie."

"I appreciate that," she commented, climbing the steps onto the bus, Bennie in tow.

"Hmm," he said, folding into the aisle seat across from her. "I guess that means ask, but no tell."

"Yeah," she replied. "That about sums this whole deal up."

Bennie narrowed his eyes. "Thanks for the vote of confidence, boss."

"Aw, don't take any of this personally," she coaxed. "Chuck is ready to chop off my head. I'm basically a pawn myself."

"Wow," he exclaimed, lifting his cap off and scratching his crown of curly, black hair, as if perplexed. "Never thought I'd see the day when Bernadette O'Neal described herself as anybody's pawn."

Wearily she quipped, "Destroys my ego, but that's reality for you."

His hearty laughter boomed over the bus's roaring diesel engine. "Well, lately reality is a moving target."

"Amen," Bern responded, her mind racing. *We'll set up with the drapes closed behind me. I'll read the message, nothing more. No explanation—as if I have one anyway. Just report the...geez...facts.*

****

"Hey, guys," Bernadette sang out as she and Bennie bustled into the women's hotel room.

Laci and Tina lolled on one bed, and Marlo paced in front of the window.

Glen rose from the desk chair, abandoning his laptop to peck a kiss on her lips. "Wandering the desert, looking for God, darling?" he posed.

"Something like that," she replied, an edge of irritation in her tone. She brushed past her husband, unwilling to engage in front of her friends—and frustrated that she apparently had developed a new hot button on the subject of faith. Reaching the window in three strides, she paused with one hand on the pull rod and said, "Hi, Mar. I hope you don't mind, but I need to close the drapes for a few minutes."

"Sure, go ahead," Marlo responded.

"Bennie, I'll just stand in front of the curtains. Can you set up now, please?"

"Way ahead of you," her sidekick said, mounting the camera on a tripod.

Laci swung her legs over the side of the bed and sat upright on the mattress edge. "We'll clear out."

"No need unless you want to," Bernadette stated. "You're more than welcome to stay and watch. This will only take a few minutes and then we'll…" During her adrenaline-fueled recent past, she hadn't given a thought to togetherness with the Belles. "Um. I don't know what we'll do," she admitted. "What have you all done since we arrived here?"

"I'm bored out of my mind," Laci groused. "It's too hot and too weird outside. TV is hopeless. Nothing but talking heads and snow, snow, snow."

"I keep calling Ramon, and he won't even pick up the phone. What a louse," Tina declared, garnering Bernadette's stunned attention.

"You go, girl," Marlo cheered Tina on. "He doesn't deserve you."

Marlo gifted Bern with a serene smile. "I was at the pool most of the morning, playing with the cutest kid," she related. "She's one of the Croatian ladies' daughters. Rosie."

Bern knit her brows at Marlo's sudden interest in children. "Where's Leo?"

"I don't know," Marlo said softly, drifting over to sit next to Laci on the bed. "Out taking pictures with his new camera, I suppose."

"That camera is radical," Bennie said. "Ready when you are, boss."

"Remind me to ask Leo about those photos, OK,

Mar?" Bernadette asked.

"Sure," Marlo agreed.

Slipping a document out of her tote bag, Bernadette plopped the bag on the floor near the blond wood dresser. "This taping will only take a few minutes, and then maybe we can all have a cup of coffee or something in the restaurant downstairs."

Bennie handed her a microphone, paced back behind the camera tripod, and held up his right hand. "We'll go on one, two, three," he said raising his index, middle, and ring finger in succession.

She fluffed her hair, deep breathed, and consciously relaxed her facial muscles during his countdown, and then she gazed directly into the camera lens. "This is Bernadette O'Neal, reporting a new development in anticipation of the predicted appearance of the permanent sign. Father Mark recounted the history of Marian apparitions in the village of Valselo, Croatia, during our telecast on the first day of snowfall. For those of you who might not have heard about the three visionaries, I'll provide a brief explanation.

"For decades, three individuals have claimed to speak daily with Mary of Nazareth who has conveyed messages concerning God's wishes and plans for humanity. Last evening, one of the visionaries, Anna Babic Robbins, asked me to read the most recent message to the widest audience possible. These are the exact words I was asked to share...

"My children, great is the love of God. Do not close your eyes; do not close your ears, while I repeat to you: Great is His love! Hear my call and my supplication, which I direct to you." Consulting the paper Anna had provided, Bernadette enunciated the words clearly, slowly, and dispassionately into the microphone. "Consecrate your heart and make in it the home of the Lord. May He dwell in it forever. My eyes and my heart will be here, even when I will no longer appear. Act in everything as I ask you and lead you to the Lord. Do not reject from yourself the name of God that you may not be rejected. Accept my messages that you may be accepted. Decide, my children, it is the time of decision." Fully aware that she stood before a world pulpit, Bern was determined to convey impartiality, and above all, create the impression that she was only the messenger, not the message.

"Be of just and innocent heart that I may lead you to your Father," she continued reading, "For this that I am here, is His great love. Thank you for being here!" Bernadette gazed into the lens again. About to sign off, the import of the few lines she had just read swirled within her mind like the universal sign outside the hotel walls. Involuntarily, she internalized the message and belief gelled. "Great is His love," she repeated.

Looking away from the camera lens, she gazed down at the floor. "I am not a religious person in my private life," she softly stated. "I'm a reporter, and it's my job to circulate facts objectively without injecting personal opinions into my work." Widening her eyes, she regarded the camera again as her pulse raced. "But after speaking with Father Mark and Anna, I'm compelled to tell you that I believe we all should pay close attention to the entreaties of the woman whom Christians believe gave birth to Christ.

"I'm not suggesting that you should change your religious beliefs in any way," she hastened to add. "The visionaries have stressed that the source of the heavenly messages is the Most High, the Supreme

Being. But during these days as you contemplate this rare snowfall, please reflect on what you have just heard."

She cast her gaze at Glen and met his eyes. "Decide, my children, it is the time of decision," she recited, not realizing until then that she had memorized the message long before Bennie had started the countdown to the shoot. "Do not reject from yourself the name of God, that you may not be rejected."

At that, Glen's eyes darkened. He turned his back on her and stalked out of the room, leaving the door ajar.

"This is Bernadette O'Neal, reporting from a remote location near the intended site of the promised permanent sign. Stay safe."

Bennie fiddled with the camera as Bernadette switched off the mic.

"Um, you want me to edit the tape before we send it in?" Bennie asked.

Her gut twisted. *We probably should.* Glen's hasty exit and the silent atmosphere in the hotel room probably predicted the world's reception of her editorializing. "Let's watch it back first," she compromised.

Anna appeared in the doorway, prompting Bernadette's spontaneous request, "Can you please take a look at the recording we just made? I'd like your opinion."

Anna peered into the viewfinder and watched the short segment, nodding in approval. Viewing her performance over Anna's shoulder only served to strengthen Bernadette's conviction that airing the unedited segment was the only course of action.

"What's the verdict, Bern?" Bennie pressed.

"Send it just the way it is," she directed.

"Chuck might have a coronary," he warned.

"He might," she agreed. "But that's OK. I think you made me a heavenly herald like you," she confided to Anna.

Anna's contagious laughter had the Belles of St. Mary's erupting in laughter, too.

Anna trained gentle brown eyes on her. "No, Bernadette. I think Our Lady has made you a disciple like me."

20

Chicago Suburbs, The Sixth Day

Marcy Timmons slammed her bedroom door. *Accidentally, Bridget, you nag.*

The reverberations hadn't quieted before the expected rebuke came, "Marcy! How many times do I have to tell you not to bang the door like that?"

She made a face in the mirror that hung on the back of her bedroom door, plopped onto her bed, and mumbled, "About a zillion times."

"Please come down here and walk Pup," her stepmother harped.

Marcy ignored Bridget, the annoyer. Her stupid stepbrother, Barry, should walk his own dog. Barry was even lamer than his mother. Who names a dog Pup? Did he have an original bone in his whole body?

And he actually thought he was so amusing. If the chocolate-eyed Labrador were hers, she would have named her something with some meaning. She'd die before she let them know how much she loved the dog.

"Marcy, please. Don't make me come up there."

Again, Marcy ignored the harpy. She opted for

passive aggression and sat at her computer, immersing in her Facebook page and then clearing emails. Her behavior would yield the same predicted results—

Bridget would clomp up the stairs and demand obedience in sugary, wheedling tones.

She could walk the dog without resistance since she secretly loved escaping the house with her canine best friend, but it was the principal of the thing. *Let her beg.*

With a smug smile, she turned off her computer, opened a book, and waited. As anticipated, a series of thuds sounded, and three gentle knocks rattled the door on its hinges.

"Come in," she muttered.

Expensive perfume wafted into the room, heralding her stepmother's entrance. "Marcy, honey, please can you walk Pup? I have a million calls to return, and I have to start dinner."

As usual Bridget looked perfect. Even after a long day at work, not a hair was out of place. She could understand her father's attraction to the woman. What she couldn't understand was why she had to live with her and her dorky son.

"It's Barry's job. Make him take care of his own pet, Bridget," she replied, butchering the pronunciation of her stepmother's name, as if it rhymed with idiot. Focusing on her book, Marcy turned a page in practiced insolence, knowing how the use of her first name, not to mention brazen disrespect, incensed her stepmother.

The queen of phony didn't rise to the bait and responded in measured tones, "Honey, I wouldn't ask you if Barry were home."

Disappointed that she hadn't provoked her

sufficiently, Marcy narrowed her eyes and cast a sullen gaze at Bridget.

Her pert and maddeningly poised stepparent smiled and said, "Poor Pup needs her walk."

In apparent response to her name, the over-sized, yellow Lab nudged open the door further with her nose, bounded into the room, and launched onto the bed next to Marcy.

"Pup, down!" Bridget bellowed, her calm demeanor disintegrating.

Ha! That's more like it.

Bridget's lips tightened as she jabbed her index finger downward and pointed to the floor.

But the Lab snuggled closer to Marcy and rolled onto her back to entice the thorough belly scratching that Marcy eagerly offered. "It's OK," Marcy asserted, delighted with the dog's defiant behavior. "I don't mind her on my bed."

"Well, I do. Get down, Pup. Now!"

The dog cast a remorseful gaze at her mistress and responded to the command. Scuttling for purchase on the bedcovers, she jumped down to the floor. On all fours bedside, she tucked her tail beneath her legs and trained sad eyes on Marcy.

Marcy reached over and ruffled the fur on the nape of Pup's neck. "I'll walk her," she conceded, satisfied with her gameplay.

"Thank you," Bridget spat out. She spun around, exited the room imperiously, and marched down the hallway, her heels clacking on the hardwood floor.

"Come on, Pup. Let's go. But no yanking the leash this time," Marcy said.

Downstairs, Marcy grabbed the chain leash from the kitchen utility cabinet, fastened it to Pup's collar, and led the dog out the back door. "Want to go to the park?" Marcy asked. She giggled as the dog's tail wagged like a metronome, and her whole body twitched with joy. Marcy secretly loved the snow that continued to fall. The tiny flakes that landed on her warm skin whispered feathery caresses along her arms as if God covered her with kisses.

Pup jumped and frolicked in the yard, her jaws opening and clamping shut repetitively to capture the flakes in her mouth.

Marcy approved of the dog's reaction to the snowfall. She believed in God big-time since the snow came, although her parents' hysterical church going the past week hadn't appealed to her in the least. She didn't care about their continuous threats to ground her if she didn't go along. What difference did religion make in the scheme of things as the whole planet was blanketed with the mysterious occurrence? Any place was church. And if the world was ending, Marcy intended to enjoy the ride.

Pup dragged Marcy behind her the two blocks to the park.

Her arm aching, Marcy squatted down to unhook the leash and let the dog run free on the park grounds. "Only ten minutes, Pup. You come when I call you."

The dog took off like a shot, galloped up a green slope, reversed to lope back down, and then ran a couple circles around the bench where Marcy perched. She rocketed away, disappeared through the trees that bordered the park, and then reemerged, racing back to Marcy's bench. Pup ran the circuit twice more and then returned to Marcy's position, depositing a well-chewed, grimy tennis ball at her feet.

"Whose ball did you steal?" Marcy laughed as she

picked up the ball.

Pup raced away expecting the throw. Marcy heaved the ball toward the canine receiver on a carefree laugh.

The jubilant dog nabbed the toss on the fly, ran the loop back to Marcy, and dropped the ball at her feet again…and again.

"OK, Pup. One more throw, and then we leave."

The sun dipped lower on the horizon. Marcy's stomach growled, anticipating dinner. She rose from the bench, wound up, and hurled the ball with muscle. It sailed over the dog's head and plummeted into the woods. The pup darted into the thicket.

Marcy stood in place waiting for the dog to return. Several minutes passed. Her patience wearing thin, she called out, "Come on, Pup. Bring it back!" Advancing several paces, she squinted at the distant tree line where Pup had disappeared.

Loud barking startled her, and she stood rooted to the spot as a tuxedo-clad man wearing white gloves stomped out of the copse.

Freaked out at the guy's creepy appearance, Marcy did a double take, her heart skipping a beat.

Pup emerged into view, her hackles up. She growled ferociously as she trailed the man and nipped at his heels.

Trusting the dog's attack instincts, Marcy's pulse raced, interpreting an imminent threat.

He raised his foot and kicked Pup.

Her pet's yelp brought a surge of adrenaline. She lunged forward, yelling, "Get away from my dog! Don't you dare kick her!" On the run, she hollered, "That's her ball. Give it back to her!" Marcy doubled the chain leash and clasped the ends in either hand in front of her body. Disregarding her own safety, she quickened her pace intent on protecting her beloved Pup.

"Call your dog off," the stranger growled as he continued stalking towards Marcy, Pup's ball in his hand.

Closing the distance, Marcy halted a few feet in front of him, trembling. "She just wants her ball, you jerk," she gasped out.

"Jerk?" He wrenched the chain out of her hand, and in a split second, cold metal encircled her throat.

Her eyes bulged as the noose stole her breath and tore into her flesh.

Flailing and powerless, Marcy heard Pup's leonine roar as her lungs burned as if they'd explode.

"Who's the jerk now?" he said as she shuddered.

The snow scape went black.

****

Joe massaged the back of his neck and gazed vacantly at the computer screen on his now pristine desk. Only a few files formed a meager stack on the corner of his desktop. Less than a month ago, every square inch of his workspace had overflowed with active files.

The hushed squad room outside his office door drove him nuts and emphasized the seemingly superfluous role of the police force. The snow continued to fall—apparently deterring homicidal and criminal acts. And Laci still would not take his calls.

Maybe I should just chuck this and get on a plane. I'm useless and stir crazy here anyway.

Worse, Laci was royally mad at him. Joe typed an airlines URL into his browser and looked for flight options. He grimaced at the screen display—the only nonstop flight to Vegas left Midway at 6:00 AM. *Why not? I'm not sleeping anyway.*

Lazing in his seat, he redialed Laci's number. Predictably, she didn't answer, and he opted to inform her voicemail, "I'm booking a flight, Lace. I'll see you tomorrow. I love you." Disconnecting, he selected the flight online and shifted to jut out his right hip and slide his well-worn wallet out of his back pocket. His partner rushed through his office door.

"Knibbe just called. They're over at a park on Twelfth. Looks like another sixteen-year-old victim," he rattled off before pivoting and striding back out into the squad room.

Joe pocketed his wallet and cell phone. Hastening out of his office, he caught up to Consuegra. Outside the station house in sweltering humidity, he jumped into Consuegra's car and rode shotgun to the scene, trying to clear the ethereal snowfall and his unreachable fiancée from his mind.

Lurching into the parking lot, Consuegra braked behind the coroner's van after the twelve-minute rocket ride to the park. Ducking under the police tape, he stomped in tandem with his partner over to what had to be the position of the body. The ME's team hovered in the vicinity and, unbelievably, the press had preceded Joe's arrival on scene.

Reporters lobbed questions at him as he stalked toward the ME, pointedly scowling and ignoring their existence.

"Is it the same killer?"

"How old is the victim? Did the Sweet Sixteen Strangler hit again?

"When are you guys going to do something to stop this murderer?"

"What do they think we're doing?" Consuegra mumbled under his breath.

Joe caught his partner's eye and clapped a hand on his shoulder. "Ignore them, Phil," Joe said. "They'll twist every syllable you give them."

Adding to the pesky buzz created by the press, a dog howled incessantly.

"Henry, what's with the Lab?" Joe posed to the patrolman, eyeing the handsome animal. The six-foot-four, three-hundred-pound cop struggled to restrain the agitated dog.

"She's the vic's dog. That's how we found the body. The dog made a commotion and neighbors called dispatch." The cop stroked the dog's back, attempting unsuccessfully to soothe her distress. "We used the tags on her collar to locate the family. They're on their way to the morgue to meet the transport and ID the body."

Joe sauntered behind the ME. "Hey, Ed, what can you tell me?"

"The body was still warm when I got here. I would peg the age between fifteen and seventeen, strangled with a dog's leash. The leash has been bagged. Don't want to get your hopes up, but he might have slipped up. Looks like there's some blood near the handle of the leash. Might be the young lady's, though." He stood, ripped off his rubber gloves, and then squinted at the sky.

"Guess the perp didn't get God's message to

change his evil ways." He grimaced and wagged his head. "I'll conduct the autopsy myself after the family's ID. This is the first murder all week. I guess some people got the message."

"That's my daughter! Let me through," a man uttered a tortured howl.

Joe whipped his head in the direction of the outburst and then sprinted to the tape where the father stood. Tears streamed down the man's face, his anguished expression a mask of agony.

"Sir, you should follow the coroner's van to the morgue where you'll be able to see the victim and determine whether or not it's your daughter," Joe said softly.

"That's our dog. It has to be my baby. I have to see her now," he wailed.

Joe spontaneously wrapped his arms around the man, intending to comfort while shielding him from viewing the body's removal from the scene.

Apparently, Joe failed at accomplishing the latter as a wail erupted from the man's core that raised the hair on Joe's arms. The dog ceased barking and emitted repetitive yelps. Joe nodded his head at the cop restraining the dog, who freed the animal.

The Lab bolted toward Joe and his grieving master. The man sank out of Joe's encircling arms, knelt on the ground, and buried his head in the dog's soft fur. "Marcy!" he screamed. He sagged against the dog's flanks. "Who did this? Who did this to my little girl?" he keened.

Joe encircled an arm around the man's trembling shoulder. "Is there someone I can call for you, sir?" His thigh muscles burned as Joe hunkered down beside the quaking man and awaited his response.

The man planted his left foot on the ground, and Joe lifted him to a standing position. Joe waited, his arms at his sides, observing the man's battle for composure.

"No, thank you," he sputtered, his throat clogged. "I want to go with my daughter. I have to take care of her," he wailed. He hung his head in his hands, and his shoulders heaved as sobs wracked him.

"Knibbe!" Joe yelled.

The officer hurried over to his commander. "Please take Mr...." Joe touched the father's arm gently.

"Timmons, Morris Timmons," he gave a muffled response.

"Please drive Mr. Timmons and his dog behind the van."

"Yes, sir." The cop led the man and his dog to the patrol car.

Depressed to the core, Joe gazed at the father's hunched back.

"This job stinks," Phil remarked, joining Joe.

"Yeah, and it's about to stink more. Do you know who that is?" Joe said, giving a nod toward the man who slumped in Knibbe's back seat.

"Nah," Phil replied.

"The mayor's new-brother-in-law," Joe informed him as he scooped out his cell phone from his pants pocket. "The vic is the mayor's step-niece. This is going to turn into a perfect storm real fast." Trudging back to Consuegra's car, Joe dialed the number and then informed Laci's voicemail, "I can't come after all, sweetheart. Another murder. I'm sorry, baby. I really am. For the love of all things holy, Lace, call me."

21

Valley of Fire, The Last Day
ATTENTION PILGRIMS

Our Lady imparted this final message for the world to Anna Babic Robbins at dawn this morning:

Dear children! When in nature you look at the richness which the Most High gives to you, open your heart and pray with gratitude for all the good that you have and say: 'I am here created for eternity'—and yearn for heavenly things because God loves you with immeasurable love. This is why He also gave me to you to tell you: 'Only in God is your peace and hope, dear children.' Thank you for having responded to my call." *Our Lady of The Roses, Final Message for the World*

Tina reread the flyer that flapped in her hand. A chill ran through her despite the already hot sand sprinkling gusts that swept across the canyon floor. The snow defied the wind and softly cascaded in linear descent. Truly, only God Almighty could bend nature and create this weeklong, supernatural phenomenon. *Final Message for the World...* She shivered again.

Epoch-making events had led Tina, her friends, and family to this moment, the seventh day of snow that promised the dawn of a new world. Her mother at her left elbow, Laci to her right, she squinted and directed her gaze to the three Valselo visionaries who stood with Father Mark, spotlighted with sunrise hues, on a stone plateau at the center of the canyon. The constant streaming snow and milling crowd around the natural, stone stage stirred a dizzying vortex of movement.

Whatever might come in the near future didn't completely terrify Tina, but the mounting anticipation that had begun seven days ago had increasingly frazzled her nerves. Antsy and jittery, she shifted from foot to foot, observing the bizarre vista and the huge assembly.

Laci frowned, her cell phone in hand, apparently picking up messages. She jerked the phone away from her ear and jammed it into her shorts pocket.

"Joe?" The assumption wasn't much of a stretch, judging from the troubled expression on Laci's face.

"Yeah," she replied. "He had my hopes up yesterday. He left a message that he was coming here. An hour later, he cancelled. The job..." she trailed off, her steely gaze and teary eyes projecting equal parts anger and sadness.

Tina rubbed the side of Laci's arm. "We're in the same boat, sweetie. Ramon is AWOL, so we girls will face this, whatever this is, without our men."

Laci trembled violently, and Tina tightened her arm around her friend's shoulders. "I've been so mad I can't even speak to him. But I keep listening to his voicemail messages over and over. I don't know how I can endure this alone."

"You're not alone, sweetie." Tina squeezed Laci's rigid arm. "And you shouldn't worry about a thing," Tina continued, her tone nonchalant despite her own nervousness and her concern for Laci. "Father Mark and everybody in the supposed know around here have said repeatedly that we have no reason to be afraid. My mother is utterly ecstatic today."

Tina craned her neck and scanned faces in the vicinity. "Where are Marlo and Leo? Have you seen them yet?"

"No. I woke up first and then left the room," she replied.

"They're here somewhere, I guess. It's so unbelievably hot," Tina groused.

Laci tugged down the visor of her baseball cap and peered beneath the brim at Tina. Her shadowed eyes cast a furtive expression on her pretty face. The sheen of perspiration on her skin and her tense posture screamed high anxiety.

She looks like she has something to hide. The realization had Tina re-spooling her memory of Laci's behavior the past week. After Bern had interviewed the priest, Laci had withdrawn markedly.

They all had, really.

Bernadette had become increasingly embroiled in the reporting aspects of the phenomenon.

Marlo had basically closeted herself with Leo. Tina made a mental note to investigate Leo. Marlo had never mentioned him romantically before, and now, they seemed inseparable.

And Laci had become a loner, completely against type. Tina had chalked up Laci's sulkiness to disappointment over the complete demise of her lavish bachelorette party. Who had a clue how to react to the incredibly impossible, anyway?

Maybe Tina's faith and her mother's unflagging belief in the goodness of the manifested miracles and those yet to come had heartened her, unlike her friends. Still, if the snow preceded God's miracle for mankind, probably every soul on earth had something to hide. Guilt over unkind thoughts of Ramon and indulgent fantasies of divorcing him nibbled at Tina's conscience.

Bernadette bounded over to where Tina stood, Glen at her side, and the ever-present, camera-hauling Bennie in tow. "Hey, Teen," she chirped.

"You're awfully lighthearted, considering whatever we have in store here today," Tina remarked, giving her friend a wry smile.

"What we have in store here is a lot of superstitious mythology and utter nonsense," Glen opined, his tone dripping sarcasm.

Bern grinned at her husband. "Maybe. But how is it, dear Einstein, that you haven't yet explained the reality of seven days of non-accumulating precipitation?"

Glen leveled a dull-eyed gaze at Bern as if contemplating an unruly child. "Experiments are ongoing. I'm sure these meteorological aberrations have their roots in global warming, tectonic shifts, a possible disturbance in the polarity of the earth, possible cosmological influences…"

"Time will tell," Bern sang out, her eyes twinkling, apparently unperturbed by Glen's viewpoint. "Actually, today will tell. Come on, guys. Let's muscle our way through this mob. I want a front and center vantage point."

Tina directed her mom and Laci to follow with a wave of her hand and then trailed Bennie's clomping feet. He ran perfect interference, the TV call letters on both sides of his camera an apparent "door opener" that effectively parted the crowd.

Situated at the base of the outcropping that served as a stage for the three visionaries and the Chicago priest, Tina spied a flat-topped boulder that would provide a seat for her mom. Rummaging in her tote bag, she unfurled a hotel hand towel and spread it over the rock. "Sit down, Mamá," she directed.

Rosa scurried over. Her parasol reflected light on her face tinting her olive skin a sunny lemon yellow. "Thank you, *mi hija*," she said as she sat down.

Bernadette stood a few feet away from the base of the rock formation. Bennie set up the camera and bustled around his gear, flipping switches and fiddling with the lens.

Jack Dunne approached to Tina's right, hastening toward the stage. He sported a bandana around his head and a dour expression on his face. Jack halted on the far side of the outcropping. His lips moved but ambient conversations obscured what he said to the priest.

Father Mark, however, responded to Jack by scuttling down off the plateau and conferring with him.

The action drew Bern's attention. She gazed in the priest's direction and then climbed up to meet him when he returned to his original position on the stage.

Bennie trained the camera on her.

After an exchange with Father Mark, Bern turned her attention to her cameraman and hollered, "Hold off, Bennie. I'll cue you when we want to start filming."

Father Mark advanced toward Anna and uttered something in her ear.

She responded with a nod and then joined the other two visionaries in apparent powwow. Simultaneously, the threesome knelt and bowed their heads.

Perplexed, Tina called out, "What's going on, Bernadette?"

She wagged her head in response. "Father Mark told me to wait…"

A loud rumbling ensued. The ground beneath Tina's feet trembled slightly, quaking shivers up her spine. In the next instant, a plume of water gushed upward from the stone plateau directly in front of the praying visionaries. The gushing fountain arced downward, pooling at the base near Tina's position and a few feet behind Bennie's tripod.

Without hesitation, Bennie angled the camera upward and trained the lens along the waterfall's trajectory and down to the rapidly rising pool of water contained within an oval of boulders on the desert floor.

Jack Dunne, beaming a smile, raced in front of the camera, a plastic gallon jug in each hand. He stooped, filled each container rapidly, and then made way for the next in a line volunteers who had emerged from the water tent at the perimeter of the crowd, bearing empty plastic jugs.

Tina gazed upward and marveled at the twenty-foot waterspout throwing off rainbows amid the swirling snowflakes.

Bernadette advanced toward Anna as the visionaries rose from their kneeling positions. "Anna, can you please explain what occurred?" she asked.

She moved the microphone below Anna's mouth.

"Mister Dunne reported that we were running out of water," Anna replied. Her eyes danced, and a wide smile bloomed on her lips. "Our beloved Lord responded to our distress. We don't have to worry about the water supply now."

"The permanent sign!" a male voice bellowed.

As if he had fired the starting pistol, the masses surged inward toward the central plateau, a jostling tidal wave originating along the circumference and cresting toward the miracle pool.

"Tina, help me, please," Rosa cried.

Startled, Tina whipped her head in her mother's direction. Stampeding humanity threatened to topple her mom to the ground. Her yellow umbrella tilted crazily back and forth as passersby snagged it in their surge forward.

Tina shoved against the opposing traffic and shouldered a path to her mother's side. Seizing Rosa's hand, she hauled her to her feet and enveloped her in her arms. Her mom clung to her as footfalls thundered and water splashed behind her. The charging crowd bulldozed on either side of her like rapids eddying around two rocks.

Dust rose, stinging Tina's eyes. Holding her ground seemed impossible as the human traffic jammed around her, a suffocating gridlock that had her swaying on her feet. She crossed herself and prayed fervently for God's protection from the aftermath of His miracle.

"Stop!"

"This is not the permanent sign!"

"Do not move!"

"People listen!"

Came the entreaties from the stage.

A slight hesitation from the crowd resulted at the outcries and then renewed shoving and elbowing battered Tina as the gathering ignored the visionaries' pleas.

"It's like Lourdes," a woman yelled. "I have to bathe in the water. I want to be healed."

"Please listen to me!" Anna screamed. "This water is a gift, so we don't thirst! Nothing more...Father Mark, do something!"

"In the name of God, stop where you are immediately!" he boomed.

Shaking uncontrollably, Tina gaped ahead openmouthed.

The crowd obeyed Father Mark's directive, and a stunned silence prevailed.

Not because the priest's command compelled absolute compliance. Not because evoking the name of God summoned the multitude's respectful attention.

The stampede ceased, and every soul present in the Valley of Fire stood mute and rooted to the spot.

Because in the same instant Father Mark demanded attention, the snow stopped falling.

Part III

The Permanent Sign

22

Bernadette stood transfixed.

The wind also stilled, as if the absence of snowfall had created a vacuum that sucked in breezes and human voices. Only the bubbling water in the mysterious, oasis pond provided sound and movement. The collective suspended animation seemed to hover in anxious anticipation. The snow was gone. What did that mean? What would happen now?

Father Mark clasped the visionaries' hands. "Dear friends," he boomed, breaking the ominous silence. "God does wondrous things to gain our attention. In ancient times, He set fire to a bush that was not consumed on Mount Sinai. Moses was compelled to investigate and because he did, his life and the world were changed forever. This week God has sent snow that did not accumulate. And you, the faithful of every religion on earth, gather here to investigate. His Holiness, the Pope says, 'The Lord has allowed you to live in this moment of history so that, by your faith, His name will continue to resound throughout the world.'"

Anna, her face glowing, beamed an ecstatic smile and said, "Thank you, Mother, for leading us here. Our beloved Lord, thank You for sending the water we so desperately need. Please continue to shelter your pilgrims on the journey to You as we wait to receive the permanent sign of Your love."

She paused, extending her arms palms up. Interpreting the gesture, Bernadette mimicked Anna's posture, poised to pray with the visionary.

"Our Father…" Anna said.

Despite Glen's pinch-lipped silence at her side, Bernadette joined the harmonious chorus of the majority of those present and prayed, "…who art in heaven…"

****

Two hours later, Bernadette, Glen, Tina, and Laci huddled in a corner booth at the hotel restaurant and ordered breakfast.

Tina fanned herself with the menu. "I'm still shaking from the crowd's reaction when the miracle water appeared. My mom has visited shrines like Fatima and Lourdes where this sort of thing is involved. She's raved about how peaceful and considerate the throngs were."

Bernadette gave Tina a head nod as she took a sip of her lukewarm diet cola. "I've been to those shrines, too, and I completely agree with her, Teen."

"You can't really label a spontaneous natural geyser a shrine, darling. That's like calling

Yellowstone's Old Faithful geyser a temple."

Glen's snide tone annoyed Bernadette. "Believe what you want, Glen," she retorted, "but I'm convinced that what you call a natural geyser is actually supernatural. And," she rushed to continue when he opened his mouth, surely intending to debate the point, "I believe that Father Mark is accurate in his assessment that we're on the threshold of a miraculous happening that will change our lives and will forever alter the future of the world."

"I'm petrified what might happen when the permanent sign is revealed," Tina said." How do you think all those people will react then?"

Tina held her thick hair up off her neck. Sweat beaded on her upper lip. "I was scared to death when the mob surged toward the fountain. Mom was almost knocked off her seat on a rock. Did you see the little old man with the cane? He pushed the woman next to him right to the ground. I couldn't believe it. If Leo hadn't helped the lady to her feet, she would have been trampled."

"Not very miraculous behavior if you ask me." Glen sneered.

Bernadette rounded on her husband. "No one asked you. It was your decision to come even though you understood the nature of what's happening here and the role I play in all this. I'm not asking you to agree with me, but for the duration, please just keep your opinions to yourself."

The rebuke had Glen stiffening his spine against the back of the booth and huffing out breath.

"I want to go home," Laci blurted out. "I can't stand being here without Joe. This is too scary. I can't go through this by myself." Tears welled in her eyes, and her clenched hands trembled on the tabletop.

"Oh, honey." Bernadette circled an arm around Laci's shoulder and gave the side of her arm a squeeze. "Why are you so upset? You aren't alone."

Tina bobbed her head in agreement. Glen gazed ahead, apparently still miffed.

"I've done some things that I'm not proud of, and I'm afraid that…" Laci trailed off. She lifted a slat of the venetian blind on the window next to her and squinted through the glass. Laci gazed fixedly out at the parking lot. Her rigid posture exuded apprehension.

"I think I understand, sweetie," Bernadette said. "Nobody's perfect. And…"

"Speak for yourself, darling." Glen interjected, grinning.

Bernadette squeezed his hand, transmitting, she hoped, her secret apology for her earlier outburst. "I'd disagree with you, Glen, but I really don't want to keep fighting with you. I'm really glad that you're here with me. I completely understand why you need Joe at a time like this, Lace. I think most of us are examining our consciences and finding that we need forgiveness. I don't know when being here changed for me from covering a fantastic story to taking personal stock," Bernadette said. "But it has. I'm interested in the multi-denominational religious services that Father Mark has arranged later this morning. For Catholics like us, he'll say Mass. Maybe we girls could go together. It might make us all feel better about things."

"Feel better about what?" Glen asked. "That you haven't gone to church for six years because you married me?"

His sarcastic tone riled her again, but Bernadette tempered her response. "I stopped going to church before I married you, Glen."

"Another happy couple," Tina teased.

Bernadette covered Glen's hand with hers. "I don't believe that anything you do will affect how God judges me. Maybe you should think about that."

Glen guffawed. "An empty exercise at best. I intend to pursue the explanation for the recent snowfall..."

"You do that," Bernadette countered. She reached across the chipped Formica tabletop and held Laci's hand. "Stay here with us?"

Laci gazed briefly at Bernadette and then looked down. "I'll think about it," she mumbled.

Unconvinced that she had influenced Laci to stay, Bern said, "You can't go home yet. We're so close to the culmination of all this. I feel deep down that we're witnessing the miraculous, and the best is yet to come." Purposefully avoiding Glen's gaze, she continued her attempt to persuade Laci. "The Belles have to be together now. This is more important than your bachelorette party, honey—more important than any experience in history. Please stay."

The waitress delivered the food they had ordered to their table.

Glen dug in with gusto, ignoring the drama between the ladies.

Laci swiped the tears away from her eyes with a paper napkin.

"There you are!" Bennie hollered from across the room. He jogged over to the booth and pulled up short, a crazed expression on his face.

Bernadette grimaced and waved a hand in front of her face. He reeked of cigarette smoke.

"Bennie, what's that smell? You've been smoking?

That's disgusting. You haven't had a cigarette in five years," she reminded him. "Are you crazy?"

"Probably. Yeah, I think I am." He waved a handful of papers back and forth, and then he handed one to Bernadette. "You tell me. Am I crazy?"

Bernadette inspected the document. It was a color print of a mammoth crystal cross seemingly erupting from the Valley of Fire canyon's floor, the water that had appeared that morning pooled around its base. "This is very artistic. How did you photo shop the cross? It looks so real."

"I didn't photo shop anything."

"What do you mean?" She furrowed her brow as she further scrutinized the photo.

"Look at these." Bennie fanned the rest of the papers in his hands. "You know how I like to take a few still shots of locations? I shot these right after the fountain of water appeared."

Extracting his digital camera from the bag over his shoulder, he turned it on and gazed intently at the viewfinder. Advancing the images a few times, he handed her the camera. "Look at that. It's the original image I shot."

Glen scooted next to her to peer at the viewfinder with her. He glanced at the printout and then at the camera. "There's no cross in that photo."

"Exactly! I attached a USB cord directly from this camera to the printer in the hotel lounge, and when the image printed out, the cross…appeared."

"That's not possible," Glen declared.

"This is proof." He handed Glen another paper. "I printed this exact digital image twice. See? A cross. Then I e-mailed this JPEG to my girlfriend at home and asked her to print it. She took a digital shot of her printout and sent it back to me."

He activated his phone screen with a thumb swipe and then jabbed the screen a couple times. Holding the phone out in Bernadette's direction, he waited for her reaction.

She widened her eyes viewing the image on the screen. "The cross is there, too."

"I'm sure there's a logical explanation," Glen said, although he didn't offer one.

"Please, please explain it to me," Bennie pleaded.

"Do you think it's a preview of what's to come?" Bernadette could not tear her gaze away from the photo. The ethereal, mesmerizing cross held her in thrall. "Maybe we should take these photos to Father Mark?"

A cacophony of bells sounded. Jingling, ringing, pealing, clanging resounded a thunderous carillon. The din overwhelmed her senses, and she jumped out of her seat in response. "Come on, Bennie!"

Responding to the resounding symbolic call, she fled the café, Ben in tow. Glen led Laci and Tina behind her. Marlo, Leo, and various St. Mary's pilgrims counted among the group huddling in the lobby.

"What's happening?" Laci whimpered.

An engine roared outside, a bus departed, and then Jack Dunne flung open the lobby door. "Father Mark, the religious leaders and the visionaries' group just left for the Valley of Fire. Hurry!" He beckoned with a wave of his hand. "Board the buses as quickly as possible."

"I have to find my mom," Tina said as the group surged forward at Jack's command. "I'll catch up with you."

****

Bernadette flew off the bus and Bennie tromped behind her, his video camera balanced on his shoulder. He trained the lens on her as he kept pace with her movements. The hair stood up on her arms, and every cell in her body reverberated with bell song.

She breathlessly improvised a commentary, running toward the central plateau where the first busload of people had congregated. "As you can hear, bells are ringing throughout the Valley of Fire, the site of the miracle of water earlier today. No church, synagogue, temple, mosque, or other place of worship is located within fifty miles of this desert state park in Nevada."

Halting at the plateau's base in front of the fountain, engulfed in the unreal sensory trance cast by invisible bells and magically appearing water, she observed Glen and her friends in the forefront of the growing crowd that faced her.

"Gathered above me," she paused as Bennie aimed the lens up at the plateau, "are the three visionaries from Valselo, Croatia, Father Mark McKenzie from St. Mary's parish in suburban Chicago, archbishops, bishops, heads of Christian ministries, rabbis, lamas, gurus, ayatollahs, pastors—basically representatives of all world religions…"

The ground quaked and a strobe light effect drew her eyes upward. Disbelieving, Bernadette gaped at the sun spinning, dancing, and pulsing in the sky. Now, outcries joined the symphonic bell choir—hosannas, screams, gasps. An ebony cloud drifted toward and then covered the gyrating sun; a total eclipse that cast eerie shadows on the sandstone formations as if extinguishing the "fire" in the valley.

Craning her neck, Bernadette vaguely registered motion to her far left. The rocky ground heaved. Alarmed, she lowered her gaze earthward and noticed that the visionaries had moved to the valley floor about ten feet away from her. The threesome stood at the edge of the fountain, their hands linked, smiling heavenward as tears streamed down their cheeks.

The bells ceased ringing as abruptly as they had begun. The waterspout that had plumed into the fountain solidified straight up in midair like a crystalline pillar as the sun emerged from the cloud. Those close enough to witness the occurrence gasped out epithets—amazing, glorious, awesome, heaven sent.

Bernadette darted her gaze and focused on Bennie. His mouth hung open, but he dutifully aimed the camera on the water that had seemingly frozen beneath a spinning desert sun.

Glen lunged forward and grasped her hand. His sharp intake of breath surprised her. He apparently had no ready explanation for the phenomenon…and she wished he did.

Incredibly, the crystalline pillar of water speared higher, piercing the heavens. The other Belles and family rushed forward and grabbed hold of each other. Marlo tucked her arm through Bernadette's and clung for dear life.

People screamed, wailed, yelled out petitions to God—a discordant uproar.

"It's taller than the Willis Tower," Marlo shouted.

The elevator-like upward momentum of the column stopped, and then horizontal beams emerged from the central pillar. The inconceivable erection of a gargantuan cross out of a pool of water and thin air progressed. When the construction terminated, the sun, now thankfully anchored in the sky, beamed down on the gleaming creation, a dazzling prism that radiated a shimmering spectrum of lights.

Tugging Glen by the hand, Bernadette raced over to Bennie. "It's your cross, Bennie," she cried. She threw her arms around him, tears streaming. "Send your images to Chuck and explain everything to him." Freeing him from her embrace, she said, "You were given a gift to share."

Returning to Glen's side she noted her husband's avid, visual inspection of the cross. "You're dying to touch it, aren't you?"

"You bet I am."

"I don't think anyone will stop you," she said.

Bennie trembled uncontrollably as he used his phone to send the e-mail to the studio. "Why did He choose me?" he murmured, his voice tremulous.

"I don't know, Bennie. I don't think anyone on earth can answer the question why about any of this."

The assembly had quieted. Prayer beads clicked and only reverential murmurs sounded.

The unexplained appearance of the fountain that morning had triggered a mob reaction. Flabbergasted by the stunning appearance of what had to be the permanent sign had the multitude reverently dropping to their knees. People whispered, bowed their heads, or chanted God's praises by His many Biblical names.

Glen staggered back to her and embraced her, trembling violently. He knelt on the ground, his arms slipping down around Bernadette's waist. Shocked, she joined him on her knees, unmindful of the unyielding rocks that dug into her kneecaps. "Without question it's a cross made of ice, over seventeen hundred feet tall, in the middle of the desert. This can't be happening. It's not...not remotely possible," he stammered.

Bernadette squeezed his hand fiercely and said, "Oh, my darling. For God, anything is possible."

23

The Judgment

Glen tilted back his head and raised his eyes, responding to an internal, urgent bidding that he perceived in every molecule of his body.

The unspoken command, "Hear me now," supplanted all other thoughts.

His soul recognized the Voice. His retinas reacted to the blistering, white light in complete reverse of their proper function as Glen widened his eyes to the limit. He hung in the thrall of this…Presence. And then corporal awareness fled as if he were nothing more than his thoughts in communion with all the Knowledge there is, was, or ever would be.

He felt utterly deconstructed by this indefinable Entity of acute intelligence. Glen retained an iota of his sense of self, sufficient to experience an overwhelming remorse. Feebly attempting to atone he said, "My Lord, I'm sorry beyond words. Please…"

You are a seeker of truth.

"Yes, I…thought…I'm sorry…I…

I am the Truth. Your vanity mocks those of faith

who accept and revere the Truth.

"I am a fool," Glen admitted. "Only You could have made that cross, brought the snow..."

In this all-powerful, all-knowing Presence, Glen was a mere spark of reflected light that he feared would extinguish forever if the Light were deservedly withdrawn from him.

But the light swelled instead, pulsing, and all encompassing. With each increasingly brighter, radiant flare, Glen was more tightly embraced as if treasured and adored. Ecstatic, he internalized the true significance of unconditional love...and knew God.

Tender guidance came. *You may continue to deny Me in your life if that is your will. But in doing so, you won't share in My eternal life. It is not My will that you separate from Me.*

Confused, Glen sputtered out, "I will continue to live?"

Yes.

Frenzied, he asked, "Do You want me to go to church? How do I come back to You...?"

Know that I Am, and love Me. I love you.

As if a shutter dropped, lightning fast, the brilliant light extinguished. Anguish shot through Glen, and he cried out, "Don't leave me. Please!"

Small rocks were imbedded in his kneecaps. He fell heavily onto his backside and sprawled on the stony ground, barely conscious of the glittering ice cross in front of him. Dazed, he gaped at the thin tracks of blood trickling down his shins that stained the linings of his gym shoes muddy crimson.

****

When the earsplitting, sonic boom came, Ramon Hernandez bitterly regretted that he had ignored Tina's entreaties to join her in Nevada the past week. His reasoning that he could escape God's wrath if he avoided the site supposedly earmarked for miraculous occurrences was fatally flawed. He was alone in his encounter with the Almighty, and he yearned to feel the touch of his wife's hand one last time before the Lord exacted punishment.

The crashing sound reverberated, and a driving wind blasted through his living room that lifted him off his feet and cast him roughly down onto the musty smelling carpet. Light extinguished as if the sun were a candle that the Lord blew out as He approached Ramon's apartment.

There was no question in his mind that he would die a tortured death in the next instant. Mortally petrified, he quaked with such ferocity that he thought his limbs might tear off his body, saving God the trouble of doing him in. Too panic-stricken to open his eyes and face the presence that seemed to envelope him like restraining arms, Ramon cowered on the floor, his head in his hands.

See Me, a thundering Voice boomed inside Ramon's mind.

"I don't deserve to look at You, my Lord," he chattered, his teeth clacking. "My sins are too great."

You are lost to Me. I love you, and I long for your return.

Shock paralyzed him. Could there actually be

mercy for him despite his actions?

"I wuh-would do any...anything," he stuttered, "to earn Your forgiveness."

Do not commit offense against My children again. Confess. Accept just punishment. You know what is right. Abide by the laws.

A glimmer of hope emboldened Ramon to open his eyes and scramble to a kneeling position. Stunned, he gaped at the floor to ceiling pillar of incandescence in front of him that radiated pure love. Swaying on his knees, Ramon basked in God's infinite compassion, feeling adored. Adoring God in return, all bitterness fell away. Ramon was reconfigured, new, and eager to atone for his sins. Perhaps he might come to deserve redemption. Although fearing the answer, he hazarded asking, "I might be with You in heaven when I die?"

If you make amends and keep My commandments, you will know Me. Or eternal separation from Me awaits.

God withdrew from him evidenced by the sudden disappearance of the column of light and the chilling retraction of encompassing love.

Ramon sank back on his haunches as sobs erupted from the depths of his soul. The offered blank slate humbled him beyond comprehension. Certain that he didn't deserve the second chance, he would greedily seize it nonetheless. He marveled at the priceless opportunity that God had provided. Intending to call his beloved Tina, he wrung his hands, trying to stop his fingers from shaking enough to dial her phone number.

****

Aghast at witnessing Glen's stricken expression when he, unbelievably, fell to his knees directly below the astounding cross, Marlo also sank to her knees. Her heart pounded a drumbeat in her ears, and her stomach heaved a nauseating somersault—even more bilious than her gut-wrenching, chronic morning sickness.

Outcries and sobbing around her suddenly muted. Then her peripheral vision blurred, and she experienced a terrifying assault of vertigo despite the fact that her knees remained anchored on the rocky earth. Her body reacted as if she poised precariously on a ledge high above ground—reeling, spinning, and petrified she'd fall any second. Unable to fathom her surreal circumstances, Marlo prayed for protection. "Dear Lord, save me," she cried aloud.

Panting, she breathed in incense-laden air that evoked memories of cathedral Masses and of her mother's funeral. A starry pinprick of light appeared far ahead that grew into a brilliant white globe that rapidly approached. As the light neared, it continued to swell in circumference until any perimeter boundaries disappeared. The mysterious luminosity surrounded and consumed her. An overwhelming sense of peace, comfort, and acceptance filled her senses. The certainty that she was in the presence of God took root as language planted in her brain.

I love you, daughter. If you love Me, you are saved.

"Oh, my Lord, I...I do love You," she blurted out.

Those who love Me keep My laws. Your intention would mock the law.

Mortified, Marlo bowed her head and wrung her hands. "I'm sorry," she wailed. "I knew...I know it's wrong. I don't think I can handle it alone. That's no excuse..."

Every creature is precious to Me, born and unborn. Each life I conceived by My will. If you choose to terminate that life, your baby will know Me in paradise but your salvation will be in jeopardy.

Shaking, Marlo internalized the dire warning. "Please forgive me, Lord." She perceived the instantaneous absolution as gorgeous warmth enfolding her as if she were cradled in the tenderest embrace. Ecstatic she rested in the arms of the Lord. Moments later, her elation was wrested away as the shimmering light withdrew and shrunk before her eyes.

"Don't leave me," she cried.

I Am with you for all time.

Weak, overwrought, and overjoyed, Marlo curled up on the hard, dusty earth, and wept.

****

Reality spun away in a flash, and Laci's world bleached colorless. A snowy field lay before her that blanked out people, things, and place. She desperately wanted to break into a run and attempt to ram through the white wall, but fright paralyzed her limbs. In her heart, she accepted that God's judgment was imminent. She hadn't doubted that this encounter would come from the first viewing of Bernadette's interview with the priest. Mankind...she would have to pay for ignoring God's existence and His inevitable tallying of misdeeds.

Acute terror mounted, and she perspired from every pore as the white light brightened, undulating as if breathing. A scream erupted from her mouth when a phrase seemed to plant in her mind.

Even so, I love you.

Her legs went to jelly and caved in. Vaguely, she registered the impact as she tumbled onto the ground. Tilting her head upward from her prone position, she focused on the light, incredulous at the loving, welcoming sensations she perceived in the Lord's presence. "I don't deserve love," she whispered. "I'm beyond redemption."

My mercy knows no bounds. Make true amends and restore your claim to know Me.

She had decided that after the wedding she would replace the money; secretly, week-by- week—the same way she had stolen the funds. Surely, the Lord knew her intentions. Would that not suffice? "Repayment will save me?" Laci held her breath and prayed that this was the right course of action.

I hear your prayer, daughter. Yes, you must return to My people in need what is rightfully theirs. And you must admit your deception and lies.

"I freely admit that I am a liar and a thief, my God. Please forgive me," she begged as the stone of dread at her core disintegrated with the confession. Her heart leapt blissful as utter peace and euphoria replaced gnawing guilt. At last liberated from years of covert embezzling, Laci sobbed—washed clean and as innocent as a newborn.

You owe debts with consequences to other of My children. True amends and true salvation lie before you.

The white light disappeared, and Laci squinted as the sun overhead pierced the desert vista and haloed the crystalline cross that loomed over her. A new terror filled her at the prospect of revealing her crimes to others. Maybe it was best that Joe hadn't made it to the Valley of Fire after all.

****

Tina abandoned rational thought as the surrounding light refracted in a kaleidoscope of every hue imaginable. A multitude of stained glass-like images played in front of her eyes, rotating, blooming out from a central point, and reconfiguring into diverse bouquets of glistening colors. Enraptured with the visual effects, she made no effort to do anything other than enjoy the awesome display. She played the jubilant spectator transported with delight at yet another inexplicable manifestation of God's power.

A parochial school teacher and a dedicated, if not overly devout, practicing Catholic, Tina remained generally content with her personal relationship with God. Father Mark had stated that God would speak to those who need to hear His voice at the culmination of prophesied events. Did she count among those who needed to hear God speak? Full of faults, she suspected that she did. But in this pivotal moment of history when the Almighty had demonstrated that He alone governed the weather, physics, the very heavens, and the earth, how would one insignificant person like her count in His individual attention?

The swirling kaleidoscope halted slowly like a carousel ride gearing down to a soft ending. Golden light suffused the contours of the scope from the center outward, expanding until seemingly endless in all directions. Tina had never experienced, could never have imagined, unadulterated ecstasy such as that attached to the rich, lemony light bathing her. She sensed rather than heard.

I love you, daughter. You do My will, and I Am pleased.

Scarcely believing the priceless favor she had found, she exclaimed, "Thank You, Father, from the bottom of my heart. I love You with my whole soul, and I'm grateful for all Your gifts."

Stunned when the loving sensation impossibly intensified, Tina prayed fervently that this moment signified the end of earthly life, and she could remain treasured in God's heaven forever.

I shall cherish you for all eternity. Keep your faith and strive to meet the tests that will come in your mortal life.

The ethereal transcendence faded with the dimming light. Crushed that she'd yet to fulfill her destiny on earth and bereft at heaven's abandonment, Tina stood on the canyon floor, her palms upturned, her gaze cast upward, praying for the Lord to come back to her.

****

Still undone by Glen's stunning reaction to the irrefutable God-made-cross, Bernadette possessed no defenses against the further demonstration of God's supreme power. She had no problem acknowledging that she was far from perfect, particularly in her refusal to let go of her stubborn bigotry. Considering herself a disciple of objective fact in her vocation, she blindly avoided analysis of her own subjective biases in living her personal life.

Bernadette didn't want to hear God's analysis of her deeply rooted hatred. She hung her head and squeezed her eyes shut, hoping that the avenging angel or whatever might come upon her in the next moments would deal with her swiftly.

Glaring white light parted her eyelids against her will, and a commanding voice filled her mind.

I love you and all my children with My pure heart.

Defensive and ashamed, she managed to squeak out, "I am sorry for my prejudice toward terrorists. But they killed my father. I don't know how not to hate."

I Am the judge. Your father knows me.

The import of the information had her heart skipping a beat. "Dad is there? With You?"

Yes. And for you to share in My eternal life like him, you must banish all resentment from your heart.

Tears streamed down her cheeks. She hadn't needed corroboration that her father had deserved heaven upon his death. But to hear evidence from Almighty God's lips? The inestimable privilege humbled her immeasurably. She fell forward onto her abdomen and lay prostrate on the ground, grains of sand snagging in her nostrils as she breathed.

Intractable opposition coursed through her veins like the same toxic loathing that had gushed through her bloodstream in the aftermath of 9/11. She wanted to heed God's warning. Of course, she wanted to be reunited with her father and loved ones when she died. But at what cost while she lived? Could she forget enough to forgive? That seemed an affront to her father's memory and all he stood for—like the thousands of people who'd died with him that day.

Do not condemn others lest you condemn yourself.

A chill ran through her. Dazed, she raised her head astonished to find that the world had righted. But it wasn't the world she had known a brief few moments earlier, despite the familiar population.

Glen sat on the ground to her left, staring vacantly at his feet. Concern at his condition snapped her out of the trance. She planted her palms on the ground and pushed up to position her feet under her. Balancing in a squat, she crab-walked closer to Glen and took his face in her hands. Gazing into his eyes, relief swelled inside, as he seemed to come back to her, his tear-filled eyes softening at her touch. She kissed him and whispered, "I love you."

"I love you, too," he said clasping her hand and rotating it to tenderly kiss her palm. "I spoke…I spoke to God!" he exclaimed.

She hitched a breath as tears streamed down her face. "I know, my darling," she whispered, gazing into his eyes. "Me, too."

Sitting back on her haunches, she took stock of her friends, and nameless witnesses of the bestowing of the permanent sign. Laci stood statue-like, gaping at the ice cross, a shell-shocked expression on her face. Tina also stood upright, her head thrown back, her eyes shut, and her palms turned up to heaven as if continuing communion with God. Marlo was curled on her side, leaking tears onto the arid ground.

Everywhere Bernadette turned, evidence mounted that every soul present had communicated with God just as she and Glen had. Her gaze lit on Bennie, hunched slightly over, peering at the video camera's viewfinder.

She rose to her feet, brushing her palms on the sides of her skirt. "I'll be right back, Glen," she said. "Hey," she greeted Bennie as she drew up to his side. "Anything new happen lately?" she joked.

He snorted resoundingly. "I left the camera recording while we all..." he trailed off. Lifting his cap off his head, he scratched his scalp and then continued, "While the Lord on High paid us a visit. I was hoping that I could actually capture God on film."

Bern burst out laughing. "Did He let you?" she asked, barely able to form the words during her fit of giggles.

"Nope. Not even a really white frame left behind," he replied, turning his attention away from the camera and gazing at her. "Just the cross, and not a shred of movement the past fifteen minutes on tape."

She arched her eyebrows and asked, "So you...?"

"Yeah, Bernie," he responded, his eyes huge. "God judged me."

Running her fingers through her damp hair, her mind raced. The thunder of a jet engine sounded overhead, triggering her curiosity. She whipped her cell phone out of her skirt pocket and dialed her contact at the FAA.

24

Tina was aware of her phone's vibrations in her pocket, but she made no move to answer the call. On the plateau in front of her, the visionaries and Father Mark riveted Tina's attention. Standing erect and exultant, the trio held hands and, smiling broadly, gazed out at the crowd. Diverse cell phone ringtones sounded from all quarters of the gathering, an eclectic symphony of chirrs, rings, and music. A few people whispered into phones or, like Tina, ignored callers altogether.

Bernadette prowled a patch of ground to Tina's right, her cell phone glued to her ear and her lips moving rapid-fire, transmitting, or possibly ferreting out urgent information.

"Dear friends in the Lord," Father Mark said into the microphone, effectively prompting the mass termination of telephone conversations.

Even her dogged reporter friend ceased talking on the phone. Bernadette gave a head nod to Bennie who aimed the camera lens at the priest in response.

A reverent silence prevailed; contact with the

outside world deemed unimportant, save Bernadette's documentation for posterity.

The three visionaries moved a couple paces behind the priest.

"We are blessed beyond imagining. Praise God with endless thanksgiving for choosing us to bear witness to the formation of the permanent sign," Father Mark announced. "We have an obligation to share what we have experienced here today…"

Grumbles of protest arose all around her.

The priest held up his hands, calling for silence. "I'm not suggesting that we share details of what we've just experienced individually. God's words to each of us should remain as private as we choose. Every single soul in the world was afforded the same preview of judgment before the throne of God at exactly the same time today. No one was left out, and this miraculous occurrence was predicted by Our Lady of the Roses and documented by the visionary, Anna, in a parchment that she presented to me three days before the snow began."

Pausing, he gazed at the audience and wagged his head. "We are all so very privileged to have been called here. I believe our mission—our sacred responsibility—now is twofold. First, we must bear witness to the creation of the permanent sign and tell everyone we meet that we are absolutely certain that God erected this cross of ice out of rock and sand—in the high summer in the Mojave Desert—right before our eyes. We must explain that this sign is God's gift to mankind as testimony to his endless love and forgiveness. It will remain until the final judgment. Second, we must convert our hearts to fully accept God's love and live from now on so that in facing this final judgment, we merit eternal life. No one knows when that time will come, but the Lord, in His merciful magnificence, has now provided each of us invaluable lessons—that if heeded, we have no reason to fear our final judgment."

Anna, Josip, and Elizabeta took the lead position on the plateau. They knelt before the cross, raised their eyes to the heavens, and led the recitation of the rosary. The vast majority of those gathered dropped to their knees, too.

Tina, along with a loud chorus, prayed the responses until the visionaries stopped speaking abruptly. Silent, Tina gazed at the trio who nodded and smiled while their lips moved in mute conversation with Our Lady. Five minutes later, they bowed their heads as if grief-stricken and resumed praying.

When Anna rose, the other two visionaries and the audience followed suit.

Anna's sweet voice sounded. "With great joy, I would like to share Gospa's message. Our Lady came, smiling with utmost happiness." She pressed a hand over her heart and sighed. "I have never seen her so beautiful, dazzling. Our Lady said, 'Dear children! I call you with complete trust and joy, to bless the name of the Lord and, day by day, to give Him thanks from the heart for His great love. My Son, through that love which He showed by the Cross, gave you the possibility to be forgiven for everything; so that you do not have to be ashamed or to hide, and out of fear not to open the door of your heart to my Son. To the contrary, my children, reconcile with the Heavenly Father so that you may be able to come to love yourselves as my Son loves you.'

"Before we leave, I invite you to come and touch the gift from Our Father. Venerate this cross as you venerate the Cross of His Son on Good Friday."

Father Mark paced to Anna's side. "And before you come forward to venerate, I'd like to say a few more words. My fellow religious..." He gazed directly at the religious dignitaries assembled. "And friends in the Lord. God sent a young girl from Nazareth named Mary on an earthly journey that began in Bethlehem. We Catholics revere her as the Queen of Heaven and Earth because we believe that she gave birth to the Savior of the world. The world has communed with God the Father, the Creator of the universe today. As His unworthy shepherd I want you to know that deep in my heart I fully believe that no matter what path you're on, God desires all people to reside with Him in heaven. I think God demonstrated today that He loves us all unconditionally, without exception—enough to show us the path to Him."

Anna smiled at the priest and then joined hands with Elizabeta and Josip. Linked together, they advanced as one towards the cross, kissed the glistening surface of the central pillar, and then stepped aside. Their families trailed them, followed by Father Mark and his family, the religious dignitaries, and finally the crowd that formed a long queue, snaking within the red rock formations encircling the canyon.

Tina lined up behind her mother who worked a string of crystal rosary beads with her fingers. The sun filtered through the looming ice monument, refracting a shimmering spectrum.

Bernadette set up with her cameraman on the other side of the cross. Pride warmed Tina as she came within earshot of Bern's broadcast. Her dear friend had run way ahead of the pack in accepting the mission to spread the word of the astonishing events the past week.

"As the priest, Father Mark stated, and reports I have received would corroborate, the so-called judgment seems universal," Bern said as she focused on the camera lens. "While experiencing this private audience with God, earthly activity suspended without repercussions. For instance, a large number of pilots airborne at the time of the global judgment experienced their personal intimacies with the Lord and then resumed navigating their flights. In other words, no planes fell out of the sky, even though the pilots attest they were definitely elsewhere for a while…"

While Tina continued to wait her turn to touch a God-given miracle, she fished out her cell phone and snapped a few pictures of the cross, intending to share them with her class at her first opportunity. She couldn't wait. What better way to begin her personal mission than by enlightening the minds of her middle school students?

Although I'll bet Now Chicago's *broadcast preempts my big news for the class by the time I get home.*

Before she pocketed the phone again, she noticed that she had three missed calls. Clicking on the icon, she verified that her home phone number was listed three times. *I'll call you later, Ramon. Just a little more me-time, and then I'll be ready to face you with an open heart.* Tina's arm shook as she knelt before the cross with her mother and flattened her hand on the solid, frosty-glazed upright post, her fingers stinging from the cold.

Rosa sobbed and blubbered, "Gracias,"

repetitively.

Moved to tears at this astounding marvel, Tina sent up a silent prayer. *Thank You, my Lord, for letting me share in the glory of this moment. I am not worthy but enormously grateful. I love You with all my heart and soul."* Reluctantly, Tina moved to relinquish her position in front of the cross as she rose to her feet and then helped Rosa stand. "I don't want to leave here, Mamá," she said, offering Rosa her arm. "I could stay on my knees in front of this amazing cross all day."

Rosa laid a hand on Tina's bicep and fell in step with her daughter. "I could too, honey. But we must follow Our Lady's example. We need to start sharing this with the world."

Lingering on the fringe of the crowd, Tina and Rosa bided time until the rest of their group paid homage.

Bernadette wrapped her broadcast and then advanced toward the cross, hand in hand with Glen.

Marlo, Leo, and Laci waited further back in line.

Father Mark directed dazed group members as they finished their devotions toward idling buses.

Tina and Rosa trundled aboard and settled in seats halfway to the back. Saturated with emotion, Tina slouched in the narrow seat and gazed out the window, still and probably forever, wonderstruck at the sight of the ice cross as tall as a skyscraper, glistening intact in one of the hottest places on earth.

The last row filled, the bus doors whished closed, and the engine growled into motion. The line of cars in front of the bus stretched toward the distant horizon seemingly without end as did the parallel line of traffic heading toward the Valley of Fire.

Bernadette had spread the word and the

unforgettable images of the permanent sign rising like crystal thunder.

People must have bolted immediately to their cars and sped to the desert.

The passengers didn't speak during the lurching bus ride back to the hotel. But the silence comforted rather than disturbed normally talkative Tina. Cocooned by what she perceived as communal love, God's voice echoed in her mind and heart.

When the buses emptied in front of the hotel, Father Mark corralled his pilgrims and informed, "Jack Dunne has worked his magic again. We leave tomorrow morning. Jack will set up a desk in the lobby. Check with him for information about your flight and seats. For anyone interested, I'll say Mass at five o'clock in the main gathering room off the lobby, and Jack has arranged a farewell dinner immediately after Mass. I look forward to seeing you all later."

Rosa kissed Tina on the cheek. "I'll see you at Mass?"

"Yes." She smiled and brushed a kiss on her mom's petal soft cheek.

Her beaming mother followed the priest into the hotel as Tina waited for the other Belles to reach her.

"What did you think of the cross, Glen?" Tina posed, immensely curious about an atheist's interpretation of God-made events.

"Of course, everything about its existence and its superficial composition is inexplicable," he retorted. "A frozen geyser that erupts through the earth's surface that isn't a puddle of water by now? It can't be ice." He wagged his head.

Marlo's mouth dropped open. Frowning, she spit out, "What are you saying, Glen? Didn't God speak to you, like me? Like all of us?" Her gaze darted from Bern to Tina, Laci, and Leo. And then she stared Glen down. "You're saying you don't believe that God orchestrated every second of the past week?"

"On the contrary, my dear, I now believe absolutely that God has engineered the inexplicable. I believe that He left this permanent sign in the desert to wake up the human race. I, for one, have gotten the message."

Bernadette squeezed his hand and smiled up at him in heartwarming adoration.

Marlo let out a breath. "Oh, good. Really, I would have questioned your sanity otherwise."

"You'll not try and break it? Dispute its source with science or whatever?" Leo baited Glen, his arm draped casually around Marlo's shoulders.

Glen gazed downward as if humbly pondering his response. "I know the truth. Only God could have made it snow and left the Cross for the entire world to remember...." His eyes brimmed with tears and Tina, understanding absolutely, touched his shoulder gently. "...to remember this day of forgiveness and take it to heart."

Laci nodded. "I agree. I can't wait to get back home and talk to Joe. Tomorrow seems so far away."

"Is everyone going to Mass?" Tina asked as her phone vibrated against her side. After receiving unanimous, positive responses, Tina extracted the phone from her pocket and clicked on the fourth missed call to connect to her home phone number.

Ramon picked up on the first ring. "*Querida*, I have been frantic to hear your voice. I miss you so much. When are you coming home?"

The clarity and strength of his voice caught her off

guard. She couldn't remember the last time he'd referred to her as *querida,* and he sounded downright enthusiastic, rather than nagging and needy.

"I haven't checked my reservation yet, but tomorrow sometime."

"I can't wait to see you. I have so much to tell you. I watched Bernadette on TV. The Cross. Is it as beautiful up close as it looks on television?"

"Oh, Ramon! I can't put into words how gorgeous it is," she gushed. "I can't believe I was on the spot when it all happened."

"I miss you terribly. Please forgive me for the way I've acted since...Well, you know. I promise I'll spend the rest of my life making it up to you. I love you, Tina."

His pronouncement robbed her breath and had her heart skipping a beat. She had longed to hear those words from him, heartfelt and given freely.

"I love you, too," she responded, her spirits soaring. "And I can't wait to get back home," she added, astounded and elated over her genuine emotion.

"Why don't you invite everyone back to our house for dinner tomorrow night? I want to hear everyone's experiences. I'll make your mom's tamale pie. What do you think?"

She did a double take and stared at her phone as if gazing thunderstruck at Ramon's face. Placing the phone back to her ear, she said, "Sounds great. Makes my mouth water, actually," she added on a laugh. "I'll ask around and let you know how many to expect."

"Great. I love you, baby."

"I love you back, *mi amor.*" Tina entered the hotel and hurried up the stairs to her room to pack. Ramon had sounded like the man who had swept her off her feet and begged her to marry him, the man she fell in love with before all the ugliness of the past few years had invaded her life.

The room looked like the aftermath of a bomb. Laci, Marlo, and Bernadette filled suitcases gaping open on the floor. Laci tossed clothes into her bag haphazardly while Marlo and Bernadette folded clothes and packed each article neatly Tina dragged her suitcase out from under the bed and joined in.

"I just talked to Ramon. He wants me to invite everyone over for dinner tomorrow night. He's cooking. Want to come?"

Bernadette widened her eyes. "Ramon is cooking? And sociable? Wow, I won't miss out on that. Glen and I will come."

"Sorry, Teen," Marlo said. "Leo and I are continuing on to New York from O'Hare. Jack was able to book a connecting flight."

"I can't commit right now," Laci chimed in. "I haven't even spoken to Joe yet to tell him I'm coming back."

"No pressure. Feel free to drop in even if you can't stay for dinner. I think I'll invite Father Mark, too."

"Speaking of, it's almost five," Bern said. "We better leave and finish packing after dinner."

****

"This is delicious." Rosa helped herself to another piece of pie. "I'm impressed, Ramon."

"Thanks, Ma. Coming from you, that means a lot." Ramon weaved his way around the tightly spaced kitchen chairs, topping off wine for Bern, Glen, Tina, and Father Mark.

Observing him play the gracious, enthusiastic host, Tina's heart swelled with affection.

"Please sit, Ramon." The priest patted the empty chair next to him. "I want to hear all about your experience."

Ramon placed the bottle of wine on the table and complied with the request. His cheeks reddened, and he sat ramrod straight in his seat like an errant schoolboy called into the pastor's office.

Apparently reading Ramon's embarrassed expression, Father Mark assured, "It's not my business what transpired between you and God. I just want to know where you were. How it happened. Everyone's story is so different and yet the same."

Tina gazed at her husband, equally interested in hearing his story.

Ramon relaxed his posture. "I had just gotten off work. It was snowing as I walked home. I changed my clothes, and as I walked past the living room window, I noticed the snow had stopped. It surprised me. After all that time, I had gotten kind of used to seeing it, you know? Then the sky started to get dark, really dark, and really fast. It scared the sh…sugar out of me."

Amused, Tina and her guests laughed.

Ramon grinned and continued relating, "Then I remember falling to the carpet. And then God talked to me. To me. I still can't believe it. I thought I was dreaming." He paused as tears filled his eyes.

Tina popped up from her seat and rushed around the table to dole out a warm hug.

"I can't believe God is giving me a second chance." He trained tear-glazed eyes up at her. "I can change, Tina, and I am going to. I promise."

She smiled and kissed the crown of his head, noticing with pleasure that his soft hair smelled clean, and his subtle aftershave smelled wonderful.

"God has given all His children a second chance. If we truly listen and change our ways, just think of what life on earth could be like with no fighting, no wars, and people loving God and each other," Tina said.

"A second Eden, paradise on earth," Father Mark concluded.

"What will happen in Valselo?" Bernadette asked. "Will Our Lady continue to appear to the visionaries?"

"I asked Anna, and they don't know. They pray that she will continue to visit them at least on their special days."

"Glen and I discussed this subject on the plane. I want to go to Valselo, and Glen wants to come with me. I've already run the idea to do a story on where it all began by my boss. Do you think you could pave the way for me with the visionaries, Father?"

"If you can wait a few days, I'll do better than that. I'm returning to Valselo as soon as I tie up a few things at church. You're more than welcome to travel with me. Let me know, and I'll call Jack Dunne. He and his wife, Beth, are going with me. I can ask him to book your tickets if you would like. He's turned into a bit of a reservations wizard."

"Yes, please ask him to include us in your plans," Glen said. "Thank you, Father."

Tina liked the "new" Glen a lot. *My Ramon is brand new, too. We all are.* She closed her eyes. *Thank You, dear God, for giving us all another chance to live our lives according to Your wishes.*

25

Laci sprang off the couch and paced to her front window for the fifth time in that many minutes. Squinting through the thin blinds, she scanned the street, awaiting the appearance of Joe's car. Belle and Mary trailed Laci, wagging their tails, evidently enjoying the game.

Back on the couch, Laci's hands shook as she bent over her phone and reread Joe's text message:

On my way. Can't wait to hold you. I love you Lace!!

Jittery anticipation propelled her to her feet again for a repeat trip to the window.

Mary dropped out of the game and lay down on the rug, but Belle persevered in accompanying her mistress.

Will he still love me after he learns what I've done? The prospect that the only man she had ever loved might not be capable of loving her now had her knees buckling. She drifted away from the window and perched on the edge of the couch, but she couldn't sit still for long. Laci resumed pacing until she spotted Joe's car swooping into a parking space down the block. A few stressful minutes later, her front door swished open.

She flew into his arms and buried her head in his chest. Her ears filled with the dogs' yipping chorus, and her mind blanked, comforted after a week of tense isolation.

"Oh Lace, baby. I've missed you so much." He squeezed her tighter. "I should have gone with you. I'll never let you go anywhere without me again." Joe tipped a finger under her chin, tilted her head back, and kissed her tenderly. He drew away and regarded her, grinning.

Dizzy and rubber-legged, Laci hung in his arms. "I love you so much, Joe. Don't ever forget that," she said, her voice tremulous.

"Why would I forget?" His gaze bored into her eyes. "You look upset. Is everything OK?"

A chill ran through her as the temporary reprieve from reality evaporated. "I'm fine," she responded tersely as she escaped his embrace and perched on the couch.

Knitting his brow, Joe sat next to her and encircled her shoulders with his arm. "I'm glad you're home again," he said. "This past week has been hell...and heaven, too, I guess." He brushed his hand up and down her arm. "What was it like being there? I've seen the eruption of the cross on TV many times the past two days. I can't imagine the whole thing in person."

"Joe, it was incredible, fantastic, amazing, spectacular..." She wagged her head. "I'm doing a terrible job describing what it was like to see that ice cross fill the sky. I guess I'll settle on breathtaking. And

I mean that literally. It would have been perfect if you were there with me."

"I'm really sorry...another murder, the mayor's relative, the job..." he stammered. "It's no excuse."

"I was furious with you for not coming after I begged."She smiled at his chagrined expression. "I'm over it. A conversation with God is a major game changer." Widening her eyes at the understatement, she added, "Anyway I forgive you."

"Thank you." He leaned closer and brushed her lips with a kiss. "I promise I'll never do anything that requires your forgiveness again. Hopefully, God's forgiveness, either."

Her gut clenched. *Oh, Joe. Hopefully, you can forgive me.* "Where were you when you heard God?" She rolled her eyes. "I still can't believe this happened to everyone."

"I know," he said nodding his head. "When it happened to me, I was sitting right here. Belle was curled up in my lap, and I don't know where Mary was. I had just taken them out for their walk. The snow stopped while we were outside. I had gotten used to snow falling, so the world seemed odd. Especially when the sky got darker and darker. I picked the pups up and ran back here.

"I thought it would start raining any minute, but it didn't. I sat here staring at nothing through the totally black window. Next thing I know, I'm on my knees on the floor. I couldn't remember kneeling...like I was dreaming. And then..." He paused, and tears welled in the corners of his eyes. Taking a deep breath, he continued, "And then I heard God speak."

Squeezing her hand tightly, he said, "After He stopped, I just sat on the floor. I couldn't move. I don't know how long I was in that state, but when I came to my senses, I jumped up and ran out of here straight to church. So many people were streaming into St. Mary's. It was standing room only, but no one acted upset or inconvenienced. It seemed absolutely right to pray there together. What was it like for you?"

Laci gripped Joe's hand. "I was trembling so badly from fright that I thought I would have a heart attack. We were all gawking at the unbelievable ice cross one minute and then on our knees on the ground the next. I couldn't stop crying and lay in the dirt like I was paralyzed for a long time after it all ended."

"How blessed are we, Lace? We get a do-over. We can change anything we need to before it's too late."

Another chance, a do-over. She loved the notion and seized it like a life raft in her bottomless sea of guilt. "I'm going to change, I promise."

"You? Change? Sweetheart, you're perfect the way you are. You don't need to change a thing."

She pressed a tender hand on his cheek. "I love you for thinking so, but I have a lot of work to do. Starting today. Let's get married."

"What? We are. In a month."

"I don't want to wait a month. I want to get married sooner. Today. Now."

He looked at her askance. "The wedding planner has called you maybe a dozen times since you left. You aren't serious."

"I'm dead serious. I already called the wedding planner and cancelled. She's only going to keep a small portion of the deposit. She says she's going to be a nun after all that's happened."

Joe snorted. "Now I know you're kidding me."

"I'm not." She popped up from the couch. "Let's

go."

Joe glanced at his watch. "It's four o'clock. Where do you propose we go?"

"How about tomorrow morning? We could try to be one of the first couples in line."

"In line where?"

"City Hall. Well, wait a minute." She grabbed her tablet off the coffee table. "It's called the Marriage and Civil Union Court, and it's in the basement of the Cook County Building."

"All right," he said hesitantly. "But what about your big white wedding? The wedding you have been dreaming about since you were a little girl?"

Laci hesitated. She had to convince Joe that this was what she really wanted. She needed to be married to Joe before she could confess what she had done. "I just want to marry you. I don't need all the hoopla. It's crazy to spend so much money on a big wedding." She read his raised eyebrows and penetrating gaze. "Don't say I told you so," she preempted him. "I know you wanted to save the money and put it to a better use. I get that now."

"You're right about that, but you've spent months planning. All the invitations have gone out, Lace."

"I don't care, Joe. I want to get married. I don't want to wait a month." Frustrated tears brimmed in her eyes.

"Whoa," he said springing to his feet. "Baby, don't cry." He circled his arms around her. "Whatever you want," he soothed. "All I ever wanted is to be with you forever," he added. "So, I guess we'll get married in the morning."

"Really?" She swiped away tears as relief coursed through her. Standing on tiptoes, she rained kisses all over his face. "I love you so much."

"I love you with my whole heart, Lace," he said.

His reassurance warmed her, consoled her, and convinced her that this was the right course of action—the only way to a new future.

****

The next morning, Laci heaved a regretful sigh as she fingered the elegant clothes hanging in her closet. Price tags dangled from at least half the items squished onto double rods. A total shame, but she had to return the lovely clothes she'd yet to wear. The days of rampant sprees at high dollar department stores with unlimited credit and utter disregard for prices were over. She'd miss the empowerment of it all, but she had a fortune to pay back and Herculean frugality going forward was tantamount.

Laci emitted a soft moan as she touched the creamy silk sleeve of an exquisite, off-white designer suit. *Hello, gorgeous.* She didn't need to consult the tag to remember the price of ownership. The jacket alone had added two thousand dollars to her credit account. When she returned the jacket and skirt, she'd apply three thousand dollars toward her charge card balance.

But that wouldn't impact the sky-high total that she owed the company, she rationalized. Today was her wedding day, and she absolutely deserved a special outfit for her special day. She hurried to the kitchen and grabbed a pair of scissors. Rushing back into the bedroom closet, she cut off the suit's price tags, and buried them in the bottom of the wastebasket.

Donning the new clothes, she preened in front of the full-length mirror hung on the back of the closet door. She knew she had made the right decision to keep the suit when Joe's admiring gaze locked on her as she opened the front door.

"You are drop-dead gorgeous," he said, his eyes gleaming.

"And so are you." She beamed as she adjusted his tie. "Perfect."

The mirror on the living room wall reflected a striking couple as they passed by on their way out the front door.

Joe steered his beater car off Wacker Drive on to LaSalle and found a parking space near the front door. "It's our blessed day." He shifted into park and gifted her with a heart-melting smile.

His loving tenderness brought tears to Laci's eyes.

"Are you sure this is what you want, Lace?"

"Positive. I want to be Mrs. Joseph Corello more than anything in the world."

"Exactly what I was thinking," he responded as he shoved open his door and set off a screechy whine from the hinges. "Stay put. I'll pry open your door."

****

Laci produced the marriage license for Berta, the name-tagged clerk who manned the counter in the Cook County Civil Union Court Office. She and Joe signed paperwork as Berta proclaimed, "It's a lovely day to get married. Good luck and please take a seat in one of the rows of chairs."

Three couples had beaten Joe and Laci in taking seats where designated. Laci inspected the institutional office's drab, grayish walls, stained carpets, and dusty fake ferns. Not exactly the ambience she had originally planned for her wedding day.

"I'm Judge Donald Garrison," the man boomed as he bounded through the door and proceeded to the front of the room. "This is a fun day for me. Let me explain the ceremony," he addressed them. "I have a Bible and if you want I will read a passage. Totally optional. Regardless, you'll repeat marriage vows after me, and if you have rings, you can exchange them after that. I pronounce you legally married, and then you're out the door." He chuckled. "Doesn't sound very romantic, ladies, does it? Since I'm a judge, I order your future husbands to make the rest of the day romantic for you. Now, let's get married. I'll take the first couple now." The judge disappeared through a doorway off the counter area.

Berta directed the first couple through the threshold.

Joe clutched Laci's hand as the third couple emerged back into the outer office, "Ready?"

"You bet." She smiled thinly.

Five minutes later, Mr. and Mrs. Joe Corello exited the building, skipped down the stairs, and raced to the car like kids at dismissal time from school.

"Wow, Lace, we're married. Wait until the Belles hear. And our folks. No one will believe this." Joe switched on the engine and edged into the slow-moving, commuter traffic toward the Chicago River rather than back toward the expressway to the suburbs.

"Where are we going?" Laci asked as Joe continued down La Salle and turned on West Erie.

"It's a surprise. I'm just following the judge's orders."

A quick right on North Orleans and Joe halted at the valet stand in front of a restaurant. The marquis read Brunch.

"Hope you're hungry, wife."

Inside the restaurant, Joe informed the hostess, "I left a message on your voicemail, requesting a reservation for Mr. and Mrs. Corello."

Her eyes scanned a computer screen. "Yep, we received it." She picked up two menus and stepped out from behind the reception desk. "Right this way, please."

Clasping Joe's warm hand, Laci followed the hostess into a private room. A bouquet of lush, white roses in a silver vase surrounded by twinkling votive candles adorned the table for two.

"We hope this meets your expectations, Mr. Corello," the hostess said.

Grinning at Laci's delighted gasp, Joe said, "It's perfect. Thanks."

Joe held the chair out for Laci, sat in the chair opposite her, and lifted her left hand. The already "charged" expensive platinum wedding band on her ring finger glistened in the candlelight.

He kissed the back of her hand and then lowered it to rest on the tabletop cupped in his.

"This place is lovely," she said. "When did you have time to arrange this for me?"

"For us," he said. "I checked the Internet. Do you like it?"

"Oh, yes."

Two waitresses approached the table, balancing silver trays laden with plates. They set dishes of Eggs Benedict, strawberry stuffed French toast, a pile of breakfast nachos, and a stack of red velvet pancakes on the table. A waiter popped the cork on a bottle of champagne, poured Joe and Laci a glass, and then nested the bottle into a silver ice bucket stand. The wait staff then discreetly withdrew from the room.

"To my beautiful wife, I love you," Joe toasted, extending his glass toward Laci.

She clinked her flute against his and took a sip of champagne for pleasure and courage. *I should say something now before I lose my nerve.* But she procrastinated, loving the meal and the man who arranged it way too much to spoil things.

The service staff reappeared to clear the dishes and pour espresso at the precise moment they both sat back, proclaiming themselves stuffed.

"I never even asked. Do you have to go to work today?" Laci said, setting the delicate cup into the saucer.

"No, I took the day off. In fact, I want to talk to you about work. I'm seriously considering quitting the force."

Laci sat speechless as she raised the coffee cup to her lips and sipped the hot brew. Joe had never voiced any other career aspiration than law enforcement since she had met him in high school.

"I've given it a lot of thought," he continued. "I want to do something more with my life. I feel like God wants me to help people like you do. Do you know of anything available at America United for me?"

Her hands shook and coffee splashed over the rim of the cup onto the pristine tablecloth.

Joe frowned. "What's wrong, Lace? Do you hate the idea?"

"No, it's not that..." Trembling, she returned the cup to the saucer and wrung her hands in her lap. This was the moment. She had to obey God. *Confess your lies and deception.* "I may not continue at America United for much longer. You see..." Her voice cracked. "I just have to pay back some money, and then I think I'll leave and find another job."

"Pay back money? What are you talking about? What money?" He clenched his jaw and gazed at her steadily.

Unnerved by his unsmiling countenance, she imagined him interrogating a real criminal and shuddered. "Don't be mad at me, Joe. I'll resolve this in time. It was nothing at first, but then things sort of, well...got out of hand. Then we got engaged, and everything with the wedding was just so expensive, and there was the bridal shower I'd always dreamed of having..." she rattled on.

"You stole money from your company?" he asked.

"Well, not exactly. No," she hedged. "I only borrowed it for a while. I'll pay it all back. No one ever has to know."

"Lace, what do you mean?" He grimaced. "You're an embezzler. I'm a cop. You have to turn yourself in."

"But you're my husband now. A husband can't testify against his wife."

Joe sucked in a ragged breath, his face a mask of pain. "Is that why you were in such a hurry to get married?" he probed in a soft voice.

She would have liked it better if he had shouted.

"Of course not…"

"You think because you tricked me into marrying you I'll turn away from what's right out of love for you?" he interjected.

Hating that he required her to defend herself, she choked out, "You just said you want to quit the force. What do you care? I will pay all the money back. I promise."

Slapping his napkin down on the table, he rose slowly.

Her stomach churned as tears streamed down her cheeks.

Looming over her, his eyes hard, he commanded, "You will turn yourself in, or I swear, Lace, I will arrest you."

26

Bernadette's piece featuring the Valselo interviews dominated the hour-long *Now Chicago* show that morning, two days after she and Glen had returned from the Adriatic village, and a week after the permanent sign had appeared in the Mojave.

Frazzled and over-worked the past forty-eight hours, Bernadette and her cohost had rolled up their sleeves to toil with the production team in sorting through hundreds of newsworthy clips and headlines that defined humanity's reaction to the Almighty's actions. In order to do the topic "Prophesied Events Come True" justice, a far longer daily broadcast was necessary, but *Now Chicago's* one hour, five-days-a-week timetable remained the total allotment, at least until the end of the season.

Since preset network scheduling posed finite restrictions, local and world news programs worked out unprecedented, information sharing scenarios with feature format shows like *Now Chicago* to air breaking news without duplication throughout each broadcast day. In the wake of universal snow and signs just about everything was breaking news.

"After a message from our local sponsors, we'll hear from Luke Middleton, leader of the grassroots movement to change the world calendar," Bernadette said, fifty-five minutes into the show clock.

Relaxing in her swivel chair behind the anchor desk as the commercial spots rolled, she gazed upward through the control booth window and caught Chuck Barton's eye. Her boss smiled warmly and switched on the booth mic.

"Excellent piece on Valselo." His compliment echoed in the studio. "After wrap-up, stick around a few minutes? I want to ask you something."

"Sure," she replied as she straightened in her seat, preparing to continue announcing when the commercial break ended.

Brock Carson, her cohost led in, "*Now Chicago* welcomes input from our viewers concerning the plan put forth by Luke Middleton, an Episcopal minister in Edinburgh, Scotland, to the United Nations General Assembly today. Middleton wants to restart the year count beginning with January 1st."

"Weigh in on Middleton's proposal to start the world calendar anew with the year 1AS on the next New Year's Day. You may vote for or against the proposition on the homepage of our website, or post Yes 1AS or No 1AS on our social media page, or you can type #1AS yes or no on our feed," Bernadette announced. "Finally, cell phone users can text Vote Yes or Vote No to the number now appearing on your screen."

"And if you do vote yes to changing the calendar next year, let us know through any of the communication modes Bernadette just mentioned if you favor AS to stand for After Snow or After Sign in keeping with Middleton's intention to symbolically formalize the impact of the recent world events," Brock said.

"That's our program for today. Stay safe, Chicago," Bernadette said.

"Blessings, Chicago," Brock signed off.

Disconnecting her body mic, Bernadette narrowed her eyes and gazed at her cohost. "Blessings? What happened to Stay Well, Chicago?" she asked.

"It just seems right to me to say that now," he explained, shrugging his shoulders.

Bern darted her gaze to the control booth; certain Chuck would rain down fury upon Brock's handsome head for introducing overt religious overtones to the telecast. But the boss chatted casually with the production team, apparently unfazed.

"Great show, Miz O'Neal," one of the grips remarked as she headed toward the steps leading up to the control booth.

"Thanks, Doug," she said. "And thank you for your great work today."

"Sure thing." He smiled at the acknowledgment.

"What did you want to talk about, Chuck?" she asked as she entered the booth.

"See you guys later for the script review," he dismissed the other occupants of the control booth.

When only she and her boss remained, he trained doleful eyes on her.

"Are you all right?" she asked, knitting her brows.

"Sure, sure," he said. "Uh...listen." He cast his gaze downward and peered at the floor a few seconds.

His tentative body language confused her. She was

accustomed to Chuck's stormy disposition and bullish movements.

"You don't look all right," she ventured.

"I'm fine. Look…" He gazed into her eyes, his expression somber.

Adrenaline shot through her. *Maybe he wants to fire me.* "Did I do something wrong?"

"Heck, no."

"Heck, no?" She tested his forehead for fever with the back of her hand. "You don't feel sick."

"I'm not sick," he asserted. "I'm supposed to be nice to you. Have I been nicer?"

A smile played on the corner of her lips. "I suppose so…"

"God told me I had to do this."

She burst out laughing. "Sheesh…God specifically said, be nice to Bernadette O'Neal or else?"

His hangdog expression prompted her to pat his shoulder as she struggled to wipe the smirk off her face. "You've been very nice to me, Chuck. I have nothing to complain about," she assured him.

"You know, every word you reported in that feature piece struck home for me," he said, gazing straight ahead as if lost in thought. "I don't intend to squander the second chance I've been given."

The sincerity of the pronouncement, especially coming from her thorny superior whose bite was a great deal bigger than his bark, impressed Bernadette—made her feel small. "I think I'll follow your example, Chuck," she said.

He raised his head and smiled. "Crazy times, huh, lady?"

"Never crazier. See you tomorrow?" she asked, seeking his approval before she left the studio.

"Yeah. Go home and get some rest," he suggested. "Brock's already on his way to the airport. He'll broadcast from the Global Summit in the morning, and you can cover commentary in the studio. Generally, just prelim tomorrow with more substance the next day, after some of the meetings have concluded."

"Sounds good. I'll be in around four thirty."

Riding in the cab bound for her Lake Shore condominium, she mentally switched off work mode and then worried about Laci and Joe. No matter how much she attempted to arrive at a calm, stable place thinking about her friend's circumstances, she couldn't reframe grief and loss into any sort of peaceful acceptance.

Tina's urgent read-me-now e-mail received while in Valselo had spurred Bern's middle of the night call to Tina to learn the facts. She could hardly believe her ears as Tina had related Laci's critical predicament. First, there was the desperate plea for bail bond money. Bern had moved heaven and earth to rapidly wire the funds to accomplish the speediest jail release.

Just when Bern thought that she could breathe easy on that score, Decadence Hotel, apparently unwilling to await the result of criminal proceedings, came after Tina, Bernadette, and Marlo to cover the expenses charged for the bachelorette party bill.

Doling out money didn't faze Bernadette. Marlo had contributed, too, so the matter had been resolved with minimal sacrifice. But her isolation from Laci and her horror in contemplating her friend's temporary imprisonment and pending trial continued to cost Bernadette peace of mind and a good measure of happiness.

She would not judge. If she hadn't learned at least

that much during her own judgment, then she might as well go straight to hell now. But her thoughts ruminated: Why? How? When? How much? Why?

Joe had reportedly quit his job and had disappeared. Where he had gone was a closely guarded Corello family secret. Rumors swirled that Joe and Laci were married, or that their marriage had been annulled, or that Joe had filed papers for divorce or annulment. Since Laci wouldn't respond to any of the Belles' attempts to communicate, only rumors prevailed.

Bernadette exited the cab and trundled along the walkway beneath her condo building's entry canopy.

"Morning, Mrs. Foster," the doorman greeted her as he yanked on the handle and swung the door wide in front of her. "Bet you can't wait to get upstairs to your family."

His enthusiasm permeated her Laci funk. "Family?" she asked dumbly.

"Yes. Dr. Foster asked me to show them in a couple hours ago."

She stared at him vacantly.

His face fell. "Did I ruin a surprise or something?"

"Uh, no. It's fine," she said, stepping inside the building and then heading to the elevator.

Glen rose from the sofa as she barged through the front door into her foyer. She hadn't understood the significance of the doorman's banter, so she was astonished at the improbable sight of her brother sitting knee to knee with a raven-haired woman on the love seat in her living room.

"Darling…" Glen stared at her sheepishly, his arms lax at his sides as if defenseless and innocent, despite her deduction that he was guilty as sin.

Glen spoke with my family behind my back? Fury and gratitude warred within her. Shaken, she gazed intently at her kid brother. Seeing him in the flesh made her realize acutely how much she missed him.

He met her gaze as he rose from his seat and then helped the woman to rise and stand at his side.

Rooted to the spot, Bernadette noted his slow, lazy smile, her dad's cobalt-blue eyes regarding her and the still visible light dusting of freckles across the bridge of his nose. Years of estrangement dissolved as she relished the sight of her sibling's familiar face.

"Hey, Bee-bee," he said.

The memory of the sunny-faced toddler with the contagious burbling laugh who could only manage two consonants to call her by name swelled her heart.

"Mickey," she whispered.

And then she flew into Michael O'Neal, Jr.'s arms for a brotherly hug nearly a decade overdue. She sobbed, her face pressed against his shoulder as his body quaked with equal emotion. Raising her head, she beamed up at him, warmed by his grin and the sheen of tears in his eyes.

"Bernadette, I'd like you to meet my wife, Madina."

Stepping awkwardly out of Mickey's embrace, Bernadette turned her attention to her sister-in-law and was faced with a lovely, open-armed woman who smiled serenely and seemingly welcomed Bernadette's affection. Shame flooded through her. How could she have turned her back on her brother and his family? How could she possibly have been so ignorant?

Her father's murder had nothing to do with this woman...or millions of men and women who would never be capable of harming another living soul.

I am the judge. Your father knows me.

Her cheeks flaming, she hugged Madina and muttered, "I'm so glad to finally meet you."

"Oh, I can hardly believe my good fortune to know you," Madina said, her Middle Eastern accent imparting a lyrical cadence to her speech. "We just watched your television program with Glen and Mother. You are so good. It is an honor to be related to you."

"Oh, gosh. I don't deserve such praise," she said before she rounded on her mother.

"Hi, Mom," she said.

Her mom held up her arms in surrender. "Don't look at me," she retorted.

Bernadette faced Glen. "How did you know I wanted...?" Words escaped her to express her gratitude fully. She could only whisper, "Thank you." And hoped Glen understood that she had never meant it more.

"You're very welcome, my darling," he said, cocking an eyebrow. "Maybe I'm a little smarter about what matters in life these days."

He gave her a warm smile as she clasped Madina's hands.

"Where are your children?" Bernadette asked, bristling with eagerness. "Can I meet them? Do they know they have an aunt? And an uncle?"

"Of course," Madina replied. "Michael tells them stories about their family and shows them photos all the time."

"We have a sitter at Mom's house," Mickey said. "Want to come back with us and stay for dinner? Would that be OK, Ma?"

Tears welled in her mom's eyes. She sniffled and

then responded, "I would love that."

"What do you say, Bee-bee?" Mickey's eyes gleamed.

Beaming at Glen and then at her brother, Bernadette responded, "Yes, we'd love to."

27

Fumbling the house keys and struggling to hang onto her suitcase and a bundle of mail, the luggage handle slipped out of Marlo's grasp. The bag thumped onto the marble floor outside her condo door and toppled sideways. She fitted the key in the lock, heaved open the mahogany door, and stomped inside.

Her cleaning lady had apparently worked her magic. The fresh scent of lemon furniture polish permeated the air.

After dumping the envelopes on her desk, she retrieved her suitcase from the hallway and lugged it into her bedroom.

Perspiring and exhausted, she plopped down on the edge of her bed and stared vacantly out the window. Central Park at twilight glittered like a forest of Christmas trees below. The magical panorama didn't infuse her with the customary peace of homecoming. Her stomach clenched. Could she go through with her plan to end her pregnancy? She could, she couldn't, and that debate had raged in her brain all week since she had returned from Vegas.

The decision to keep the baby had seemed firm before the past week's photo shoot. But her mounting professional success cracked her resolve. The *Vanity Fair* cover was a dream come true. Everything she and Leo had worked toward bore fruit. Filming the pilot for their television show would begin next week. The allure of fame and money, especially the money, influenced her flip-flopping decisions concerning abortion.

She fluttered a hand over her stomach, dismayed that logic edged out sentimental notions of motherhood. *I can't have a child. My career is too demanding, too important. Pregnancy weight gain is absolutely out of the question.*

Before she changed her mind again, Marlo rummaged in her purse for the business card, dialed the clinic's number, and made the appointment to have the procedure the following day. Relieved that at least she had taken decisive action, she sprawled on the bed and closed her eyes.

Her chirring cell phone interrupted her rest a few minutes later.

"Hey, Leo," she answered after a quick glance at the caller ID.

"Hey, doll face, just checking in. How was the flight?"

"Amazingly easy. The limo let me off at my building before I was even supposed to land. How was the meeting with the big brass?"

"Amazingly easy," he parroted. "Maybe not as easy as your flight, but they agreed with the changes we wanted and everything is moving along. Can you believe it, Mar? It's really happening for us."

"It's hard to wrap my head around it all." She

closed her eyes and massaged her forehead. "I have to pinch myself to make sure I'm not dreaming."

"Speaking of, you must be exhausted. How about we meet tomorrow for lunch? Let's say Aldinato's at noon? I can bring the paperwork from today's meeting."

She wagged her head as a knot formed in her stomach.

"I can't. I have something tomorrow morning," she responded praying that he wouldn't question the nature of the schedule conflict.

"OK. I can wait. How about a late lunch or even dinner?"

"Late lunch, it is. I'll meet you at two."

"Sounds perfect. Get some sleep. Love ya."

"Love you, too." I really do, she thought as she disconnected the call. Experiencing the appearance of the permanent sign had changed Marlo. What had irritated her before about Leo's behavior didn't matter in the least anymore. And her affection for Leo had outgrown the confines of friendship. He was with her when Bern had called asking for money for Laci's bail, and he had immediately written a check to split the amount, no questions asked.

The Cross had changed Leo, too. They never argued anymore. He was attentive but never smothering. Surprising, but true, Marlo was increasingly physically and emotionally attracted to the man and even indulged in fantasies about marrying him.

But how would he feel about impending fatherhood? If he knew about her intention to abort their child, would he view her differently? Hate her? Agree with her?

Leo would never know because she would never tell him. All the pamphlets preached that a woman had the sole right to choose what happened with her body. She intended to exercise that right. Her baby would dwell with God in paradise.

Modeling was all Marlo knew in this life. Her entire livelihood revolved around her body's flawless condition. Surely the man whose livelihood was intertwined with hers wouldn't oppose the abortion.

Afterward, she'd atone and beg God's forgiveness. God always forgave.

Her still perfectly flat stomach growled, empty after a day that had started with morning sickness and had ended with a dry salad on the plane. She rose off the bed and headed toward the kitchen where an impulse-buy of ice cream called her name.

Standing in front of the open freezer door, frosty vapor wafted in her face. *Oh, why not?* Tomorrow she'd eliminate pregnancy cravings and force herself to be happy with the decision and satisfied with a diet of lettuce and cucumbers. *Tonight, I'm still having a baby.*

She seized the pint of ice cream and then grabbed a soup spoon out of the cutlery drawer. Standing at the kitchen counter, she popped off the carton's top and shoveled up a heaping spoonful of dark chocolate-laced ice cream. As the sweet confection melted in her mouth, tears streamed down her cheeks.

****

Marlo scrawled her name on the sign-in sheet on

the reception counter and peered through the window. "Good morning," she greeted the receptionist.

"Good morning," the woman behind the glass responded without glancing up from her computer screen. "I'll be with you in one minute."

Normally, the minor delay in receiving attention wouldn't faze Marlo. But standing at an abortion clinic's reception window, she wanted to jump out of her skin waiting for the receptionist to execute a few clicks on the keyboard, print out paperwork, and affix it to a clipboard.

The window slid open, and the woman jutted the clipboard and a pen out toward Marlo. "Here you go…" She glanced down at the sign-in book and then added, "Ms. Waters. Please fill out these forms. And I will need a copy of your insurance card."

"I don't have insurance. Here's my credit card."

Marlo waited for the woman to process the card, having predetermined to forego any insurance company record of the procedure.

She signed the charge slip and then slumped into a molded plastic chair in the waiting room, her heart pounding. Dressing that morning, she had stuffed her mane of black hair under a Yankee baseball cap and donned a pair of wraparound sunglasses—her attempt at a disguise. Probably no one would recognize her regardless, but why take the chance?

A nurse in blue scrubs called out, "Ms. Waters!"

Marlo popped up and approached the woman who held her patient clipboard in hand. She smiled, held the door open for Marlo, and then led her into a small examining room.

The chrome table gleamed under the fluorescent light. A butter-colored hospital gown lay folded on the corner of the table. Marlo's hand trembled as she took the specimen cup the nurse held out.

"My name is Shirley. If you need anything or have any questions, I'll be with you for the next few hours."

"Thank you, Shirley. My name is Marlo."

"Nice to meet you, Marlo. Now we need you to change into this hospital gown, and we'll also need a urine sample. The bathroom is behind that door." Shirley pointed over her shoulder. "I'll wait here until you're finished, and then I'll draw some blood to check your RH factor and your blood count."

Marlo shuffled into the tiled bathroom and closed the door. She had expected the clinic to have a more forbidding vibe—maybe a dark office, sinister, a place of destruction. But the serene green painted walls, spotless equipment, and glaring florescent lights simulated a gynecological visit, routine, ordinary.

She donned the gown, peed in the cup, and then emerged from the bathroom zombie-like to take the next step.

Shirley directed her to sit on the side of the examining table, wrapped a stretchy tourniquet around her upper arm, drew the blood, removed the tourniquet, and then applied a small round bandage to the site of the needle prick.

"You can lie down on the table now. Dr. Cole will be right in to perform an ultrasound to establish the extent of pregnancy, and then she'll answer any questions."

Marlo swung her legs onto the table and lay down, casting her gaze to the ceiling. Sick with dread, unanswered questions spooled in her mind. *What am I doing here? Is this the answer? Should I be alone now? Should I have told Bern or Tina or Laci? Leo?*

The door burst open and a petite, blonde woman burst into the examining room. Hovering over her, the woman said, "Good morning. I'm Dr. Cole. How are you feeling?"

"I have to admit I'm nervous, doctor." Marlo's voice cracked.

"Totally normal," she said as she lifted up the gown, squirted gel on Marlo's skin and slid the ultrasound wand around her abdomen. The doctor gazed fixedly at the ultrasound equipment.

Marlo couldn't see the monitor. No invitation was extended to view the baby in utero, marvel at tiny features, or watch a beating heart.

A switch flipped off, and Dr. Cole offered a handhold to pull Marlo up to a seated position on the table.

"Let me explain what comes next," the doctor said. "We'll walk to the operating room where we'll give you twilight sedation. This will make you feel drowsy, but you'll remain awake for the entire procedure. You might experience some discomfort or cramping. It won't last long. The procedure takes about seven minutes. Then you'll be in the recovery room about three hours. It's just precautionary. We do not expect any complications."

Doctor Cole paused a beat before asking, "Any questions? Are you comfortable with your decision?"

Marlo heaved a ragged breath as certainty finally gripped her. "Yes, I am," she replied. "Totally comfortable."

****

Her phone pressed to her ear, Marlo stood at the empty maître d's stand and surveyed the bustling restaurant.

Leo waved his arm from their favorite corner table.

"Bye, Bern. Good luck. I think you'll need it," Marlo said acknowledging Leo with a wave of her hand.

"Thanks a lot, Mar."

She laughed as she ended the conversation with Bernadette and then wove through the tables topped with red-and-white checkered linen.

Leo stood to pull out her chair and kissed her cheek as he seated her at the table. "Who was on the phone?" he asked as he occupied the chair across from her.

Marlo placed the checkered napkin in her lap. "Bernadette. Would you believe she's babysitting for her two nieces and nephew? They're having a sleepover in Bern's condo."

"Are they the good doctor's family?"

"No. They're Bern's brother Mike's kids. Mike has been an absolutely taboo subject with Bern for years. All I know is that she hadn't met Mike's wife or kids until last week. Now they're staying overnight. Crazy, huh?"

"Not crazy. Sounds like more miracle in the desert stuff to me." He took a sip of water. "Speaking of the miracle, I have something I want to talk over with you."

"Uh oh."

"I don't think you'll have a problem with this." He

glanced downward and then he leveled his gaze at her. "At least I hope you don't. I want to become a Christian."

Marlo did a double take. "Wow. I didn't see that coming. What will your parents think? I can just hear Sophie now. Where did we go wrong, Saul? Our bubala is going to be a goyim." She giggled.

Leo gagged on his ice water and coughed loudly. "I'll have you know that when I spoke with Sophie this morning, she told me that she really wished I'd embrace the faith of my birth, but she loves me no matter what I choose."

Marlo clenched her hands against her chest in a fake heart attack pose.

Leo smiled. "I know. I thought she would explode. But after everything happened, everyone has changed. I spoke with Father Mark before you arrived, and he has lists of people who want to convert. My becoming a Christian will make it easier for us, too."

She furrowed her brow. "In what way?"

"We promised each other that if we're not married by the time we both hit forty, we'll get hitched."

"And how drunk were we when we did that?" she teased. "Don't worry. I won't hold you to it." At his pained expression, she blinked. "All right. You're serious," she said softy.

"Yes, of course. Now we could marry in your church."

His sincerity stole her breath. Tears brimmed in her eyes as she broke eye contact and stared at her lap.

"What's wrong, Mar? What did I do? Please don't cry." He reached across the table to clasp her hand.

"You didn't do anything. It's me," she blubbered. "After I tell you about my morning, you might want to rethink our marriage pact."

She sobbed into her napkin. A chair leg scraped along the floor, and then his arm wrapped around her shoulder. Raising her head, she gazed at him. The tenderness she read in his soft brown eyes spurred her to cry harder.

"You can tell me anything." He waved away the waitress. "Please just give us a few more minutes."

He squeezed Marlo's shoulder. "Tell me about your morning."

"I had an appointment..." she trailed off barely able to breathe. She gulped. "An appointment to get an abortion," she sobbed, tears streaming down her face.

"Whoa. Are you OK? Shouldn't you be lying down or something?"

Dabbing under her eyes with the napkin, she composed herself. "I didn't go through with it. I couldn't."

"Why are you crying then? Having a baby is a blessing. Have you told the father yet?"

"I'm telling him right now."

He widened his eyes and gaped at her. "Me? I'm the father? How? When?"

"Do you remember Hawaii about two months ago...?"

"Uh...I guess."

"That's when. And I'm sure you can figure out how all by yourself."

"I can't believe it." He jumped to his feet.

Marlo bowed her head reconciled to his leaving the restaurant, and most probably her life, after the bombshell she had delivered.

"I'm going to be a daddy!" he bellowed.

Cheers arose from surrounding tables in response

to his outburst. "And this beautiful woman is going to be the mommy," he shouted.

Marlo tugged on his arm. "Sit down, please," she begged, prickly from the glare of attention. "This is not the reaction I expected."

Even more unexpected, Leo went down to the floor on one knee.

"Good grief," Marlo exclaimed. "You're crazy."

"Marlo. I have loved you since I first laid eyes on you in the restaurant. I know you don't feel the same way about me, but I will love you enough for both of us. And I want our baby's parents to be together. Please say you will marry me." His voice cracked, and tears glistened in his eyes.

"I do love you, Leo. But I don't want you to feel you have to marry me just because I'm having a baby."

"You are not just having a baby; you're having my baby. And I would have proposed a long time ago, but I was afraid you would say no."

Her heart leaped. "I say yes. Yes, I will marry you!"

He launched off the floor, wrapped his arms around her, and lifted her to her feet. His eyes danced as he cupped her face with his hands and kissed her.

28

Tina luxuriated in one of Bernadette's Barcelona chairs, positive that she lacked absolutely nothing in her life. Ramon had transformed into the caring, funny, romantic man she had married. Every night since her return from Nevada, cocooned in his arms, she had given thanks and praise to God on high for that miracle.

Bernadette had never seemed happier. Joking with her eight-year-old nephew in the kitchen, Bern's smile alone could light up the room that evening. The penthouse condo that her friend had purchased when she'd married Glen had always seemed sterile and almost uninhabited with its angular modern furniture and architectural vibe. Now, just a couple weeks after Las Vegas, Bern's home was filled with children's high-pitched voices and bursts of adult laughter.

The doorbell chimed and Bernadette called out, "Teen, can you get that, please? It's Laci. The security guard at the front desk just told me she was on her way up."

"Sure,'" Tina replied. She heaved up out of the

low-slung chair and counted yet another blessing anticipating seeing Laci.

Hurrying towards the foyer, she reached the door and swung it open. In the next instant, she flung her arms around Laci and hugged her fiercely.

"Oh, Teen..." She trembled within the embrace as overcome with emotion as Tina.

Bern, Glen, and Ramon hovered behind Tina.

"Come on in, Lace," Bernadette said. "Glen has already poured you a glass of your favorite wine."

"That sounds perfect," Laci responded, her voice husky.

Tina slipped an arm around Laci's waist and ushered her into the living room trailed by the cluster of adults.

Bern whisked Laci away, drawing her into an enveloping bear hug. Bern's eyes closed as she said, "Oh, honey, I've been so worried about you." She held Laci at arm's length and peered at her face. "How are you holding up?"

"I'm doing OK," she said weakly.

Glen appeared with the glass of wine. Handing it to Laci, he invited, "Please, sit."

"You just sit there and relax," Bern added. "Tina, Ramon, and Glen will keep you company. I'll be right back. I'm almost done cooking dinner."

Glen perched on a leather ottoman, and Ramon settled into the chair behind him.

Laci sat alone on the sofa, heightening her tiny stature, frail appearance, and the awkwardness of her recent estrangement.

Raising his glass, Glen proposed a toast as Tina returned to her seat. "Blessed be to God for bringing us all together tonight."

Laci's jaw dropped, and she gaped at Glen as he calmly sipped some wine.

Apparently amused at her reaction, he continued, "Laci, you won't believe what I did this morning."

His eyes twinkled as he gazed at Laci, and his pleasant smile drew a smile from her in return.

"This is mysterious. I'll bite," she teased. "What did you do?"

"I went to church," he replied in a deadpan tone.

The women hooted in unison.

"Last thing I expected you to say," Laci remarked. "Um, did you enjoy it?"

"Pretty much," he said, his expression serious. "But some churches drag out things. So far, I like the Catholic Mass the best."

"He went to the synagogue yesterday," Bern sang out from the kitchen.

Glen nodded, his expression composed and serene as if it were the most natural thing for a confirmed atheist to frequent places of worship. "Right. Talk about dragging things out."

"I take it you've changed your religious views?" Laci asked.

"A complete one-eighty," he tossed out. "Hearing God's voice kind of clinched it for me."

He winked and then grinned at his wife as she squeezed onto the ottoman next to him. "Glen's heading up a scientific expedition to analyze the permanent sign," she said.

"Why?" Tina said. "I mean, wow, Glen. You were right there. You don't think that the ice cross is miraculous? "

"On the contrary," he replied forcefully. "I want to document proof of the miracle in the annals of world history."

Silence. Surely people who had experienced the Valley of Fire first hand would have more to say to one another. *It's Laci*, Tina thought. *We're glad she's here, but we don't know what to say to her.*

"So...What's new with you, Ramon?" Bern asked, pointedly refraining from questioning Laci.

"I'm good." He flashed a radiant smile at Tina. "Enjoying life."

Bernadette winced as her gaze darted toward Laci.

Laci apparently interpreted Bern's guilty expression accurately. "Guys, there's no need..." She paused, gazing out the window as if lost in thought. "I am scared, and I don't really know how this will all turn out. Probably prison, and I'll be in debt to my former employer forever. But I have a lot to be thankful for. It's an enormous relief for me to have finally cleared my conscience. I'm ready to pay the price for my actions and put it behind me. I'm grateful to my mom who insisted on helping me with legal expenses, and I'll never be able to thank you for helping me with bail and the whole bachelorette party thing...I'm so ashamed." Bowing her head, she sobbed. "The hardest part is living without Joe."

Bernadette and Tina flew toward Laci. Each took a seat next to her on the sofa and draped an arm behind her—Belles of St. Mary's bookends intent on shoring up Laci's spirits.

"It will be all right," Bernadette said, massaging the side of Laci's arm. "We'll be there for you, won't we, Teen?"

"Absolutely," Tina affirmed. "Is there something we can do to contact Joe?"

Wiping away tears with the back of her hand, Laci

replied, "Actually, he called me after I posted bail. He said that he's glad I listened to him and turned myself in. And spared him from having to arrest me..." Her voice hitched. She sniffled and a smile played at the corner of her lips. "He said he's trying hard to forgive me."

Bernadette frowned and her blue eyes darkened. "It's not much, but I guess it's a start."

"It's huge, Bern," Laci contradicted. "We're still married, and he hasn't tried to change that. I'm praying that after I've faced this and served my sentence, we might still have a future together."

"We'll rev up the prayer chain for that intention, Laci." Tina gave her shoulder a gentle squeeze. "In the meantime, we'll help you any way we can."

"Auntie Bee," Shara O'Neal sang out as she zipped into the living room.

"Yes, love." Bernadette regarded her six-year-old niece affectionately.

"There's a lady on your video on the computer. She said I'm so pretty I should be a model."

"Marlo!" The Belles chorused as they shot off the sofa and hustled into Bernadette and Glen's home office.

Tina beamed at Marlo's smiling countenance on the laptop screen. Leaning over Marlo's shoulder, Leo wore a Cheshire grin matching Marlo's exuberant expression. Somehow, they fit together despite Marlo's exotic, stunning features and his shaved head, retro glasses, and three-inch-shorter height than her five feet eleven inches.

"Kids, why don't you go see your Uncle Glen in the kitchen?" Bern requested. "There are some pretzels and cheese for you. As soon as we're done with this computer chat, we'll have dinner."

The children tore out of the room, and the Belles clustered around the laptop screen.

"Hey, guys, you're all together," Marlo said. "Oh wow, Laci, too! This is perfect."

A chorus of greetings sounded.

"What's up?" Tina asked, her intuition screaming that romance was afoot. "You look beautiful, by the way."

Marlo smiled. "Thank you. I wanted to share our news."

Her eyes gleamed. "Actually, I'm about to explode I'm so happy. Are you guys up for another Belles bachelorette party?"

Laci's eyebrows shot up. "No way," she declared.

"What?" Bern shouted. "Are you two getting married?"

"Uh huh." Marlo brandished her left hand in front of the camera, and the solitaire on her ring finger shot off sparkles. "We went to Tiffany's a little while ago. My head's still spinning."

The women shrieked with glee.

"Congratulations!"

"Fantastic news!"

Laci's brow furrowed. "Have you set a date? I'm not allowed to leave Chicago," she said.

"We're having a family wedding with Leo's family only. Then after the baby's born and Leo has converted to Catholicism, we're going to have a church wedding."

"A baby!" The Belles chorused.

"Well, duh! That's why you were so sick in Vegas!" Bern exclaimed.

"This is unbelievable! Why didn't you tell us?" Laci

asked.

"I didn't want to hog your spotlight," came Marlo's unconvincing reason.

Her gaze averted from the camera, and Leo squeezed her hand.

"Mar? What is it?" Tina said.

"I was going to have an abortion, and I didn't want anybody to talk me out of it," she admitted.

Bern knit her eyebrows. "Oh, honey. You should have said something. No matter what, the Belles support each other."

Laci grinned sheepishly into the computer camera. "I can attest to that statement."

"I couldn't go through with it, and after I left the clinic, I told Leo he was going to be a father."

Leo beamed a smile. "And then she made me the happiest man on earth when she accepted my proposal."

"I want to do the baby shower here," Bern volunteered. "Is that OK?"

"Oh, yes!"

"We're going to be aunts!"

The women raised a racket that brought Glen and Ramon racing into the office. The Belles shed copious, joyful tears while the men gaped, alarmed at the women's behavior.

Tina patted Ramon's arm as Bernadette signed off with Marlo. "We've just had wonderful news. We'll tell you all about it over dinner."

****

Changing clothes at home that evening, Ramon posited, "God told Laci to come clean." He gazed at Tina intently. "Don't you think?"

"Hmmm," she said, buttoning her pajama top. "I would think so. But Joe really gave her no choice. He said he'd arrest her if she didn't turn herself in…because it's the right thing to do."

Ramon nodded, his eyes downcast. Irrational foreboding gripped her as she noticed his clenched hands and rigid posture.

"Is something bothering you, Ramon?"

He raised his eyes and stared at her. A chill ran through her at the foreign, sinister expression on his face and the sheen of tears in his eyes. He clenched his jaw and clasped both her hands. "You're scaring me," she whispered.

He gulped. "I have to tell you something…"

Tremors vibrated off him and caught her up in his distress. Something awful hung in the air. Desperate to prevent her world from destruction, Tina pressed her right index finger against his lips, "Shush…"

"No, Tina, I have to," he said, his hot breath puffing against her finger.

She frowned and tried to shake her left hand out of his grasp, certain that she didn't want to hear this confession, but he held tight.

"I did it," he said between clenched teeth. "She forced me…I had no choice. It was the only way to shut her up…"

Mystified, Tina struggled to interpret his rambling. "What did you do? Who is she?"

His face fell, and he gazed past her as tears streamed down his face. He wet his bottom lip with his tongue and then responded, "I killed Jodi Weller."

Dumbfounded at his false admission, her mind raced. Jodi Weller, the teen who'd cost Ramon his teaching job, the one who'd sent him into a downward spiral was very much alive. *How could I have missed this? He's out of touch with reality. What do I do? Dear Lord, help me.*

"No, *mi amor*," she said, clasping his elbows. "Jodi Weller is alive. You didn't kill her. You couldn't kill any…"

Her voice caught in her throat as he shook off her hands and gripped her arms, viselike.

"I did kill her over and over and over," he chanted, tilting his head side to side. "In the playground, on the Prairie Path, the park, over and over. She won't stay dead."

Taking ragged breaths, she sagged on the bed. Her uncontrollable trembling rattled the bedpost against the wall and drummed a sickening beat. Unbearable revulsion came with dawning knowledge. She wailed. "Are you saying you're the Sweet Sixteen Strangler? How could this be…? Ramon, no!" Anguished and sobbing uncontrollably, she buried her face in her hands. Animalistic lowing sounded, and she yanked her hands away from her face.

Ramon huddled on the floor, facedown and humpbacked, dissolved in hysteria.

Instinctively, she rushed to kneel next to him and enfold his quaking form in her embrace.

"God will forgive if I pay," he said gutturally. "I want to go to the police. I want to pay."

Opposition rose in her throat like a stranglehold. *My husband is a serial killer. My husband! My husband? No. No. No. He'll never leave jail. Or they'll kill him. He's insane. He needs help.*

I shall cherish you for all eternity if you continue to meet the tests that will come in your mortal life.

"No, no," she said, squeezing his shoulders. "Ramon, come on. Sit up. Look at me."

She sat back on her haunches as he unfolded from the fetal position and trained red-rimmed eyes on her. *Forgiveness. God wants me to forgive Ramon just like He does.*

"We're going to start over. We'll leave here. We'll..." Focusing on an action plan, the steps emerged. "We're going to move to Wisconsin. There's a teacher's license reciprocity agreement in place. We'll find an apartment, find jobs...I'll research doctors."

He knit his brow and gazed at her intently.

"Trust me," she said. "This is best. This is what God wants us to do. I know it. You just have to promise me that you'll forget about Jodi Weller. Never, ever think about her again. Do I have your word?"

He shook his head. "What about paying? Look at Laci. She said she's glad she cleared her conscience..."

Giving his shoulders a shake, she insisted, "Laci's different, Ramon. You have to see that. She'll have a life after...you won't. Unless you listen to me and promise that you'll start over."

He nodded, obedient. "OK, Tina, OK. Yes, I promise."

Epilogue

January 1, 2AS

"Happy New Year, Chicago," Bernadette said on camera. "For those of you just joining *Now Chicago,* the guests on our panel this morning are Archbishop Mark McKenzie, Anna Babic Robbins, fondly called The Rose In The Desert, and Dr. Glen Foster.

"We'll hear from Dr. Foster who has spearheaded the analysis of the phenomenon popularly known as the Fire and Ice Cross in a minute, but first a summary of the first half hour of our program today.

"Archbishop McKenzie related the highlights of the post-universal sign era with respect to the unification of world religions. Lines continue to blur between religious denominations and between religious leaders and government officials. The peace initiative continues to gain disciples.

"The Marian visionary Anna Babic Robbins discussed her ongoing work in sharing the continued messages of Our Lady of the Roses. The central and urgent themes of these frequent messages are to heed the Lord's wishes that He imparted to each of us, to never forget the universal sign or the inspiration of the everlasting sign, and to be prepared to account to God again. Anna alluded to secrets yet unrevealed. The new Eden is imminent, and all will be judged worthy or unworthy of abiding there soon.

"For a transcript of our guests' comments or to view video presentations, please visit the *Now Chicago* website."

Bernadette straightened a sheaf of papers against the desktop and then gazed into the camera lens. "Now we'll hear from Dr. Glen Foster, the 1AS Nobel Laureate in Physics for devising the protocols to analyze the composition of the Fire and Ice Cross—the prophesied permanent sign that appeared in the Valley of Fire after the cessation of the week-long universal sign.

"Dr. Foster, thank you for participating on our panel today."

The camera panned the panel and focused on Glen's torso in profile as he sat behind the desk, facing his wife. "Glad to be here, Bernadette." He grinned and winked at her.

Amused, Bernadette said, "Dr. Foster and I are married, so please forgive the familiarity. Glen. Tell us about your team's findings."

He faced the camera that swung in his direction. "I led the forensic team endeavoring to determine the physical properties of the permanent sign. The names of my esteemed colleagues are listed on this slide. As you see, the team's credentials are superlative, representing a brain trust in the scientific fields of physics, chemistry, photonics, molecular biology, and etcetera.

"We employed both sophisticated and

commonplace tools to investigate the structure such as lasers, spectrographs, and even a chain saw in the attempt to literally chip away at the cross and its mysterious existence in an environment as hellish as the Valley of Fire.

"The compendium of the forensic team's test results, observations, and conclusions is available free to all world citizens on the Fire and Ice Cross website, on the *Now Chicago* website, and via online book retailers."

"What were your final conclusions?" Bernadette posed.

"The cross is composed of water molecules, the covalent bond of one oxygen and two hydrogen atoms—H_2O in solid form. Ice. This is the basic and simple scientific explanation of the intricate, inexplicable, and impossible existence of a skyscraper of ice in a high temperature atmosphere. The cross doesn't melt. Pick axes and chain saws can't penetrate it. The Fire and Ice Cross is unmovable and indestructible. It stands as a monument that God spoke, and we're not to forget that. I had the opportunity to investigate minutes after this permanent sign had erupted out of the ground because I was there with you in the Valley of Fire, Bernadette. There was no doubt in my mind that this represented a gift from God."

Bernadette gazed at her husband, remembering the events of that day in vivid soul-stirring clarity. "Then why did you organize the forensic team, Glen? Wouldn't that testimony from you and others present have sufficed?"

The camera focus pulled in for a close-up of Glen. He beamed a smile and said, "I wanted to see the expression on the faces of the scientific community when the facts lined up as I knew they would." He chuckled and then added, "And I thought it essential to provide salient facts, so that the team's findings could incorporate into world history for all time."

The camera switched to Bernadette. "Thank you, Doctor Glen Foster, for your work, and for your participation on our New Year's Day panel.

"Finally, in other news, a Chicago Police Department spokesperson announced cooperation with authorities in Watersmeet, Wisconsin, in supplying evidence connected with a serial killer, active in the Chicago suburban area during the seven-day universal snowfall, who was never apprehended," she said.

"Watersmeet Sheriff Joseph Corello, a former CPD homicide detective, is leading the investigation into the murder of a sixteen-year-old girl by strangulation in that community. A possible connection with the murderer known as the Sweet Sixteen Strangler is suspected."

Editor's Note

Rose in the Desert is a story that shares what willful obedience versus willful disobedience can do in our lives. Each of the characters in this fictional tale, received miraculous messages from God, who spoke to them about their sin and the direction of their lives. God wanted repentance and, in correlation to that, action. None of us are worthy of grace. Romans 3:10 declares, "None are righteous. No not one." Romans 3:23 tells us "For all have sinned and come short of the glory of God." But we have hope, as Romans 5:8 shares, "But God commended His love toward us, in that while we were yet sinners, Christ died for us."

In Rose in the Desert, we are shown an extension of God's love through this miraculous happening. God reminds the characters of their sin and declares a means by which their sins can be forgiven. Of course, without the acceptance of Christ, there is no forgiveness, so each had to humble himself and admit that Christ was Savior. Then, having that acknowledgement, they were to obey.

Rose in the Desert brings to life the truth of God's saving grace. God's messages to the characters were an extension of His love. Whether the individuals in the story understood Christ or had accepted Christ, they still needed to repent, amend their ways, and do as God said. God even reached out in love to the vilest of all: a serial killer. God had a specific message for the killer, and that individual was ready to do what needed to be done to make his life right with God. But something terrible happened. The consequences are seen in the last paragraph.

Another character received little condemnation but an admonition to meet the tests that would come into her mortal life. This one to whom little condemnation was shown, failed the future tests, and her willful disobedience has the greatest impact in the story.

The last paragraph of Rose in the Desert is not meant to be a cliffhanger for the reader. The ending is made to stop the reader, keep them from closing the book and thinking it just another good tale. My hope is that it causes a moment of reflection.

I was struck by how much my willful disobedience may affect others. In this case, another person died—a physical death. But what if my willful disobedience was more subtle? What if I encouraged another to be outside the will of God? What would the consequence be? Just like the actions of the character, my disobedience could cost a life—a life that should have been dedicated to God, a life who might not come to know God because of my actions.

The ending of Rose in the Desert was a reminder to me that God is gracious, God is good. He is longsuffering and patient. Yet, my actions, if not attuned to His will, can come at a cost I, and others, cannot afford.

What were your reflections?

Publisher's Note

Many years ago, when I read KM's precursor to this novel ("Jewel of the Adriatic") I was intrigued by the manner in which KM wove inspirational and supernatural aspects into an entertaining and thought-provoking story. These novels, as KM tells it, were inspired by approved Marian apparitions as well as the purported Marian apparitions at Medjugorje. While the Medjugorje visitations have never been deemed as authentic messages from Jesus (through His mother, Mary), as a backdrop for KM Daughters's novels, these and approved Marian apparitions do pose several interesting questions regarding the supernatural and how God can choose to interact with His creation.

It is never my intention as a publisher to confuse readers or to lead them into something that would pull them away from Christ, so it is important to remember that KM's novels are a work of imagination and not a statement regarding the supernatural. We'll leave such weighty things to the theologians. But, as a piece of fiction, KM's works are not only entertaining stories, but also make a person think about salvation and all that Christ has to offer...and pondering all that Christ has to offer is always a worthwhile endeavour.

God speaks to us in many ways, but most widely through the Bible, which is His inerrant word. As with any private revelation, it is always important to tread with caution and to test the spirit/message/inspiration. God will never provide any revelation that contradicts what He has already revealed to us. He will never ask us to do something evil. (The end does not justify the means!)

So, as you have read this novel, I trust you have enjoyed the story for what it is: an entertaining work of fiction. But I also hope it has caused you to think about your own journey of faith and has helped to bring you closer to Christ in some meaningful way.

Thank you

We appreciate you reading this White Rose Publishing title. For other inspirational stories, please visit our on-line bookstore at www.pelicanbookgroup.com.

For questions or more information, contact us at customer@pelicanbookgroup.com.

White Rose Publishing
Where Faith is the Cornerstone of Love™
an imprint of Pelican Book Group
www.PelicanBookGroup.com

Connect with Us
www.facebook.com/Pelicanbookgroup
www.twitter.com/pelicanbookgrp

To receive news and specials, subscribe to our bulletin
http://pelink.us/bulletin

May God's glory shine through
this inspirational work of fiction.

AMDG

You Can Help!

At Pelican Book Group it is our mission to entertain readers with fiction that uplifts the Gospel. It is our privilege to spend time with you awhile as you read our stories.

We believe you can help us to bring Christ into the lives of people across the globe. And you don't have to open your wallet or even leave your house!

Here are 3 simple things you can do to help us bring illuminating fiction™ to people everywhere.

1) If you enjoyed this book, write a positive review. Post it at online retailers and websites where readers gather. And share your review with us at reviews@pelicanbookgroup.com (this does give us permission to reprint your review in whole or in part.)

2) If you enjoyed this book, recommend it to a friend in person, at a book club or on social media.

3) If you have suggestions on how we can improve or expand our selection, let us know. We value your opinion. Use the contact form on our web site or e-mail us at customer@pelicanbookgroup.com

God Can Help!

Are you in need? The Almighty can do great things for you. Holy is His Name! He has mercy in every generation. He can lift up the lowly and accomplish all things. Reach out today.

Do not fear: I am with you; do not be anxious: I am your God. I will strengthen you, I will help you, I will uphold you with my victorious right hand.
~Isaiah 41:10 (NAB)

We pray daily, and we especially pray for everyone connected to Pelican Book Group—that includes you! If you have a specific need, we welcome the opportunity to pray for you. Share your needs or praise reports at http://pelink.us/pray4us

Free Book Offer

We're looking for booklovers like you to partner with us! Join our team of influencers today and periodically receive free eBooks and exclusive offers.

For more information
Visit http://pelicanbookgroup.com/booklovers